10-18-05

To Amy,
I wish you health, happiness, and success! Your kindness and understanding will always be remembered.

[signature]

THE LAST SEASON

THE LAST SEASON

Joseph J. Bradley

iUniverse, Inc.
New York Lincoln Shanghai

THE LAST SEASON

Copyright © 2004 by Joseph J. Bradley

All rights reserved. No part of this book may be used or reproduced by any means, graphic, electronic, or mechanical, including photocopying, recording, taping or by any information storage retrieval system without the written permission of the publisher except in the case of brief quotations embodied in critical articles and reviews.

iUniverse books may be ordered through booksellers or by contacting:

iUniverse
2021 Pine Lake Road, Suite 100
Lincoln, NE 68512
www.iuniverse.com
1-800-Authors (1-800-288-4677)

This book is a work of fiction. Names, characters, places and incidents are the product of the author's imagination or are used fictitiously. Any resemblance to actual events, locales or persons, living or dead, is coincidental.

ISBN-13: 978-0-595-35647-8 (pbk)
ISBN-13: 978-0-595-67252-3 (cloth)
ISBN-13: 978-0-595-80124-4 (ebk)
ISBN-10: 0-595-35647-8 (pbk)
ISBN-10: 0-595-67252-3 (cloth)
ISBN-10: 0-595-80124-2 (ebk)

Printed in the United States of America

This book is dedicated to my son Ryan and daughter Taylor who have given my life purpose and meaning.

Acknowledgements

I offer my sincere thanks and gratitude to Anthony Bradley for his continued support and encouragement in all projects and feats I have undertaken throughout my life. My respect and admiration for Anthony is one beyond compare. I would also like to thank Lois Darcy my copy editor for her diligence and expedience in helping to prepare this book for publication. Thanks to Judi Hershel, assistant copy editor and Miriam Gonzalez and Louis Pagano for all their help and support. I would like to thank Yvonne Marshall for her love and encouragement, and her contribution in writing the Spanish dialogue, which has given the story its flare. Most of all I would like to thank God. For I truly believe the words are his and I am just the messenger.

***Human Metamorphosis** is*

a hope that can be realized

—*Joseph J. Bradley*

Foreword

Saint Anthony, Patron Saint Of Lost Souls

Saint Anthony Claret's Mission

On July 5, 1866 a poor man knocked at Arch-bishop Anthony Claret's door. His porter was under strict orders that no poor person was ever to be turned away without an alms-even if they kept coming back. The porter opened the door and gave him some money. "No, that's not enough," the poor man said. "I want to speak to the archbishop himself."

The man did wait, and the porter told Claret's secretary about his uncommon persistence. "Let him come in," said the archbishop.

The poor man kissed his ring and said, "Your lordship, I'm down and out and very sick. The doctor says I should take mineral baths for treatment. But I have no money to get to the spa or pay for the baths. Will you help me, for God's sake?"

Archbishop Claret called the steward. "Give this poor man the money he needs to pay for his trip and the baths."

The steward said, "I'm sorry, your lordship, but we've already spent all of this month's allowance giving away alms and books. There is nothing left to give." Claret lifted off the archbishop's cross that hung around his neck. "Never let a poor man go away from my door without the alms he needs. Take this cross to the jewelry shop of Don Victor Perez, on Lope de Vega street, and tell him I want to sell it. Bring back what he gives you for it, and help this man."

The poor of Madrid, both natives and migrants, always found their way to Archbishop Anthony Claret's door. Whoever called on him found one or more sick or needy persons waiting. He gave away most of his salary in alms and was often lacking the few necessities of his own meager standard of life.

The life of Saint Anthony Mary Claret is full of such striking variety that a rapid glance scarcely reveals the thread that links everything he did. This 19th-century saint-whose achievements point to the 20th century-was a missionary, a religious founder, an organizer of the lay apostolate, a social reformer, a queen's chaplain, a prophet and wonder-worker, a writer and publisher, an archbishop, a target of calumny and persecution, and a promoter of devotion to the Immaculate Heart of Mary. What, then, is the thread that ties together these and the many other aspects of his career?

A clue is to be found in the poor man asking for money-an episode like thousands of others in his lifetime. The thread of unity, the dominating passion of his life, was his apostolic drive. Saint Anthony Claret had a quenchless thirst to help the poor and rescue souls.

Anthony Claret's Childhood

This passion showed up very early in his life. One night in 1813, when he was only five, he had just said his prayers and climbed into bed when a sober thought struck him. He sat up, serious and still, heedless of the iron bars of the bedstead pressing into his back. The day before, in catechism class, he had learned that in hell there is eternal fire and that many sinners are condemned to go there.

This observant boy had already seen that there are many in this world who suffer-the poor, the aged, the sick. He did not want people to suffer. So that night as he was about to close his eyes the thought of the suffering in hell came back to his mind. He began conjuring up pictures of long ages of time, of cycles and aeons of tremendous duration, throughout which the sufferings of the damned must continue. But the endlessness of it he could not grasp.

This fearful realization stamped itself on his memory for life. With it came the lasting desire to save souls from such a fate.

Anthony was the fifth of the eleven children of Juan and Josefa Claret. He was born on Christmas eve, 1807, in the village of Sallent, in Catalonia, Spain. As a child he was remarkable for his piety, modesty, and obedience. He took great delight in receiving and visiting the Blessed Sacrament, in making pilgrimages to the Shrine of Our Lady of Fusimanya, near his village, and in reciting the rosary.

Notwithstanding his piety, the boy was harassed by two severe temptations. The one, against chastity, he resisted. More recurrent was a curious urge to rebelliousness against his mother and against his Heavenly Mother Mary-a cruel mental torment. Over this, too, through prayer, patience, and humility, he eventually triumphed. Throughout his early childhood, Catalonia was frequently overrun by the troops of Napoleonic France, burning and pillaging. The townspeople often had to evacuate Sallent. One such time, when he was five, he refused to flee with his family but stayed to take care of his elderly, half-blind grandfather and lead him to safety. From the first Anthony wanted to be a priest. With this in mind, when he had finished his primary schooling he enrolled in the Latin school of Father Juan Piera. But shortly afterward, the teacher died, and there was no other way in sight for Anthony to advance toward the priesthood.

His Youth

The family business, a weaving shop, needed his help. He developed a keen interest in weaving and textile machinery and soon learned everything his father had to teach him.

So at 17 Anthony was sent to work and study in a large plant in Barcelona. He encountered the temptations of the city and saw that some of his companions succumbed to them. He, too, met crises, but the Blessed Virgin Mary, his beloved patroness, obtained him the grace to persevere.

His constant preoccupation with problems of weaving was the means God used to redirect him to his true vocation. He writes this in his autobiography: "In the last days of the third year of my stay in Barcelona, while assisting at Mass, I had great difficulty in banishing the thoughts that assailed me. Although I enjoyed thoughts of my art, I wished that they would not come to me during Holy Mass and my other prayers. I wished to be occupied only with what I was doing, so I tried to avert these distractions, but in vain. I could not curb my imagination....

"In the midst of this flood of distractions I remembered having once, as a child, read the gospel maxim, 'What will it avail a man if he gain the whole world and lose his soul?' The remembrance of this made a deep impression. It was an arrow that wounded me. Suddenly changed, like Saul on the way to Damascus, I began deliberating what I should do. I could not decide...I directed myself to St. Philip Neri, or rather to the Fathers of the Oratory...."

Father Amigo, an Oratorian priest, listened to Anthony's story and approved his resolution to pursue Holy Orders. The priest advised him to begin by resuming the study of Latin. Now the young man's spirit became serene. He began to study Latin, often with the book propped before him at his loom.

Where he would study for the priesthood Anthony did not know, but as he was unhappy with the life of the secular world, he was quite sure he wanted to enter the seminary of some religious congregation.

Unknown to him, an acquaintance of his had recommended him to the Bishop of Vic, a city north of Barcelona, and the Bishop invited him to enter the diocesan seminary there. In the conflict of his desires he went to Father Canti, of the Oratorians, for advice. Father Canti settled it for him very simply: "Go to Vic." He went there, and the Bishop immediately said to him, "My son, you are admitted into my seminary. Be a good seminarian." Claret was an exemplary one and was ordained on June 13, 1835.

The Young Priest

His first appointment was as assistant to the pastor of his hometown, Sallent. But though his work there was fruitful, he felt himself called to be a laborer in the foreign missions. With this view in mind, and impelled by a desire to shed his blood for Christ, he went to Rome to consult the Prefect of the Propagation of the Faith. As the Prefect was out of town, he began his annual spiritual exercises under a Jesuit director.

After this retreat he was invited to enter the Jesuit novitiate in Rome, and he gladly accepted. But after some months of happy community life with the Jesuits catechizing, preaching to convicts, ministering to hospital patients, he developed a chronic, crippling pain in his right leg. The General of the Society of Jesus pronounced this a sign that God had other plans for Father Claret.

By the time he reached his next assigned post, the mountain parish of Viladrau, Catalonia, he found himself cured. That district, despoiled by the recent Carlist civil war, was still scourged by robber bands. The doctors had abandoned the town, and sickness and misery were everywhere. "What else could I do," the saint wrote, "but become a doctor of corporal as well as spiritual ailments?"

By applying simple herbs and salves he cured the most severe and varied diseases, even in people at the point of death. The cures, he believed, were God's way of calling attention to the importance of the Word of God, which he, God's missionary, was preaching to them.

Early Mission Journeys

Late in 1842 Father Claret was appointed an Apostolic Missionary to all of mountainous Catalonia, with its 13 cities and 400 towns. Religious practice there had suffered much from the French invasions, the Carlist war, and the shift of political power at the hands of the antireligious Liberal party. To demonstrate against the rising vice of greed, Father Claret always traveled from mission to mission as the poorest of men. His baggage consisted of a razor, a pair of socks, a breviary, a map of Catalonia, and half a loaf of bread. He never carried money. He never went by carriage, or even by mule, but always walked: often by backroads, trails, and across country in rain, snow, and burning sun.

He put each of his missions from three days to nine or more days long, in the hands of our Blessed Mother and before beginning a sermon, would have the congregation recite the rosary with him. Then, he would begin to preach, perhaps on one of the four last things, the gravity of sin, perseverance in virtue, or on the conversion of St. Mary Magdalen or St. Augustine.

As much as he hated and dreaded sin, he did not scold, ridicule, or terrify sinners. He learned that only suavity and gentleness could win them to repentance. And with these softer qualities, in which he trained himself, he touched their hearts. Of help to him, too, were his eloquence with the Catalan language and his apt metaphors drawn from life in Catalonian cities and countryside.

People came from miles around to hear him preach. Once they heard him, they waited outside his confessional for hours, even for days, with lunches they brought from home. Often he could read the consciences of these penitents far better than they themselves could. The pulpit, the altar, and the confessional took up almost all of his day. He ate and slept very little. Sometimes he squeezed in a session of apostolic writing, or of planning for his project, the Religious Publishing House.

For 30 days in a row people packed the huge Church of St. Stephen in Olot to hear his three hour sermons. Though he himself heard confessions as long as 15 hours a day, in Olot 24 other confessors were kept busy also. And three priests spent the entire morning distributing Holy Communion. In these years of traveling and preaching in Catalonia, Father Claret worked countless wonders of healing, both bodily and spiritual. On his way to one town, to deliver a scheduled sermon, he was crossing a mountain pass when two armed robbers stopped him and searched him for money. Angry that he had none, they said, they were going to kill him.

Father Claret was unafraid, and asked them, as a favor, to wait. He had to preach to the people who were expecting him. When he had done that, he would return and put himself at the bandits' disposal, and he promised he would not bring the police. The robbers let him go. The next day, at the same hour, he was back. The robbers, overcome by his faithfulness to his word, did not shoot him. They knelt and confessed their sins to him.

Claret's Overseas Mission

Throughout the lifetime of Saint Anthony Claret, Spain was plagued by misery and strife. Riots, revolutions, intrigues, and general privation made government and life itself precarious. Christian living was difficult, and as Father Claret constantly found, so was the work of the traveling missionary. During the time of his Catalan mission, England, France, the Spanish queen mother, and other factions were scheming to choose husbands for the young Queen Isabella II and her sister. In October of 1846, Isabella was induced to marry her cousin, Duke Francisco of Cadiz, and her sister simultaneously to marry the son of the French king, Louis Philippe.

This political stroke enraged the archconservative Carlists-supporters of Don Carlos, the rival claimant to the throne. The Carlists now staged their second revolt. The center of the uprising was Catalonia, Father Claret's mission territory. To make trouble for Father Claret, his anticlerical enemies falsely accused him of plotting with the rebels.

This endangered his life. Father Claret was not troubled about that, but his bishop was. Bishop Casadevall seized an opportunity to send his missionary to the Canary Islands, a Spanish possession off the coast of West Africa.

Mission to the Canary Islands

Father Claret reached this post in March of 1848 and took up the same life and work he had pursued in Catalonia. Though now he had to preach in Spanish-with a Catalan accent which some scoffers mimicked his success was once again overpowering.

On May 1, 1848, he opened a 28-day mission in the town of Telde, on Gran Canaria Island. There was a great drought, and the farmers were preoccupied with fear for their crops. He said to them, "I can promise you, brethren, that before this mission is over there will be a plentiful rain that will revive your plants, quiet your homes, and rejoice your hearts." While he was preaching the closing sermon, the rain began. Morals were lax in Telde; theft was especially prevalent. But the mission of Father Claret wrought a great change. As the pastor wrote to the bishop: "This town has never seen the like of it. The most bitter enemies have made peace. Scandals, both public and private, have been terminated and amends made. Broken marriages have been mended. Restitutions have been made. Why? Because no one can withstand the fire of his preaching, the kindness and liveliness of his manner, his forceful reproofs…and the impact of his reasoning. The appeal of his words breaks his listeners' hearts, and everybody, even the proudest nature-falls at his feet weeping."

But it was not only his preaching that won the veneration of the townspeople for Father Claret. Many of his penitents made it known that in the confessional he had seen into their consciences, reminding them of sins that through ignorance or forgetfulness they had failed to mention. And there were droves of penitents. He began hearing their confessions at dawn because they started lining up the evening before.

Here at Telde he also performed two striking cures. One was that of Antonia Hilaria, 25, afflicted with epilepsy from early childhood. During her convulsions, six to eight men were required to restrain her. The most casual event could bring on one of her spells. One occurred during an evening service at Father Claret's mission. As he came into the sacristy, he asked what the crowd of people was doing there.

"My sister is having a nervous spell," a man said, "and when that happens she needs the help of all of us." Father Claret took the girl's handkerchief, dipped it in holy water, and then said to the people holding her, "Let her free! Let her free!" They could not, they replied, for she would throw herself on the floor and hurt herself.

"Let her free," Father Claret insisted. "No harm will come to her." They did so. He put the moistened handkerchief on her eyes. The girl sat up and was quiet. "Take the cloth from her eyes," Father Claret said. Usually her eyes were glazed and bulging after an attack. Now they were calm and natural. She walked home, slept peacefully, and shortly afterward was able to take a job. She lived many years, but never had another epileptic spell.

Then, throughout the plaza, the voice of Father Claret was heard: "Don't be frightened, brethren. The demon has put out the lanterns. The demon has thrown them to the ground. But be assured, not one lantern has been broken. God has not given him permission for that. Just pick them up and relight them." They did, and to their surprise not a single lantern had been broken.

Father Claret kept writing books and pamphlets for his Religious Publishing House throughout his 14 months of labor in the Canary Islands. The venture was successful, but his coworkers were anxious for him to return to Spain and confer on business problems. The second Carlist revolt ended in the spring of 1849, and Claret returned to Spain.

His Mission Congregation

The party which considered the church an ally, the Conservatives, had maneuvered itself into power, displacing the Liberals, who considered the church an enemy and had restricted it in every way they could. Consulting with his bishop and with trusted advisors, Father Claret decided that the time was ripe at last for the realization of a hope he had nurtured for years: the founding of a religious congregation to aid him and to follow him in the vast work of the missions. He had already helped several other founders in starting their congregations and was familiar with the canon law and the practical difficulties involved. Five young priests, aged 27 to 32, heard of his intentions and sought to join him. Father Claret was 42. With the bishop's permission, they assembled in a room in the Seminary of Vic, in recess for summer holidays, on July 16, 1849. As the Immaculate Heart of Mary was so powerful a help in his own mission labors, he proposed as Article I of their Constitutions: "This Congregation...shall be named the Congregation of the Sons of the Immaculate Heart of the Blessed Virgin Mary, and it shall have her as its Patroness." The others agreed.

Article II was read: "Its aim is to seek in all things the glory of God, the sanctification of its members, and the salvation of souls throughout the world...." Then the remaining articles were read and discussed, all of these intended as aids in accomplishing the great purposes of the Congregation embodied in Article II. The following three weeks, the new Congregation spent making the Spiritual Exercises of Saint Ignatius, under the direction of Father Claret. A Dominican priest, Father Dominic Costa, saw the infant Congregation as they were completing their Spiritual Exercises and wrote, "It seemed as though these Fathers were coming out of the Cenacle. It was a re-enactment of Pentecost."

Assignment to Cuba

But one of the group, Father Claret himself, was even then undergoing a great test. Ten days earlier he had been summoned from the Exercises to report to Bishop Casadevall. The bishop showed him a paper from the Ministry of State in which Queen Isabella II had appointed him Archbishop of Santiago, Cuba. This was an honor, a promotion, but a most inconvenient one. His heart and his hopes lay with the toddling Religious Publishing House and with the newborn Sons of the Immaculate Heart of Mary.

But in this, as in all matters, he wanted to act under holy obedience, not according to his own preference. So he laid the case before several good and prudent priests and asked them what he should do. Their judgment was that God's work required his presence in Cuba. On October 6, 1850 in the Cathedral of Vic, Anthony Mary Claret was consecrated Archbishop of Santiago, Cuba. The following February he arrived in Cuba and was installed in his See.

As he embarked on his trip to Cuba in December of 1850, Claret was saying goodbye to friends in Spain. At dawn one day, he took a stagecoach to visit the Archbishop of Tarragona. When the coach drew into Villafranca del Panades early in the morning, all the priests of the town were there to meet it and begged Archbishop Claret to interrupt his journey and come to their aid. As soon as he heard their story he dismounted and sent word to his host that he had been delayed. Four criminals were to be executed there that morning, three boys in their late teens and a man of forty, and all four had refused to confess and receive Communion. The pastor of the town pressed Archbishop Claret to have a quick cup of hot chocolate and hurry over to the prison. No, the Archbishop said they must first go to the church and place the affair in God's hands. When they had done that, they went to the prison, and the missionary was at once let in to see the condemned men. Claret's warm, fatherly pleas soon conquered the three younger criminals. They made their confessions, and the chaplain prepared to administer them Viaticum, the last communion. He asked the young men, according to the custom, if they forgave all who had injured them. Two replied yes. The third said yes, he forgave everyone except his mother.

Claret prostrated himself and kissed the boy's feet. "My son," he said, "if you do not pardon your mother, you will be damned. For God's sake and for my sake, I beg you to forgive her."

"No," the young man said, "it's because of her that I'm in this trouble. If she had punished me in time, I wouldn't be here. I don't forgive her." The four prisoners were covered with execution robes, mounted on mules, and led to the scaffold. The moment before his sentence of death was carried out, the unforgiving youth shouted, "I forgive my mother from my heart. Pray for me!" Then the older man, the toughest of the four, held up his arms and asked to confess. Seated on the bench, with his head covered, he confessed and was absolved. Then the four men were put to death.

Revelation 22.21

See, I am coming soon; my reward is with me, to repay according to everyone's work. I am the alpha and the omega, the first and the last, the beginning and the end.

Chapter 1

▼

It was a day like no other. The wind gently blew the oak and maple leaves that had fallen down to dance in the sun. A tiny twister slowly turned round and round holding captive several leaves and a paper bag. One could smell the crisp, clean air and the changes that occur during autumn in New England. It was a new day that offered hope, a future and life.

Beth sat on a park bench taking in deep breaths of fresh air, a cool breeze awakening her every sense with the soothing warmth of a contradicting sun against her face. She ran her gloved fingers across a heart that had been carved in the bench seat. Next to it read "Pat and Jack forever." Beth wondered whom they were and if they were still together. The roar of a trash removal truck suddenly disrupted her attention as it screeched to a halt at the intersection of Lincoln and Temple streets. A short, round black man wearing a pile cap and a dead cigar stub between his teeth hopped off the back of the truck, snatching up one barrel and then another, leaving them lying on their side empty and moving on with little enthusiasm.

The streets were calm on this early Tuesday morning. Beth had been sitting on the bench for some time. On this day she needed extra waiting time to think about the future and what life would offer the child that she carried deep inside her. She was a beautiful woman, olive complexion and dark brown flowing hair that rested on her shoulders. Her body was firm and being an avid runner kept her in excellent physical condition. Beth had a unique physical characteristic that set her apart from most. She had big, bright, light blue eyes, eyes that drew the attention of anyone in her presence. Her mother used to tell her that her eyes were a gift from the angels so others could see the reflection of their pure soul.

Beth never really understood what her mother meant; she hoped one day she would.

She gazed across Temple Street at the building she was waiting to gain entrance into. The building was three stories high with light brown colored brick that had been laid over a hundred and fifty years earlier. The windows had faded with time and were secured with steel bars. The sight of the building brought Beth back to a place she lived as a child, a cold, dark place where she was overwhelmed with loneliness, Saint Anthony's home for orphaned girls. The days there seemed to linger on as if time had stopped. There was very little comfort and enjoyment there and Beth had kept herself occupied by playing with her imaginary friend. Victoria knew Beth better than anyone and listened to her thoughts and understood her feelings. None of the other girls paid much attention to Beth, except to make fun of her. Victoria was her best friend and kept her company at night when the lights went out. She was afraid of the night, and the darkness brought the awful feeling of loneliness that plagued her since her parents abruptly vanished off the face of the earth and left her to reside in the heavens with God. Beth was the only child of a happy and charming young couple whose lives were cut short in a tragic automobile accident when she was four years old. With no other relatives known, Beth was turned over to the state of Vermont and transported to St. Anthony's Orphanage where she lived until she was adopted three years later. The loss of her parents left a scar deep inside her that would slowly dissipate with time but would never completely heal. It was like a part of her was missing and it was a pain matched by no other, a lingering pain that had no end, a teardrop that never dried.

Sam and Nancy Brown were extraordinarily happy and caring people. With no hope of having a child of their own they had decided to adopt a baby girl. The drive from Boston to Vermont was an exciting adventure for them. It was a cold winter day and the landscape was covered with snow. The contemplation of a new addition to their family had added a permanent smile to their faces. It was the missing link in their life's chain that would offer them complete contentment.

The driveway into St. Anthony's was a long narrow road with towering pines lined up on both flanks standing erect like soldiers in a parade. At the end of the drive it opened up to a four acre yard with an old square brick building that housed twenty-nine girls from four months to fourteen years of age. To the right of the building was the soccer field with young girls clumsily flocking around the ball in an attempt to lure it toward the goal. The Browns had driven to Vermont with the intention of returning to Boston with a baby girl, but, as fate would have it, things changed. As they walked toward the entrance to the building they found a little girl sitting alone at the base of the statue of St. Anthony. As they approached, Mrs. Brown noticed how gorgeous the girl's eyes were and was compelled to stop.

"Hello there. What is your name?"

The little girl looked up, surprised that someone cared. "Beth," she replied.

"Well, Beth, what are you doing out here all by yourself?"

"I was praying to Jesus, asking him if I'll ever see my mommy and daddy again."

At that moment Mrs. Brown became overwhelmed with a strong feeling of sadness and compassion for the little girl. She turned to her husband and could sense he felt the same. Without taking his eyes off the child, he said, "I believe we have found our daughter." They both reached down, took her by the hand and started toward the building.

As they drove back down the long driveway leading away from the orphanage, Beth kneeled on the back seat of the Brown's new 1967 Chevy and looked out the rear window. The building grew smaller and smaller until it disappeared from sight. Until that moment it never occurred to Beth that she would ever feel safe and comfortable riding in an automobile.

Mr. Brown was a social worker and a genuinely good-hearted man. When he wasn't working, he did volunteer work at the homeless shelter or the hospital. Mrs. Brown was a housewife and Sunday school teacher. They were simple, caring people who gave to others and asked for nothing in return. Beth had been blessed that day in Vermont, for her new parents loved her unconditionally and offered her a wonderful childhood. On that afternoon, Beth left her friend Victoria behind at St. Anthony's, never having to speak to her again.

Chapter 2

▼

The cell was five feet wide by seven feet long. Inside, a metal toilet and sink with a narrow steel bench for sleeping. The bars were covered with plexiglass to prevent detainees from attempting suicide or passing bodily fluids outside the cell. Daniel had been locked down for nine weeks, awaiting trial for the murder of a street thug who had allegedly attempted to rob him outside an automated teller machine (ATM).

Daniel was a tall, ruggedly handsome man with long dark hair that nearly touched his shoulders. He had brown eyes and a long, straight prominent nose. There was a scar on his cheek just below the left eye, where he had been struck with a beer bottle in a bar room fight. He took seven stitches and his opponent a broken arm and jaw. Daniel was a strong, God-fearing man, the son of an army major. He had spent most his youth living in the foreign countries where his father had been stationed throughout his career. Daniel had very few long lasting friendships growing up, because he was seldom in one place for very long.

His brother Seth was his only sibling. Daniel loved his brother but had never felt love in return. Seth, a tall thin young man, six years older, applied himself academically and spent most of his time reading and doing research projects. He once built a rocket that was a magnificent army green, three-foot high missile that he had launched in a remote wooded area while living in Germany. The missile blew up at launch and scattered into three pieces about ten feet apart. Seth was humiliated in front of his schoolmates. He started to curse and blamed the steel, stating it was made in Germany and less than adequate. Seth never attempted to build another rocket nor did he ever speak of it again.

Seth despised Daniel, as he was his father's favorite. Daniel could do no wrong in the often-bloodshot eyes of his father. His father was a drunk who had been passed up time and time again for promotion. With lingering allegations of sexual harassment and drunken misconduct, he never had the opportunity to advance to Lieutenant Colonel. Daniel's father never accepted responsibility for not advancing through the ranks. It was the political bureaucracy of the military that had been responsible for his stagnant career. He also blamed his ex-wife, for if it weren't for her leaving him, he would have had help raising the boys and could have devoted more time to advancing his career. The Major never got over his wife leaving him. His drinking increased after she left. Daniel could see his father trapped in a downward spiral, leading into an abyss. Watching his father drowning his pain away caused Daniel extreme anxiety and he vowed never to pick up a drink for the rest of his life.

For a period of two years, letters addressed to Seth and Daniel would sporadically arrive post-marked from Florida, and then Arizona. Daniel was nine years old when the last letter arrived from Las Vegas, and that would be the last time either of them heard from their mother. Daniel's world was falling apart. His mother was gone, dad was a drunk, and his only brother lived in a vacuum. A year passed by since Daniel had last heard from his mother. He had mailed several letters to her but they all came back stamped "Return to Sender." One day fell into the next and Daniel plunged into a life of loneliness and despair. He was a lost soul in a world filled with emptiness.

The following year the Major had been transferred to Seoul, South Korea, and he was excited because the liquor and whores were plentiful and inexpensive. He had put in for Korea several times, but his requests had always been denied. This was his chance at a new life, a chance to forget the past and start over.

Seth remained in the United States with his Uncle Harry to prepare for college and it came with a ten-thousand dollar price paid by the Major. Daniel wasn't prepared to move again, but he didn't have a say in the matter. It was a new chapter in a book that was forever changing. The pages offered no consistency or substance. In Daniel's eyes it was a book that appeared to be a tragedy.

Chapter 3

▼

Daniel could hear the guards approaching. As they passed each cell the detainees would shout out obscenities and ask for blankets, food and coffee. One of the guards was a very large black man who could easily be mistaken for a New England Patriot linebacker and the other was a frail white man with wire rim glasses and short greasy hair.

"Dan, you have a visitor," the large man said. He jammed in the key and slid the cell door open.

"You know the drill." His expression was fixed and his words in monotone.

Daniel held his hands out and had handcuffs secured on his wrists. Simultaneously the thin guard struggled to get the restraints around his ankles. The sound of handcuffs being administered was a sound not to be mistaken by any other. It was a sound Daniel had been hearing much too often and each time was just as degrading as the last.

The thin guard was fumbling along. "Damn restraints," he muttered, "bout time they bought some new ones. These must've been used on Sparticus."

After being secured, Daniel shuffled down the long hall with a guard on either side clinging onto his triceps.

The visitation room was nearly full as Daniel was escorted in. It was a long, narrow room with yellow painted walls and a wooden stool placed in front of thick bullet proof glass and a phone hook-up, to the right of the window. From a distance he could see her eyes as he approached his station. They were eyes filled with love for him and no other. They had met at a Karate tournament one Saturday morning at Brandeis University in Waltham, Massachusetts. Daniel, who was there as a competitor, noticed Beth observing from the bleachers. She had been convinced by a friend to go along for a day of superb martial arts competition. Daniel was infatuated from the moment he laid eyes on her. Beth was not overly attracted to Daniel at first. He had long hair and looked as if he just returned from a safari. While watching him in the finals, she saw how graceful he moved for a man over six feet tall, and was intrigued by his ability. With his persistence she agreed to have dinner with him. They began seeing each other on a regular basis and their relationship flourished. They were engaged to be married nine months later.

As Beth sat in wait for Daniel to arrive, she was rehearsing in her head how she would tell him about his child growing inside her. She was excited about the pregnancy, yet scared for Daniel at the same time. Beth knew he was innocent. Daniel was a kind man filled with compassion and a zest for life. He could not deliberately kill anyone. She was praying that Leo Schanz, Daniel's attorney, would prove that in a court of law. Daniel sat down on the stool and raised his cuffed hands to pick up the phone. Beth already had the phone to her ear.

"How are you doing, Honey? I miss you so much."

"I'm doing ok," Beth said. "The days are long without you near. I miss you."

"I know," Daniel said. "It won't be too much longer. The trial starts soon and Leo is very optimistic that we can get the jury to see that it is a case of self-defense and not voluntary manslaughter. The DA is being a real pig-headed ass on this case. He is not willing to budge on the manslaughter charge. Leo says if he was a prosecutor instead of a wannabe politician, the charges would have been plead down to involuntary manslaughter. Apparently he has his eye on the mayor's seat and wants the public to see how tough he is on violent crime."

"Yeah, at your expense," Beth replied. "How are they treating you in here, darling?"

"Well, the food is awful and I've stayed in rooms with a better view. I feel like an animal in a cage. No privacy. The days drag on with nothing to do except sleep and hope that I will win this case and have you back in my arms soon. I love you, Beth, more than you'll ever know."

"I love you too, Daniel. Darling, I have some good news. I went to the doctor yesterday and he told me that I'm," Beth hesitated for a moment, and she was nervously trembling. "We're going to have a baby."

"What, it can't be!" Daniel said. His face changed and wrinkles defined his forehead. He felt as if he had just been run over by a truck. "Are you sure? It has to be a mistake!"

"No darling, it's true. We are going to have a baby. I'm eleven weeks pregnant."

"Beth, I told you that I was unable to produce children ever since the accident I had when I was a kid. It can't be mine." Daniel had a look of sadness you might see in the eyes of an abused puppy.

"It has to be, I haven't been with anyone else. Your doctor must have been wrong."

"I was examined again when I was nineteen and the doctor assured me I would never be able to impregnate anyone." The phone grew heavy as he held back his tears.

"Well, Daniel, you have and I'm proof of it." She placed her hand against her stomach.

Daniel stood up with a look of disgust on his face. "I have been impotent since I was 11 years old, Beth. What have you been doing out there while I've been locked up? It will be easier on both of us to forget about each other and move on." The room seemed to be spinning. "I may be in here for a long time, Beth. Forget about me and get on with your life. I have to go. Goodbye Beth."

Daniel turned and shuffled away. Beth just sat there, eyes filling with water and her hand on her abdomen.

Chapter 4

Essex County Superior Courtroom number two was a magnificently architectured room with twelve rows of solid oak benches that flanked the center aisle. The aisle began at the entrance and ended at the attorneys' tables in front of the seating area. The judge's bench stood five feet high in the front center of the room. To the right of the bench was the witness stand, and the jury box ran along the front right wall. In front of the judge's bench was a small desk and chair where the clerk of courts sat to assist with the daily task of organizing the case files and court documents. Just to the clerk's left, the stenographer's recording machine lay in wait for the tired fingers of the stenographer to once again pound its keys. Behind the bench were rows of red and green law books. The walls stretched up to a ceiling twenty-one feet high. The first five feet consisted of beveled oak wall panels. There were several large portraits of judges who had heard cases in that very room dating as far back as 1836. The walls they hung on were painted a dull light green. The floors were faded hardwood that had felt the repetitive pounding soles of defendants, witnesses and attorneys coming and going throughout the years.

    Daniel sat at the defendant's table situated on the left side facing the bench. Directly across on the right side was the prosecutor's table. Seated to the right of Daniel was Leo and to his right was John Carney his assistant, a recent law school graduate who graduated in the top three percent of his class at Harvard Law. John, while preparing to take the bar had been chosen by Leo to help him with the mundane tasks that Leo found too menial to bother with. Leo would send John to the library to research case law and run him around the courthouse filing motions and other daily chores that interfered with his luncheons and cocktail parties.

John was a thin young man who stopped growing physically in tenth grade, but continued to soar intellectually by the minute. Sporting short dirty blond hair and gold rim glasses, he looked like a prince sitting next to Leo Schanz, who was a large balding man in his late fifties, who for nearly two decades had not seen the shoes on his feet while standing.

The prosecuting attorney was assistant district attorney Michael Alberto. Everyone called him Mickey except for his wife, who deeply despised him. He was a pudgy, round-headed man who had very few friends. Mickey had loyalty to no one except himself. The only thing that concerned him was his political agenda, and he would try and take down anyone who stood in his way. When he wasn't working he could be found at a local restaurant drinking and eating with his cronies, most of whom resented him. Sometimes he might be found on the golf course with a cigar in his mouth, cheating at every chance. His wife of seventeen years knew he had been unfaithful ever since he started working in the DA's office, but for the children's sake, she put up with it.

Mickey had one thing on his mind, and that was becoming the Mayor of Boston. He had graduated from a small law school in Western Massachusetts and finally passed the bar after failing the first two times. Using his family connections, he was given a job working in the district attorney's office. Mickey wasn't the brightest of lawyers, but he was relentless in the trying of cases. With absolutely no integrity, he would prosecute a case using any means necessary in order to win, even if it meant participating in unethical activity.

Mickey had asked Devon Williams to assist him in prosecuting Daniel. Devon was delighted to assist, for this would be his first murder case. Most of the cases he worked were domestic related or assaults. This is the case that would put Devon on the charts. Mickey had no intention of considering anything Devon had to contribute to the case. He had brought him on board as a token for the jury to roll around between their fingers during the trial. Part of the strategy Mickey had planned, was to prosecute the case that involved the killing of a black man with a black man on his team. Every time the jury would look at Mickey they would see Devon, a clean-cut black man, educated and well dressed. In Mickey's eyes it was a brilliant approach because this was a tough case to prove. He had to get the jury to feel sorry for the victim, to see him as a human being with potential, not only a victim of murder, but a victim of childhood neglect and abuse, a poor soul who never had the chance to become a Devon Williams because his life was cut short in a deliberate act of violence perpetrated against him. It didn't matter to Mickey that Staples had a long criminal career, including a conviction for armed robbery. He knew Staples was most likely guilty, but it was a murder case and he was going to win.

There were three bailiffs assigned to courtroom two. The largest of the three was standing directly behind Daniel. The other two were situated at the entrance to the courtroom and by the door leading to the judge's chamber.

"All rise, court is in session," said the guard standing next to the bench. The judge entered the room, acknowledging the clerk and stenographer with a slight bow of his head. "Be seated," said the guard in a low scratchy voice.

Judge Thomas J. Murphy was a stern but fair man with thinning short, white hair. His black robe concealed a solid physique for a man nearly sixty-one years old. He kept in shape slapping a ball around a court that had no bench, no law books and no pictures on the walls. This was the court he enjoyed most, just walls and glass. He found refuge in the empty court. In that room he forgot about all the cases and all the lies. He never thought about the young men he sent to prison or the guilty ones he set free, all the lawyers who would do anything for a buck and the few with a conscience who had been stepped on along the way. This was the place that helped him keep in check. Four days a week he started his day in the empty court, just a handball and two men.

Judge Murphy looked as though he had heard a million cases. He knew the law and he did not deviate from it. Taking a minute to examine the people sitting at the tables in front of him, he started.

"Bring in the jury," Murphy said.

The guard opened the chamber door and a jury filed into the room, taking their place in the jury box. They slowly walked in with their heads facing forward like children in parochial school during the nineteen fifties. They took their seats and gave Murphy their full attention.

"It has been said that the law can be interpreted in many different ways," Murphy said. "Well, I don't believe there is more than one way to interpret the truth. After all, isn't that what the law is all about, the truth? This is a clean courtroom and it will remain that way as long as I wear this robe. I hope I make myself very clear, councilors?"

"Yes your honor," Mickey said. Leo just smiled and nodded.

The jury had been carefully selected and Mickey was pleased with the final outcome. Judge Murphy had instructed the jury and this was the day for opening arguments. Mickey felt confident, smiling at the jury while running his index fingers and thumbs down the lapel of his fifteen-hundred dollar Italian made suit.

He was proud of his suit and only wore it for special occasions. He would joke with his boys at the bar about how the suit fell off the back of a truck. Mickey liked people to think he had very high-level connections with the mob. In reality, they used him to fix small cases and disclose information on upcoming sting operations and indictments. The local wise guys knew Mickey was never going to amount to anything and he was often the subject of their jokes. Mickey was Italian and that was it. He was not smart enough to ever be in a political position of power, so they kept him at a distance, but made him feel as though he was accepted. Mickey had an ego so big, it was said, that court officers had to grease his fat head so he could make it through the courthouse door.

The jury was made up of three African Americans, two of whom were men. Two Hispanic men, one Korean woman, and the remaining six jurors were white and four of them were women.

Mickey liked the idea that there were six females in the box for he had a belief that most women were liberal and could easily be convinced that the victim, being black, was a subject of discrimination and repression.

"Mr. Alberto, your floor," Murphy said.

Mickey stood and started toward the jury.

"Good morning, ladies and gentlemen. You all know who I am? I'm Mickey Alberto, assistant district attorney. Charles Staples was not an angel. He had his share of troubles in life. You will hear from the defense team that he had a record of criminal misconduct and convictions, that he was a bad guy and had offered very little positive contribution to society. You will hear that the defendant killed Charles Staples in self-defense during an attempted armed robbery. The Commonwealth will show beyond a reasonable doubt that Charles Staples did not have to die at the young age of twenty-six. We will show that this was not a robbery, but a drug deal gone bad. We will also show that the defendant, trained in the martial arts, could have easily subdued Mr. Staples without the use of lethal force that maliciously caused his death. We will prove beyond a reasonable doubt that on the night of August thirty-first, the defendant committed murder."

Mickey nodded to the jury and walked back to his awaiting chair. Daniel sat there feeling like his world was falling apart. He wished it was all a bad dream and he would wake up and have Beth lying next to him. His normal life would continue, free from anxiety and complications, just a happy, healthy life filled with contentment and peace of mind. The thought that Beth may have been unfaithful had been a dagger through the heart, and now the chance that he may go to prison for a murder he didn't commit was the slow turning of the blade. He knew Beth was in the courtroom but he dared not look in her direction. There were also two representatives from the Iron Workers Union sitting in the room. Daniel had been an Ironworker for seven years and a foreman for three. Schanz leaned over and said, "Our turn." Leo was not wearing an Italian suit but he was flashing a gold Rolex and a two-carat diamond ring. He walked slowly toward the jury and stopped just short of the box. After a short period of silence he started.

"Mr. Alberto went and spoiled my whole opening statement. He told you what I was going to say, and I spent three days rehearsing it. So now I'll have to say it verbatim. It really all sums up to the same thing, though. The defendant sitting over there could be you. It could be me or it might even be Mr. Alberto. It could be any law-abiding citizen who stopped at the ATM to withdraw money so he could take his wife out to dinner on the eve of Labor Day. We all have the right to defend ourselves. He had a right to defend himself." Leo pointed to Daniel.

"In a struggle over a knife that Mr. Staples used to rob my client, he was killed. This is not murder. This is self-preservation. This is instinct. This is justified. This, ladies and gentlemen, is an innocent man. Thank you."

Leo had captured the attention of the whole courtroom. The room was completely silent as Leo made his way back to his chair. For a brief moment Daniel felt that there might be hope for him. Leo patted Daniel on the shoulder and took his seat. Daniel lowered his head and began to pray.

Chapter 5

Mickey started his campaign by calling the first police officers that arrived on the scene to the witness stand, one at a time. He moved to enter the knife into evidence as exhibit A. They both testified as if they had spent the past three days rehearsing, with Mickey as the bandleader, baton in hand. Testimony from the police officers amounted to eighty percent of his case so Mickey knew he had to make it as dramatic as possible. Both officers stated they found Mr. Staples lying on his side with a knife protruding from the right side of his abdomen. There was a discrepancy as to who was performing CPR on him when the ambulance arrived, and Leo capitalized on that. He attempted to question their credibility but found out once again how difficult it was to convince a jury that police officers are sometimes less than honest.

The next line of questioning by Mickey related to the contents the officers found when conducting an inventory of Staples belongings. One of the officers testified he retrieved a wallet, a set of keys, a cell phone, two dollars and thirty-seven cents, two condoms, a comb and thirteen small packages of marijuana, referred to as nickel bags. Mickey entered the marijuana into evidence as exhibit B.

The victim was dead on the scene but it wasn't official until a doctor at the emergency room examined him. During cross-examination, Leo questioned a testifying officer, asking him if Daniel's fingerprints had been found on the weapon, and he reluctantly answered, "no, only the victim's."

Mickey called one of the arresting officers to the stand who had taken Daniel into custody after he turned himself in. During that line of questioning Mickey kept pressing the fact that Daniel had initially fled the scene of the murder. He asked the officer, "Have you ever had an innocent man flee a crime scene of such a serious nature in your tenure as a police officer?" The officer answered, "No," without hesitation. Leo quickly jumped up and asked the police officer if Daniel had voluntarily turned himself in once he learned that Staples had died from the stab wound. The officer answered, "Yes," and began to finish with his own conclusion when Leo cut him off shouting, "That will be all, Officer Conway."

The next witness for the prosecution was Kerry Windfall, a probation officer to whom Daniel had reported several years back. Mickey was clear in pointing out that Daniel had been convicted of possession of marijuana, and had reported to Windfall at the city probation office for two years. Murphy overruled most of Leo's objections. The judge wanted to hear the whole story and didn't allow any room for speculation.

As the case continued into the second week, Mickey called Arthur Burbough to the witness stand. He testified as a video surveillance and photography expert. Mickey was excited to enter exhibit C into evidence. The altercation had been caught on tape by the ATM camera, and the tape was entered into evidence after it had been projected on a screen for the jury to watch. During the showing of the tape, Burbough stood up and snapped his retractable pointer into full extension like he was a gladiator entering the Coliseum in Rome. He began pointing out the offensive stance Daniel had taken during the confrontation. He repeatedly kept using the word "aggressive," and Mickey was having a parade inside while observing the jury's reaction to Burbough's testimony. During cross-examination, Leo attempted to discredit the observation of Dr. Burbough, stating an automobile obstructed the camera view and the darkness rendered the tape unclear.

To put the icing on the cake, Mickey convinced a local martial arts instructor to testify as an expert witness. His line of questioning was based on his theory that a person trained in the martial arts could subdue a non-trained person without the use of lethal force. He also mentioned twice that Daniel had the option to run away; this seemed to capture the full attention of the jury.

It wasn't long before Mickey was running out of witnesses. Leo had called some character witnesses to the stand to testify on Daniel's behalf. John Carney kept pushing Leo to divulge the long list of crimes committed by Staples, but Leo didn't want the jury to think he was slandering the dead. He took a more subtle approach and it became clear to the jury that Staples was not an altar boy.

After two weeks of testimony, it took the jury less than three hours to return with a verdict. They found Daniel guilty of voluntary manslaughter. Judge Murphy was not pleased with the verdict, but he never openly conveyed his thoughts.

However he made it clear in his sentencing. He sentenced Daniel to a minimum term of eight years at the Commonwealth of Massachusetts correctional facility at Cedar Junction. He would be eligible to petition for parole in five years.

Daniel stood before the judge and listened to the sentencing. He didn't look at the jury, nor did he see the reaction from the prosecutor's table. He just stood with his head lowered looking at the floor, showing no emotion.

Chapter 6

The living room in Beth's apartment was usually well lit, with the sun beaming in and brightening up the room. She had purposely rented an apartment with lots of windows, hoping the sunshine would help brighten up her less than cheerful existence. She needed all the help she could get to forget the dark, gloomy despair that invaded her life. On this day, Beth didn't welcome the sunshine. She sat with the curtains blocking out the world. Her wedding photo album lay next to her on the sofa. A year had passed since Beth and Daniel were married and she sat thinking about how heavenly her wedding day was. They were both so happy and in love. It was all right there in the photographs. It was real. Now Daniel wouldn't even speak to her. Her letters were returned; her calls unanswered. Beth was falling into a state of depression. She knew she had to be strong with the baby growing near full-term, so she continued to find serenity by pounding the pavement. She had kept running to help maintain her sanity, but it was becoming more difficult as she blossomed. The run had changed to a fast walk and eventually a moderate stroll.

Most of her friends tried to support her, but she had passed on invitations to the parties and gatherings. Watching all the happy couples together that she and Daniel used to spend time with was too much to bear. It was just she and the child she carried inside. That was all she had now. Beth began to drift back to the days at Saint Anthony's; the loneliness that plagued her as a child had returned.

Nancy Brown sat in a plane that was descending toward Logan International Airport. It was a direct flight from West Palm Beach and Nancy couldn't wait to feel the earth under her feet. She had a fear of flying and had avoided it her whole life. It was a week earlier that she had called Beth and insisted that she fly up and spend time with her. Beth had told her mother she was fine, but Nancy knew better. After sparring a couple of rounds, Beth threw in the towel and agreed that Nancy could fly up and visit for a few weeks. Beth missed her mother terribly but didn't want to burden her. Nancy had enough of her own heartache, with the loss of Samuel six months earlier. Her husband's heart stopped beating while he slept. It was a peaceful passing, and Nancy had told Beth he had a smile on his face the morning she had found him. Nancy had many friends in Florida and she kept busy playing bridge and shuffleboard. The tennis racket was beginning to weigh heavily on her arm so she retired it to the closet. She kept herself busy in order to keep her mind occupied, but she missed her husband desperately. At night when all the lights were off she lay in bed remembering all the wonderful times they shared. Often her smile would turn into a frown and she would cry herself to sleep.

Beth stood in the baggage claim area waiting for Nancy and her luggage to arrive. In the distance Beth saw her mother approaching. For a brief moment, she was a little girl at St. Anthony's sitting at the base of the statue needing comfort and security, needing a mother.

Chapter 7

Life as Daniel knew it had ended. He knew great troubles lay ahead. The coverage of the trial had been broadcast all over the local news stations and was on the front page of the Boston Globe. Daniel was a white man convicted in the stabbing death of a black man. How could his life have turned around so drastically, so fast, he thought. He missed Beth terribly, but the thought of her having sex with another man tore deep into his core. Daniel was stubborn and tried to put her out of his mind. How could he ever forgive her or face her again. She would be better off getting on with her life anyway, he thought. It would be easier for him to do his time without thinking about her and what she was doing on the outside. He wondered if he was making the right decision. He wasn't sure.

"We're coming up on the Pole now," said the correctional officer driving the prisoner transport van. Daniel was shackled in the back. He couldn't see where they had taken him because there were no windows in the van. The vehicle screeched to a halt and Daniel could hear the driver being cleared through a checkpoint. When the van reached its destination the two officers got out and opened the rear doors. Daniel slowly climbed out observing a whole new world, a world he had never seen. He had no idea how evil this new world would be.

One of the officers muttered, "Welcome to your new home." Daniel just looked at him in disgust.

Cedar Junction housed the worst criminals in Massachusetts. Daniel had overheard two prisoners talking about Cedar Junction while awaiting trial in the county lock-up. What he heard was that it was hell on earth, and without the right protection some inmates never made it out alive.

Daniel wondered if he would be able to make it. He wasn't sure he wanted to. The jury had taken everything from him. He had never really understood the concept of freedom until now. His freedom was a distant memory, and if he were to survive, he would have to forget the past and future. He would take every day as it came and make it through that day, just like Alcoholics Anonymous, one day at a time. If he did that he figured one day he might be able to walk out of prison a free man.

The compound was enormous. It was surrounded by a twenty-foot high wall wrapped with five strands of electrical wire at the top. There were nine observation towers that were manned with armed sentries. The facility was a level six prison that housed over ten thousand inmates and five thousand correctional officers and employees. It was constructed to replicate Alcatraz and there has only been two successful escapes since it opened for operation in South Walpole, Massachusetts in nineteen fifty-five. One thing is for sure, Daniel thought, there was no way out until an inmate completed his sentence. Daniel had finished orientation, was processed and was being ushered to his cell located on the third tier. As he walked down the tier inmates were yelling obscenities at him from their cells. It was lock-down and all prisoners were secured in their cells.

"Hey, white boy, you did the nigger? You a dead man." Daniel just kept walking.

"Hey, faggot! Come suck my dick," shouted another inmate.

"Pretty boy, I like your hair, you can be my bitch until Dog takes you."

When Daniel made it to his cell, he was humiliated, angry and scared at the same time.

"Open twenty-three," the guard commanded.

The bars slid to one side and Daniel entered the cell.

"Close twenty-three."

The sound of the cell door slamming shut was like a gunshot and Daniel had been hit dead on.

"I heard you was coming in today. I was hoping it wasn't true. I was getting used to having my own crib. I'm Hector." He sat up from the top bunk. "What do you call yourself?"

"No offense to you, but I don't want conversation," Daniel said.

"Okay, man." Hector lay back down.

Daniel did the same but he didn't sleep. Hector woke up the next morning to find Daniel sitting on the floor to the right of the toilet with his legs folded, forearms resting on his knees with his middle fingers lightly touching his thumbs. His posture was correct and his eyes were closed.

"Good morning, Grasshopper, were you sitting like that all night?"

"No," Daniel replied, opening his eyes and standing up. "I would not have been able to meditate through all your snoring."

"Is that what you call that, meditation?"

"It's called Chi, a Chinese form of meditation."

"Your into the arts?"

"I've trained a little."

"I hope your good, man, because I think you're going to need it. Word is out that you're marked. The brothers say you killed one of theirs. Between you and me, watch your back. Dog is looking to take you out."

"Yeah, who's Dog?"

"Dog runs the show in here. He's a bad dude, did three on the outside that they know of and one in here."

"Sounds like a real nice guy."

"When he comes at you he'll come with help. He has a posse in here, man."

"Why are you telling me all this? You don't even know me."

"Dog carved up my amigo Juan two years ago. He got paroled four months ago but still has serious stomach problems."

"Did they discipline him for the stabbing?"

"Discipline, Dog doesn't get disciplined. He has most screws in his pocket. Money talks and bullshit gets squashed in here."

"What does he look like?"

"You'll know him when you see him. He looks like Mike Tyson with a big-ass nose ring. The dude is crazy and a racist."

"What are you doing in here, Hector?"

"Armed robbery, man. I was the driver in a bank heist. Got a nickel for it. I have a year and a half to go. What about you, man, how much time did you buy?"

"Eight years."

"What happened?"

"I don't want to talk about it."

"Okay, man, it's almost chow time anyway and I'm hungry. You're going to love the food in here, man. Just like Mama's home cooking."

A few minutes later the guards sounded out that it was breakfast time. They started with the first tier and worked their way up to the third. The block consisted of three tiers on both sides of the main hall. Each tier had fifteen cells.

"Stand clear, opening three," the guard announced.

The doors all slid open simultaneously. Daniel followed Hector out of the cell and stood next to him.

"Turn left," the guard barked as if it were programmed in his brain.

As they walked down the tier in single file, Daniel glanced down to the lobby floor. It was about thirty-feet down and there were several guards looking up at them. Daniel wondered how many inmates had taken the fast way down. It was a short walk to the chow hall and Daniel's stomach was growling all the way. He had not been eating well in the past several months and had lost fifteen pounds. He was hungry yet nauseated at the same time. As they filed into the mess hall, Daniel was amazed by the size of the room. It was huge, he thought. There were guards standing along the walls at both ends of the mess line. A guard armed with tear gas stood in watch in a tower that reached high up to the ceiling. Most of the inmates had dark skin and many of the guards as well. Daniel felt out of place and all alone.

"Eggs and grits," Hector blurted out.

An overweight black dude wearing a chief's toque drenched in sweat plopped a couple of spoonfuls on his plate and he moved on to pick up a bagel. Daniel looked at the eggs and kept walking. He decided to go with two boxes of Cheerios, a bagel and a banana. The utensils and plates were made of plastic for safety purposes. As they walked toward the tables, Hector turned to Daniel, looking somewhat embarrassed and said, "Find a spot man, you can't sit with me."

Hector went off and sat with several Hispanic inmates. Daniel looked around and located a table with two guys eating as if it were their last meal. He sat down and they both immediately got up and moved to another table. Daniel knew something was wrong. He had very good intuition, and more importantly, excellent peripheral vision.

"How old is your daughter?"

"She's eight. Last time I held her she was five. She's going to be a vet, she loves animals."

"What's her name?" Daniel asked as he flushed the toilet.

"Maria," Hector said, while sitting on his bunk sketching a landscape.

"Do you have any kids?"

"No"

"Kids are the best, man. When I was a kid I never had any real holidays. One gift at Christmas, that was about it. After Maria was born I was able to re-live all the holidays through her eyes. It gave me real happiness to see those holidays I missed as a child. She is so beautiful. I miss holding her and the way she smells. I could just sit and watch her play all day long. I miss her smile and the way she laughs. Her mother takes her to visit once a month. Man, I live for those visits. They only live an hour away and that bitch will only make the drive once a month. I know it's because Maria hounds her, otherwise she wouldn't come at all. She's too busy fucking Renaldo, my best friend, if you can believe that. When I get out of here I'm going to move in right next-door so I can spend all my free time with her. She is going to know her father. Not like me, I never knew my father. Even when he was around I was just a burden to him, always in his way. The only time he showed any emotion toward me was when he was yelling at me."

"So how long have you been drawing?" Daniel asked.

"Since I was a kid. It keeps my mind off this place. This is where I want to take Maria to live with me one day. It's a village in Puerto Rico right on the water, called Salinas. My grandmother took me there once when I was eight." He handed Daniel the sketching pad. It was good work, Daniel thought. It was a colored drawing of a cottage surrounded by palm trees, and an old sailboat resting on a beach.

"I'd give my right arm to be there right now," Daniel said. "You are talented."

"You think so, amigo?"

"Absolutely."

Hector knew he was right. The walls of his cell were covered with drawings of Maria from when she was a baby until the present. There were drawings of automobiles, boats and landscapes.

"I believe everyone has a God-given gift of their own. Everyone has a gift. Some people choose to take advantage of it and others ignore it, but it's there," Daniel said.

Hector just sat, deep in thought, nodding his head in agreement.

Lunch was not much different than breakfast. Daniel sat alone and picked at a greasy grilled cheese sandwich, which was left on the grill much longer than its life expectancy. He accepted the reality that his only friend in prison was his cellmate, but the only time he could enjoy his company was in their cell. In the yard he would be all alone again.

The yard was a wide-open arena of activity and Daniel was delighted to be outside. There were prisoners playing basketball, weight training, punching a heavy bag, running around a mock track and just gathering together playing games and talking. Daniel was stretching when a guy came strolling over from a group of fourteen skinheads that were lifting weights. They looked like a Yul Brynner fan club, Daniel thought.

"Sally, get your hair cut and you can hang with us," the bald-headed guy said. "We will watch your back. As you can see we are outnumbered in here so we need to stick together. Without protection, the niggers and spics will cut your heart out in here."

"Thanks, but I can take care of myself." Daniel was stretching his legs.

"You think so? Numbers, they come at you in numbers. Doesn't matter how tough you are. They will wear you down."

"I'll take my chances. Besides, I look awful without hair."

"Good luck then. When you change your mind, the name is Shoe."

He walked away and Daniel headed toward the heavy bag, which just became free. Daniel pounded the bag like smooth flashes of lightning and loud cracklings of thunder. He moved around the bag as if it were a dance partner, jabbing, straight cross punches, and hooks, which came from the earth. He was fast and hit hard. The combinations came in groups of three to six without flaw. He began to draw the attention of the inmates in the yard, and one in particular, who was watching him very closely.

Tyrone Spence was an evil man filled with hate. He grew up in Roxbury, Massachusetts and fought his way to the top of the gang chain. His first murder was at age twelve when he shot a neighborhood boy on a dare because he was outplayed on a basketball court. He walked up to the kid, who was a year younger, and put the gun against his throat and pulled the trigger severing his spinal chord. Tyrone was infatuated with the power and control he had realized that day while watching his victim fall to the ground clutching onto his neck in an attempt to stop the blood from spurting out. With his first victim's life ending, a new one began, a life with a thirst that could only be quenched by the spilling of blood. As his prey fell, he became stronger and widely feared. He had no compassion, no remorse, just hatred and a desire for control, power and blood. He was an animal that would not give up until he hunted his prey and took their life. This earned him the name Dog.

Daniel punched and kicked the heavy bag until he was exhausted. When he was finished, it felt as if a hundred pounds had fallen off his shoulders. This was the first time he had been able to take out all his frustrations since his arrest. For Daniel, it was therapy, and he was off to a good start.

While walking past the bleachers, Daniel noticed a very large black man playing chess and he stopped.

"Mind if I challenge the winner?" Daniel asked.

"What do I have to gain by playing you?" The large man responded.

"Knowledge about the game. Besides, how are you so sure you'll be the winner?"

"I haven't lost a game since I've been here," he said with pride as he stared into Daniel's eyes without blinking.

"So, you're going to teach the Master how to play chess?" asked the man playing with him.

"Did I ask you to be my spokesman?" Master asked.

"No." His opponent responded.

"Then shut the fuck up."

"So you're going to teach me how to play chess?" Master said with his hand on his chin.

"Maybe we can both learn something from each other," Daniel said.

"One game?"

"One game," Daniel said. "Black or white?"

The con quickly got up and hurried off.

"I always play black," Master said.

Daniel played the master for the next three days after he finished working the heavy bag and running. Every game ended up with Master in checkmate. On the Fourth day, Master didn't show up so Daniel decided to lift some weights. He was lying on the flat bench pushing up a barbell. As he lowered the bar, Dog appeared behind him and he wasn't there to spot him. Dog reached down, grabbed the bar and rolled it up to Daniel's throat while pushing down.

"You like to kill niggas? Try killin this nigga, mother fucker."

He pushed harder and Daniel began choking.

"Kill his ass, Dog," Bitch said, a tall, lean, muscular, light-skinned man wearing an orange jumpsuit with a number on the left chest and back, like the rest of the inmates at Cedar Junction. Bitch followed Dog around the cellblock yard kissing his ass at every chance. Whenever you saw Dog, Bitch was with him. That's how he earned the nickname Bitch. There were rumors of homosexual relations between them, but the talk was kept to a low whisper.

Still holding onto the bar, Daniel was pushing up while Dog was leaning over, pushing down with his weight on the bar. In a desperate attempt, Daniel pushed his feet off the ground and rocked his weight backward in a sudden upward motion putting both knees into Dog's face, fracturing his nose. Pushing the bar up enough to slide his head under, Daniel got back on his feet as Dog was getting up. Daniel reacted as another attacker threw a right-handed sucker punch at him from the right. It was as though his attackers were moving in slow motion.

Daniel was able to tell when an attacker was going to strike by the initial flinch of the shoulder or weight shift of the lower body. Daniel buried a side thrust kick into his solar plexus before the punch found its mark. With a snapping sound, his heel felt like it had penetrated bone and the attacker buckled over holding his mid-section. With both hands on the back of the guy's head, Daniel thrusted his knee upward finding his attackers mouth and knocking out his two front teeth.

Daniel's footwork was so smooth, it was like he was gliding along the ground, sidestepping his opponent and striking before his foe realized what had occurred. As his attacker fell to the ground, Daniel blocked a right-handed hook punch from Dog with his left arm. Then, with the precision of a cat, he grabbed Dog's nose ring with his right index finger and ripped it out. Dog began to scream in anger and charged Daniel, getting him into a bear hug. He picked Daniel up off the ground and buried his teeth into Daniel's throat. With both hands cupped, Daniel simultaneously struck Dog's ears, causing a suction that ruptured one eardrum and injured the other. Dog immediately dropped Daniel holding onto his left ear. With a fierce front snap kick, Daniel found Dog's groin, followed by a three-punch combination fracturing Dog's cheekbone. From behind, Bitch punched Daniel in the back of the head. Daniel spun around like a whirlwind, delivering a shuto knife-hand chop to Bitch's throat, crushing his esophagus. Bitch fell to the ground choking on his own blood. As Daniel turned to face another attacker he was struck on the head with a twenty-pound dumbbell that was thrown at him from a coward, too afraid to confront him. Daniel could hear the guards coming as he fell to his knees. He could not maintain consciousness and the daylight faded.

Chapter 8

Daniel began training in the martial arts while living with his father in South Korea. After being in the country for a few weeks, Daniel had met Kim Yung He. In the few short years he lived there, they would become the best of friends. Daniel was thirteen and Kim was a year older when they met in Munson on a very hot summer day. In Korea summers are scorching hot and the winters are extremely cold. Daniel was curiously strolling along the streets of the village attempting to understand their culture. Most people traveled on foot and some were riding around on bicycles. The majority of motor vehicles on the street were taxicabs, and the drivers made New York City's cab drivers look responsible. The streets were paths consisting of gravel and dirt, and the hooches where they lived looked as if they were made of hardened clay. The village was crowded and entertaining; women carried laundry and oversized bowls on their heads while hurrying along to do their chores. There were groups of men gathered together on the street corners, just squatting there with cigarettes hanging from their mouths, chatting away. Daniel wondered, if he had a chair to offer, would they accept. Along came the outhouse man pushing a cart of feces he had collected, going from hooch to hooch. There were no plumbing or kitchen appliances in the village. The hooches consisted of one-room flats with makeshift beds on the floor. Each little complex housed three to five apartments, and the occupants shared a common area with an outhouse and well for drinking water, bathing and laundry. There was usually one television per complex and they would all gather together at night and tune into one of two channels that offered a decent signal. The constant stench of manure lingered from the rice paddies and into the village. In the marketplace whole chickens and dogs hung in the windows by their legs, gutted and headless. It was a primitive place. Daniel found it interesting, yet sad.

It came without warning, and out of nowhere. Daniel felt the sharp and painful blunt trauma of a four-inch rock as it struck him on the right side of his head. He managed to remain standing but knew he had been hit hard. There was a painful ringing in his head and he could feel the blood pouring down the back of his neck. Although he was disoriented, he knew it wasn't an accident. A moment later he took a blow to the stomach, which buckled him over. Two Korean boys had attacked him and thrown him up against the wall. The only words in English he could understand were, "Yankee" and "money." Daniel held onto his pocket, clutching the few dollars he had as they kicked and punched him in an attempted robbery. It was then that a struggle ensued with a stranger and the two boys. He looked up and saw a younger Korean boy kick one of his attackers in the face with a roundhouse kick followed by a spinning back kick to the mid-section. As the boy bent over from the kick, he was finished off with a cross elbow strike to the nose. The other boy didn't wait around to see the outcome. He was gone in an instant.

The boy helped Daniel to the nearest market where he asked for a towel and offered it to Daniel. As they walked down the village street Daniel felt battered but safe. He held the towel hard against his head and could feel the bump growing under his trembling fingers.

"I am Kim Yung He, call me Kim," said his new friend.

"My name is Daniel," he responded. "Call me Daniel."

"Where did you learn to fight like that?"

"I learned from Sa Bum Nim Park, Master of Hapkido. Would you like to meet him?"

"Yes, yes I would. Where did you learn to speak English?"

"I learned from my uncle. He lived stateside for five years, New York City."

"What type of karate do you practice?"

"It's not karate. Karate originated in Japan. It is called hapkido. It's better than karate."

"What is so different about hapkido that makes it better than karate?" Daniel asked.

"Hapkido has the kicks, strikes and blocks of tae kwon do and also the fluid, smooth motion of aikido," Kim said proudly, with his chin held high. "It has side-stepping and sweeping movements. It also offers joint manipulation and weapons defense techniques. It is a well-rounded form of martial art totally geared toward self defense."

Daniel was impressed by Kim's ability, confidence and dedication. Kim had earned a black belt just one month earlier and wore it with undeniable pride.

Daniel started training in martial arts the next day with Master Park, and he continued training hard for the next three years in hapkido. With Kim as his mentor Daniel learned fast. He was a natural. He would leave Korea with a first degree black belt in hapkido and it would only be the beginning of a life dedicated to the martial arts.

Master Park stood five feet seven and weighed one hundred sixty pounds. He was the son of a fisherman, who began his training thirty-three years earlier with the founder of hapkido Choi Yong Sool. Park was solid as a rock and lightning fast. He was a former Republic of Korea (ROK) Special Forces soldier who had instructed the elite unit during the Vietnam conflict in the ways of hand-to-hand combat. Park had survived two tours in Vietnam and had received a medal of valor equivalent to that of the U.S. Silver Star. He was a soft-spoken man who quietly battled the demons of his past. It wasn't until Daniel attended a seminar in Pusan that he realized how good Park really was. He was a true master. Daniel watched in awe as Park ran and jumped over a standing man's head in a flying sidekick motion. His knife defense techniques were fast and precise. Three attackers with knives lunged at Park from different angles as Park disarmed them and finished them so fast that Daniel could barely comprehend what had taken place. It was done with smooth, fluid technique and excellent timing and form, and more importantly, without injuring anyone. Daniel learned to respect and love Master Park like a father. He trained three to four hours a day, six days a week at the school, and on Sundays, Daniel would go up to the mountain with Kim to spar and practice Chi. They were some of the best years of his life. They were the most peaceful.

Chapter 9

▼

"Doctor is running about twenty minutes behind. She'll be with you shortly," said the receptionist.

"That's fine," Beth said as she flipped through a Cosmopolitan magazine. She started to read an article about love lost and found, and wondered, would she ever find true love again and if she did, would it be with Daniel or another?

"Beth, Dr. Kowalski will see you now."

Beth struggled to get on her feet while pushing up on the armrests of the chair as if she were doing dips at the gym. She made it to her feet, maintaining her balance as she started toward the door. She was ushered to an examination room where the nurse took her temperature, checked her blood pressure and timed her pulse. She was asked to disrobe and put on a gown. Beth changed and began perusing Dr. Kowalski's graduate school certificate that was so proudly displayed on the wall. Harvard Medical School, she must be good, Beth thought.

"You must be Beth," said the doctor as she entered the room. "Nice to meet you."

"Nice to meet you as well, Doctor."

"Sorry to hear about Doctor Harris. I never met him but I understand he was an archive." The doctor said.

"Yes, it was very tragic and sudden."

"Heart attack?" The doctor asked.

"Yes, he died on the golf course. He was very old." Beth responded.

"Well, I don't play golf, so hopefully I'll be here to see you through your full term," the woman said with a slight smile.

She was thirty-five years of age but could pass for thirty. Her dark hair was pinned tight to her head and she wore glasses that seemed to barely cover her eyes. She was thin and stood a couple of inches shorter than Beth.

"When did you last see Dr. Harris?"

"Two weeks ago."

"When was the last internal exam?"

"Oh, that was a while ago," Beth said. "Maybe four or five months."

Dr. Kowalski looked up in surprise as she began the internal examination.

"He pretty much asked me how I felt and did external exams. He asked me if I was feeling any real pain and if I was taking my vitamins. I have felt fine, actually stronger than a few months ago."

"Something seems unusual," the doctor concluded. "How long have you been married?"

"Thirteen months," Beth responded with a look of concern.

"Have you been having regular intercourse?"

"No," Beth was feeling uneasy.

"When was the last time? I know these questions are hard, but as your doctor I need to know certain things and this is one of them."

"Actually, my husband and I are separated and we have not had sex in quite some time."

"I'm sorry to hear that, Beth. When was the last time?"

"Eight months ago."

"You are eight months along in your pregnancy," the doctor said. "So this little person was the result of that?"

"Yes."

"Before that, did you have regular intercourse?"

"Are these questions necessary?" Beth was getting agitated.

"It appears that your hymen has not been ruptured."

"What?" Beth looked her straight in the eye.

"When did you lose your virginity?"

"After I was married."

"You were only married four months before you got pregnant?"

"Five. Where are you going with this Doctor?"

"This is very unusual." The doctor was baffled. "This is the first time I have examined a pregnant patient with her hymen intact."

"Daniel was very gentle with me. Most of our sex was touching and oral copulation. It hurt me to have intercourse. He was very understanding. When we did have intercourse, it was very gentle and easy. Is it possible to become pregnant without having your hymen broken?"

"It is possible, but extremely rare. Let's have some pictures of the baby taken tomorrow," Doctor Kowalski suggested.

"Have you found out the gender?" Kowalski asked.

"No, I want it to be a surprise."

"I want to see you next week. You can get dressed." The doctor patted Beth on the shoulder and moved on to her next patient. She would make time that night to conduct statistical research on the probability of pregnancy occurring with a woman who has a non-ruptured hymen.

Beth left the doctor's office and went directly to her church. Beth felt safe there and found that time spent in the pews gave her a feeling of hope and peace. During her lifetime, Beth had experienced several divine visions at night. While lying in bed looking toward her bedroom window, the light peaking through the window had brought colorful visions of angels and the Virgin Mary. Beth wasn't sure if she was dreaming or if they were messages sent from the heavens. They seemed to come during times of great despair. As time passed she realized they were not dreams. There had been so many signs, and too many occurrences that had enlightened her. Some people believe in God. Beth knew in her heart the truth about His existence, but had always kept it to herself. She believed that signs from God are there for many people to see, but most people write them off as coincidences or choose to ignore them. Who would believe her? She would be deemed a liar or insane. Beth knew better and accepted this as her secret, her gift.

Chapter 10

"Welcome back, man, glad to see you made it out alive." Hector was drawing as Daniel was escorted back to his cell.

"Good to be home," Daniel said sarcastically.

"You are the man in this joint, everybody is talking about you. You're a star."

"Why is that, because I took a dumbbell on the melon and can still eat without a bib?"

"You kicked Dog's ass. What really pissed him off was that you took half his nose off and he lost his ring. He looks like shit. He spent three days in the hospital, and Bitch still hasn't come out. I hear he had surgery on his throat. And the other brother has a ruptured spleen; he's rooming with Bitch. I didn't see it, but I heard you kicked ass. Most everyone was happy to see Dog get dusted. Too bad you didn't kill that pendejo. How are you feeling?"

"I'm okay, had a concussion. Took a few stitches where he bit me."

"Be careful man, Dog has vowed to kill you."

"Thanks, Hector, I will." Daniel said, as he patted him on the shoulder.

As Daniel walked into the yard many inmates were grinning at him. He received a thumbs up from one guy and a high five from another.

"Nice going, bro," said a black inmate as he walked past.

"Can I hold the bag for you while you hit it?" asked another.

"No thanks, I like it to swing natural."

Daniel hit the bag for a while, but started to get a headache, so he decided to stop. He walked over where Master was playing a game of chess.

"This game is over," Master said to his opponent. Without hesitation, the man got up and walked away.

"Take a seat." Master gestured to the bench and Daniel sat down. "Black or white?"

"I thought you always played black?" Daniel said.

"I always do, but maybe I should change up with you. It might change my luck."

"I'll take white," Daniel said.

It wasn't long before Daniel had trapped Master with his queen and two horses.

"Where did you learn to play like that?" Master was agitated.

"My father taught me. He was an excellent strategist. Anyway, it was a game he could play without interrupting his drinking."

"My pop was taken by the bottle, too. He was a good man when he was straight. Problem was he was hardly ever straight. The only time he ever showed he cared was when he was drunk. I think that was the only time he had the courage to show his feelings. He didn't say much at all when he was sober."

"I guess we have something in common besides chess," Daniel said. "Can I ask you something?"

"Yeah."

"What is your real name?"

Master hesitated, and then responded. "Harold Carter, but don't you tell anyone that."

"Alright, mum's the word," Daniel said with a nod of his head.

Master was an unusually large man who stood six feet, seven inches tall. He weighed in at two hundred eighty-nine pounds of solid muscle. He had a scar across his forehead and the sun beamed off his glowing head like a smooth rock protruding from the ocean sand. He had received a life sentence for killing a Pastor who headed the county church in a small town in Mississippi where he was a member. Although Master was reluctant, he eventually agreed to do his time out of state for his own safety. Pastor Phillips was a pedophile that Master surprised while molesting a ten year old boy in the recreation room one Saturday evening. Master strangled the evil out of him until he lay lifeless on the floor. Pastor Phillips had deep connections with the prosecuting attorney, who pushed for the maximum penalty after receiving the case. They had gone hunting together every year and all the secrets that Pastor had learned from his parishioners would spill out over brandy by the lodge fire. He would tell the prosecutor how Mrs. Campbell was having an affair with Mr. Schultz, and how Joshua Urlick was the one who broke into the hardware store and stole several fishing poles and hunting gear. He divulged to the prosecutor the person responsible for bringing into town the marijuana that the kids were smoking. Violating his pastor-parishioner privilege came easy to Pastor Phillips. He was a man who lacked moral integrity.

"One day I will beat you," Master insisted.

"I hope you do," Daniel said.

Daniel walked away and Master gestured to a short stocky Asian inmate standing by the wall. The convict came over in a real hurry.

"What is it, Master?"

"Find Dog and tell him I want to see him."

A few minutes later Dog came strolling over with three of his boys. Master was sitting, staring at the board, and pondering how he was taken so quickly.

"You wanted to see me?" Dog Asked.

"I hear you're fixing to ice Daniel?"

"What? I can't hear so good, that mother fucker popped out my drums."

"I said I hear you are going to kill him." Master raised his tone.

"That's right, look at my nose, man. White boy put the Bitch in the hospital too."

"I don't want him touched." Master demanded.

"What, you protecting that white punk?"

"Since I've been in here I have never lost a game of chess. He came along and beat me four games straight. I don't like losing." Master said.

"So that's more reason I should off his ass," Dog muttered.

"No, I'm going to beat him. You leave him be, or you won't have a nose at all. Do I make myself clear?"

"This is bullshit, man. You call yourself a brother?"

Master stood up and slowly walked up to Dog, quickly reaching out, grabbing him by the throat, and choking him.

"Understand this, you ain't my brother. You're a piece of shit. If you or any of your punks lay a hand on him, I'll fucking kill you."

Master pushed Dog away as he released his throat.

"Alright man, but once you beat his ass in chess, he's mine, and I'll be watching the games real close. Let's get outta here man."

Dog and his posse walked away and Master sat back down to his board.

"What do you think of this sketch?" Hector asked, handing it to Daniel. "I drew it while you were in the hospital."

"Very nice."

It was an animated fight scene with Daniel tearing out Dog's nose ring and a couple guys lying in puddles of blood at Daniel's feet.

"Are my arms really that big?" Daniel asked with a slight smile and a flex of the bicep.

"Not really, but I need to make it look real fantastic like."

Daniel chuckled and lay back onto his bed.

"You asked me what really happened the night I killed Staples?"

"Yeah," he had Hector's full attention.

"I was going to the ATM to get some cash, when he approached me with a knife. I had just taken out a hundred bucks and he said he was going to stab me if I didn't give him the money. I told him to get out of my face or he was going to get hurt. He took a swipe at me and almost cut my chest. That's when I knew he was serious. So I told him if he wanted the money he was going to have to take it. Just then he lunged forward toward my stomach. I grabbed his wrist and forearm, ducked my head under his arm as I swung around in a circular motion and the knife ended up in his stomach. Apparently it entered his liver and he died on the scene.

"That was self-defense, man."

"That's not the way the jury saw it. The DA, who had political ambitions, turned the whole story around and the jury bought it. Assistant District Attorney Mike Alberto, the scum of the earth. He entered the tape from the ATM camera into evidence and the angle was not very favorable for me. Apparently Staples had several packets of pot packaged for sale in his pocket. Six years ago I was arrested for possession of marijuana and he turned it into a drug deal gone sour. He also played the martial arts card, stating that I was an expert and could have overcome Staples easily without the use of deadly force, or simply run away. With all that he was able to get the jury to convict. He had picked the right jury and I didn't see it coming."

"You got railroaded, man."

"Yeah I did." Daniel had a sad expression on his face. It wasn't self-pity but a gut-wrenching disappointment in the system.

"Do you think you could have gone easier on the dude or maybe ran away?"

Daniel sat up in bed and looked at Hector without blinking an eye. "When a man pulls out a knife and tries to take something from you, he better be ready to die."

Hector didn't say a word. He just lay there thinking about what Daniel had said. He was in agreement.

Chapter 11

▼

Beth glanced over at the clock. It was 11:30 PM. She put down her book and with the aid of the chair arms pushed herself onto her feet. She figured she was either getting weaker or heavier; she knew it was the latter of the two. A warm, wet feeling came over her and she looked down to find her nightgown soaking wet. Her first thought was to clean the small puddle on the floor and then she quickly came to her senses and realized what had occurred. She felt frightened and excited at the same time. Making her way to the guest room where her mother was staying, she knocked on the door and in a calm voice began speaking.

"Mom, my water just broke."

"Are you sure honey?" Nancy bounced out of her bed like a marine recruit in boot camp giving her full attention.

"Yes, I'll be ready to go in a few minutes."

She cleaned up in the bathroom, brushed her teeth and changed. Her hospital bag had been packed for weeks and was sitting in the closet full of everything she would need for the next three days. Beth had read so many books on pregnancy, childbirth and child-raising that she felt she was nearly an expert on the subject. She had picked out some names for the baby but wasn't sure on a boy's name. If it were a girl, she would name her Victoria.

The baby arrived at 3:34 AM that morning. Beth lay in the hospital bed with her new son in her arms. He was beautiful and weighed in at 8 pounds 2 ounces. Once Beth saw him, she knew his name.

"Justin, meet your grandmother. Do you want to hold him?" Beth asked.

"Of course I do."

Nancy took Justin into her arms and was overwhelmed with a sense of joy. Beth could see it and they both began to cry.

"He has your eyes. Well hello there, little Justin. You're such a handsome little guy."

Beth was smiling ear to ear. And though she was delighted to see her son alive and healthy, tears were rolling down her cheeks. Daniel wasn't there with her to see the miracle that had just happened. He wasn't there to welcome his new son into the world. Beth was thankful her mother was with her, but it just wasn't the same. She still loved Daniel and she missed him terribly.

Nancy stayed for a month to help Beth get settled with Justin. She helped Beth paint his room sky blue and they hung colorful kites on the walls and ceilings. The time they shared together was special for both of them. They were able to catch up on everything that had happened in their lives since Nancy moved to Florida. Nancy asked Beth to consider moving to Florida so they could be closer to each other, but Beth declined, stating she wanted to raise Justin in New England, so he could grow up with four seasons. Beth was so grateful her mother was there with her. Justin slept most of the time, which allowed for long walks and conversations. This was a time Beth would treasure forever. She had missed her mother's company and always kept her close in her heart. Every night she said a special prayer for her mother asking God to keep her healthy and happy. Nancy was a unique and special woman and Beth felt she was the luckiest daughter in the world.

"Beth, dear, have a seat, your eggs are done."

Beth took her place at the kitchen table.

"I need to get a plant for the kitchen." Beth said.

"Why don't we do that today? It will be a gift from me for the new member of our family."

"That sounds like a plan, but you don't have to buy it. You need to watch you're spending. You could live for another twenty years and who knows if social security benefits will still be available by then. The way our government spends money we may both be living under a bridge in our retirement."

"I think I can swing a few bucks for a plant. Honey, when are you going to tell Daniel about Justin?"

"I called the prison a few days ago and asked the lady in inmate affairs to give Daniel a message that we had a healthy baby boy and we are both fine. He still refuses to take my calls or letters so that's all I could do. I just want him to know he has a son and his name is Justin."

"He still refuses to take responsibility?" Nancy asked.

"Yes, he doesn't believe the baby is his. He keeps going on about his childhood accident and is convinced that Justin isn't his child."

"I think he's living in denial, honey, and he needs to take responsibility. I think it's time to take this to court. Maybe after he gets a DNA match from his and Justin's blood, he will wake up and admit Justin is his son."

"I don't know, mom, maybe I should try and forget him and move on with my life. I am so angry with him for the way he is behaving. How could he ever think I would cheat on him?"

"Give it some time, Beth, maybe he will come around," Nancy said, putting a positive spin on it.

"Maybe you're right, mom."

"Have a court order for a blood test and hopefully that will get him back on track."

"I'll call the lawyer tomorrow and get advice on what steps to take to get a court order for a blood sample."

"So, are you ready to continue teaching after the holiday break?"

"Yes, I spoke with Tom Reynolds last week and they are looking forward to seeing me back at work. They have been so understanding and patient. It will be good to get back in the classroom again."

"Is everything all set with daycare?"

"Yes, I'm a little nervous about leaving Justin all day, but they all seem really nice and they appear to be responsible. They should be, for what they charge."

"What does daycare cost these days?"

"Two hundred dollars a week while he is in diapers."

"Wow, they really don't like changing diapers today, do they?"

"Mom, how are you coping with the loss of dad?"

"I miss him every day. He was my best friend for thirty-six years. He was the kindest man I have ever known. I often wonder why the good people are taken so early in life."

"I think God takes people when their work on earth is done," Beth said.

"I suppose you're right. I believe everything has been written and we are all destined to do what we will in our lives before our time is up. And the more good we do the more God rewards us in life. It is the selfless thoughts and the good deeds that we do for others that give us the most joy in life. As we continue to live this way throughout our lives, God rewards us ten-fold."

"I guess you're right, but sometimes it's hard to see the sunshine through the clouds," Beth said.

"It doesn't always happen right away, but it will when the time is right. When you need Him the most He will be there for you. Never stop believing and always keep the faith." Nancy offered.

Beth got up and embraced her mother. "I love you so much, mom."

"I love you too, honey. Do you want me to move up here and live with you and Justin? I can help take care of him."

"It's too cold up here for you. Your arthritis is bad enough without dealing with the New England winters. I appreciate the offer though."

"All right, but I really think you could use the help." Nancy was shaking her head side to side. "Two hundred dollars a week."

Chapter 12

"Bitch, how's your throat, and shit?"

Dog gathered Bitch and a few of his cronies together in the yard.

"It fucking hurts" he mumbled.

"What?" Dog asked.

"Man, between his fucked up throat and your fucked up ears, you two better forget about trying to communicate by talking. Write that shit down on paper or something," Carl said.

A few of the inmates started laughing and Dog snapped and grabbed Carl by the shirt with one hand and started punching him in the face with the other.

"Easy, Dog! he was only joking," Simms said, a tall, skinny, dark skinned man with a recurring stammer. He had a huge flat nose and a seventies style afro. He could easily pass as a Jackson family member.

"I aint in the mood for no mother-fucking jokes," Dog backed off. "That Uncle Tom punk, Master, told me not to fuck with white boy."

"I don't mean to disrespect you, Dog, but why do you have it in for that boy so hard?" Simms was stuttering.

"The brother he took out was a homeboy from Roxbury. My homey Leon did time with him in Gardner. Said he was an okay brother. So he went and stabbed my homeboy, that's why. Any more mother-fucking questions?"

"So what are we going to do?" Simms asked. "If Master says not to touch him, we can't touch him. You don't want to fuck with Master. He has most screws in his corner, bro."

"Maybe I'll take that big bitch out then. I'll think of something," Dog said, as he rubbed where his nose ring used to hang.

Daniel took his seat across from Master and the game began. It was hot out and Daniel had just finished pounding the bag and was still sweating. Master never asked Daniel any questions about why he was locked up or when he would get out, and Daniel respected that. He never asked Master any questions, either. Their relationship was based on the game and mutual respect for another human being who had been sentenced to a life of seclusion and despair. Daniel enjoyed his time sitting across the board from Master. It was a time free from all his troubles. Free from the thought of how badly life had turned out for him. He temporarily forgot about Staples, Alberto, and his murder conviction. For a short time, while tactically plotting his strategy, he didn't think about how he had lost Beth, or the child she had given birth to. He only concentrated on the game. The game had gone on longer than normal and Master was determined to prevail.

"Check." Daniel moved his king.

"Check." Daniel moved his bishop to block Master's queen.

"Checkmate." Master trapped the king with his horse.

"Well, you finally beat me," Daniel said.

"I got lucky." Master managed a slight smile.

"No you didn't, you outplayed me."

"Listen," Master said. "I don't want anyone to know about this."

"About what?"

"That I beat you, okay? This is between me and you."

"Okay, if that's what you want."

"That's what I want. Don't tell anyone I beat you."

"You got it. Good game." Daniel reached over and they shook hands.

Three days passed and Daniel was reading in his cell when Hector came in from his job, making license plates.

"How was your day at work?"

"It sucked, like always. I work my ass off for fifty cents an hour, man."

"Well at least it keeps you busy. I may look into working myself."

"Yeah, you should. It ain't that bad, man," Hector said. Daniel laughed.

"I got called into the hospital today. I was ordered by the court to give blood for a DNA test."

"Why?" Hector asked, as he took off his boots.

"My wife had a baby and she say's it's mine. But I'm sure it isn't."

"Are you sure it's not yours? How do you know?"

"I can't have children. I had an accident when I was a kid."

"What kind of accident?"

"I suffered a severe laceration and rupture after falling off a roof and landing on a picket fence."

"Damn! that must have hurt like a bitch!"

"I have definitely felt better."

"So, she was stepping out on you?"

"Yeah, she must have been."

"Is there a chance the doctors were wrong? They might have made a mistake, man."

"I had it checked out when I was nineteen and it was confirmed then."

"Sorry to hear that man. Is it a girl?"

"No, boy."

"Well, the DNA will prove that it's not yours, right?"

"Right."

"She hurt you bad, didn't she?"

"It cuts deep. It's the worst kind of pain. Physical pain is much easier to take, if you know what I mean."

"You still love her, don't you?"

Daniel didn't answer. He rolled over on his side clutching his pillow, pulling it close to his head and closing his eyes.

Chapter 13

It had been raining for five days straight. The air was growing warm and the days long. Soon the flowers would be blooming and the birds would be singing in full chorus. Nancy had flown back to Florida and Beth was feeling lonely again. She had not seen her friends very often over the past year. With Daniel in prison and refusing to see her, she wouldn't know how to explain to them everything that had happened and she didn't want to. She was glad to be teaching again, but was looking forward to summer vacation so she could enjoy more time with Justin. Beth loved teaching world history and she was very good at it. After school she allowed time for an hour run before she picked up Justin. This was her time alone to vent, to forget. It was her private sanctuary.

Justin was the light of her life. He brought her so much joy. She never realized she could love someone so much until he came into her life. Beth would sing to him at night and he would lie there listening, while staring up at her lips. It was as if he knew the song. Every day she would have conversations with him and at times he would respond in baby talk. She loved to hear his little voice. It helped her to forget the past.

Beth and Nancy talked on the phone at least three times a week. Nancy kept asking if she wanted her to come up to stay, but Beth declined, not wanting to impose on her. All of Nancy's friends were in Florida, and Beth knew it would be difficult for her to watch Justin day in and day out. She was retired and this was her time to enjoy life.

Raising a baby alone and working full-time had been a lot for Beth to handle. She kept telling herself, "The days are long but the years are short." This helped her to cope. She knew she didn't have a choice, so she tried to be positive and maintain strong faith.

It was Thursday night. Beth had put Justin down and she finally got to her mail. She looked at the letter from the court and immediately knew what it was. She sat down just staring at the envelope for a moment. Beth opened it to find the result. As she read, her hands began to tremble and she had an awful feeling in the pit of her stomach that moved up to her heart and spread throughout her whole body. Daniel and Justin's DNA was not a match. Beth started to cry hysterically. She threw the document on the floor and fell back onto the sofa. She would call them in the morning and have them do another test. How they could make such a terrible mistake, she wondered. How could they be so incompetent?

It was three AM when Beth woke up to a beautiful light that beamed through her window from the outside. The colors were magnificent. There was a beautiful woman holding a baby in her arms. Beth knew it was the Virgin Mary. It was so clear. It was real. She just stared at the window. Beth didn't ever want that moment to end. She was at peace like she had never been before. She was safe. She was loved. Beth reached out to her and she faded away.

Chapter 14

One day seemed to fall into the next. Summer and autumn had come and gone without incident. Daniel had gotten back the DNA results months earlier and it only reassured him of what he already knew to be true; the baby was not his. A part of him was hoping it would come back a match and he could call Beth and tell her how much he loved and missed her. He could tell her how sorry he was for everything that had happened in their life. They could still be a family and one day be together again.

Daniel was practicing Chi when Hector entered the cell.
"How did it go at work?"
"Okay," Hector lay down on his bunk.
"It's really cold out today huh?"
"Yeah, a hot shower will feel good tonight." Hector said.
"Yes it will," Daniel replied.

Daniel was washing his hair in the shower. His long hair was lathered with shampoo. It was a time he looked forward to three nights a week. It was as if all his troubles flowed down the drain along with the water running off his body. All the dirt disappeared for fifteen minutes while the hot water pounded his body. He began rinsing off the shampoo when he felt a sharp punch in his lower back and then another. As he spun around with a strike, he could barely see with the shampoo in his eyes. A second attacker plunged another blade into his side, piercing his liver, and again into his abdomen. Daniel fell to his knees in a pool of blood, and then came the blade into his neck. He fell backward sitting against the corner wall. He could not move, and his life was flowing from his body as a red river of blood was streaming toward the drain. Daniel looked up and realized what betrayal really meant. He was confused. He didn't understand why; he was heartbroken. The last words Daniel heard were, "I'm sorry, Daniel, please forgive me. God, forgive me." Hector stood in front of Daniel holding a bloody knife, weeping like a child.

The investigation into Daniel's death had not led to the indictment of any suspects. Two weeks had passed, and several inmates and correctional officers had been questioned, but no solid evidence had come to light. The officer who had the washroom post the night of Daniel's murder was the focus of the questioning, but he stuck to his story that he didn't see anything out of the ordinary until he found the body.

Tuesday morning was the same as any other morning at Cedar Junction. First check was at six AM. The guard walked down the tier, glancing into the cells half asleep. As he passed Hector's cell he saw the silhouette of a man upright against the bunk. He quickly got on his radio and within minutes the officer in charge and several others arrived on the tier. Hector had hanged himself from the top bunk with a bed sheet. On the ground by his feet was a photograph of his daughter posing between two black men standing by a park swing. The back of the photograph had a note that read. "Your cellmate dies or my boys cut Maria's throat after they fuck her skinny ass ragged." K9

Six days after Hector's body was found, Dog had choked to death in the mess hall on several small razors and glass that had been slipped into his drink. The investigation into Daniel's death had been closed. A new investigation into Dog's death had begun.

Master was in the yard in front of his board. It was snowing outside and very cold. He sat looking up to the sky. The white flakes were landing on his face and he felt as if he were trapped, sitting in the bottom of a snow globe he remembered as a child.

The yard was quiet and most inmates had stayed inside secured in the dayroom. A tall white inmate approached Master standing erect looking down at the big man. He had just arrived at the Pole two days earlier.

"Can I challenge you to a game?"

"Are you any good?" Master asked.

"I used to play a lot when I was a kid."

"Where did you learn to play?"

"My grandfather taught me."

"Just one game," Master said.

The inmate sat down across from Master. He sat there in awe of his size.

"White or black?"
Master looked up and said, "It really doesn't matter."

Chapter 15

Beth sat in her backyard sipping Chardonnay. The northeast had been in a heat wave for over a week and there were no signs that it would let up any time soon. There were hundreds of deaths attributed to the heat, and the number kept climbing. She kept a hand towel close by to dab the sweat off her forehead while she worked in her garden. It was the first garden she had of her own, and she had a hard time keeping anything worthwhile alive long enough to eat.

The heat didn't stop Beth from running. Every morning she would drop Justin at her neighbor Allison's house for an hour while she timed her six-mile run. Justin was napping and she was reflecting on the past year and a half since she received the news of Daniel's death.

The news of Daniel's murder knocked Beth into a severe depression. She had lost over ten pounds before her mother convinced her to see a doctor. She was reluctant but knew she had to do something, if not for her sake, then for her son's. The doctor prescribed Zoloft, a mild antidepressant. Beth had agreed to take the medication for the short-term, just to get her over the hump. She had not been sleeping well and the doctor assured her it would help. After four months, Beth had weaned herself off the drug.

The funeral was kept very simple. Daniel had once said to Beth he would want to be cremated, should he die before her. Beth made sure his wish was realized. The service was short and there weren't very many people in attendance. Daniel was more of a loner and had only a few close friends. His father had passed away a few years before Daniel's incarceration and Daniel's brother didn't care to keep the family bond. Seth had moved up the corporate ladder and became the CEO of a mid-sized publicly held company in Chicago. Daniel had always been the one to make the call, to put in the effort. As time went on Seth didn't bother returning the calls. It became clear to Daniel that Seth wanted to break the tie. Daniel had never known where his mother was, or if she was still alive. There were a few co-workers from the Iron Workers Union in attendance and some friends from his martial arts school. Many of Beth's friends had come to pay their respects. Some of them knew Daniel and some didn't, but the people who knew him loved and admired him.

Nancy had flown up to attend the service and comfort her daughter. She offered to watch Justin for the entire day so Beth could spend time alone. Beth needed time to think about what she would tell Justin about his father. She had to tell him the truth, but she wanted to do it in a gentle way. How do you tell a young boy his father was murdered in prison while doing hard time for a murder conviction? He would not understand that Daniel was a good man who had been unjustly convicted. Beth decided to wait until Justin was old enough to comprehend the entire truth of the matter. She decided to tell him his father was killed in an accident. This did not sit well with Beth, but for now she needed to preserve the memory of Daniel and the mental well-being of her son.

When the service ended, Beth drove to the south shore to a place she and Daniel had gone together when they first started dating. Hingham was as beautiful as she remembered it. It was a very cold winter day, and Beth sat on a rock looking out at the ocean until she became numb. When she had cried all her tears away she tossed Daniel's ashes into the bay and drove to the restaurant where they had dined on their first date. Beth wasn't hungry, so she sat and drank three glasses of wine while listening to Chopin's nocturnes being played on a grand piano by a young man who couldn't have reached his twenty-first birthday. His fingers were magical and with each sip of wine he became better and better. When Beth had her fill she walked the streets until her face was stinging from the cold. It had been the one of the saddest days of her life, yet she knew she would survive, she had to.

To Beth's surprise, Daniel had kept up with his life insurance premiums and union dues. He had asked co-worker, Vinny Marsetti, if he would continue paying a few bills for him while he was in prison. He had written a check to Vinny in order to keep up with his automobile payments, union dues and life insurance. He had not changed the beneficiary, so Beth had received a check for three hundred thousand dollars for term life insurance, two hundred thousand from Daniel's individual benefit and one hundred thousand paid by the union. Vinny was kind enough to pay Daniel's bills and store his car in his garage. The car had been paid off two months prior to Daniel's murder and Vinny drove it over to

Beth's apartment a week after the funeral. Daniel had a little over seven thousand dollars in his savings and twenty-two hundred that Vinny had left over from the money Daniel gave him. Beth insisted that Vinny keep the twenty-two hundred. With three hundred and seven thousand dollars in her hands, Beth knew what she had to do. This was Daniel's last gift to her and Justin. He would have wanted them to move out of the apartment and into a house, to live in a house with a yard where Justin could play, a neighborhood with other young children his age whom he could grow up with.

Daniel had over fifty thousand dollars in the bank when he was arrested and Leo had taken most of it defending him. Beth figured Leo would drain Daniel financially. She just didn't know to what extent. She didn't trust lawyers or politicians. She felt they were self-serving, for the most part. There were a few exceptions, but very few.

Home prices in the Boston suburbs were way too high according to Beth's standards. She took her time looking and she and Justin toured houses on the weekends. What she was finding in her price range were small three-bedroom capes and ranches. Some of them were priced at nearly a half million dollars and Beth was astounded at what was offered for the prices listed. It was more important to Beth that she find a good neighborhood than a fancy house. Beth finally found a home she adored in Arlington. It was a three bedroom colonial with a fenced in yard in a very quiet neighborhood. The house was white with black shutters and a finely trimmed landscape. The floors were hardwood and there was a brick fireplace in the living room. Justin's room had a window seat that overlooked the back yard. The house sat on a side street where children rode their bikes along the sidewalks. The house was perfect for them, Beth thought. She had spent more than she had anticipated but knew it was the house she wanted as soon as she laid her eyes on it.

It didn't take Beth long to make a new friend. Allison was Beth's age and lived two houses up the street. Allison Sharpe was a mother of two, a boy, Tannon, who was five years old and a girl, Monica, who had just turned two and was six months older than Justin when they moved in. Allison's husband Tom was a project manager for Information Technology at a financial consulting firm in Boston. He worked sixty hours a week and Allison was beginning to wonder what his secretary looked like. Beth had taken a liking to Monica from the start. She was always offering to help with Justin, so Beth could go running or shopping. Allison was a housewife with an undeniable zest for life. She would sing and dance around her kitchen as if she was on stage performing in front of fifty thousand fans. She loved music and lived as though it was a major part of her life and without it she would be lost. She had always wanted to be a music teacher and maybe even play in a band, but it never came to fruition. Allison began piano lessons at the age of seven. Her instructor was an eighty-one year old woman who had lost forty percent of her hearing ten years before. This didn't stop Allison from learning at a pace that left the twelve-year olds in the dust. She had moved on to *Moonlight Sonata* while the other children her age were still practicing *Twinkle Twinkle Little Star*. Her lessons continued until the instructor died six years later. As the years passed by, she would sit down behind the ivory keys at least once a week for an hour of practice. She continued to be famous in the eyes of her children and friends who gathered around her piano at the parties she hosted several times a year.

Beth was intrigued that Allison knew nearly all the artists and most titles of the songs on the radio. Her CD collection was enormous and Beth had gotten the updated scoop on the music scene and had listened to many of the great musicians. Allison always said the best rock and roll and rhythm and blues bands came from the 70's and 80's era. "That was real music, not like today," she always said. She was an attractive woman of five-foot-three inches with short light brown hair and brown eyes. She was thin and kept in shape doing Tai Bo in her family room in front of the TV. She wore black-rimmed glasses which she despised. Contacts bothered her eyes so she suffered the pains of wearing glasses. Beth thought they made her look more attractive. "You have a perfect face for glasses," Beth told her. Allison was a good-hearted person and Beth was glad to have her as a friend.

It was on Thanksgiving that Beth met Douglas Brady. Allison insisted she and Justin attend Thanksgiving dinner with her family. Allison conveniently forgot to mention to Beth that her husband also invited Doug, a friend with whom he played tennis once a week. Doug was fairly new to the area and didn't have anyone to spend the holiday with. Knowing this, Tom invited him to their house.

Allison knew Beth would have declined had she known Doug was going to be there, so she never brought it up. Allison had met Doug on a couple occasions and thought he and Beth might hit it off. Doug was a bright, handsome man with short black hair. He stood five foot eleven and weighed about one hundred seventy-five pounds. Running and tennis kept him in good condition and he excelled at both. He had dark blue eyes and wore glasses while reading and when his eyes grew tired. Doug was an electrical engineer at a fiber optic company located in Waltham, just west of Boston. He had graduated at the top of his class at MIT, and it was there that he started having to wear glasses. The doctor said it was the strain on his eyes from long hours of studying that had caused his vision to blur. Doug had never been married, but he was engaged twice. He had backed out both times and the second time he nearly left the bride-to-be standing at the alter. Doug had felt bad about backing out with such short notice, but he wasn't in love with her. He had been pressured into marriage and was going into the partnership for all the wrong reasons. He knew it wouldn't have lasted, so he backed out a week before the ceremony. It was a costly decision, but would be worth the price in the long run.

Doug never believed in love at first sight until Thanksgiving Day. The moment he laid eyes on Beth, he knew he wanted her. She was the most beautiful woman he had ever met. If he could have drawn a picture of the perfect-looking woman, it would be she. Beth found Doug to be a gentleman. She knew right away he was attracted to her. It was obvious by the way he beamed when speaking with her. This was not unusual for Beth; most men were attracted to her and it became bothersome after a while. Since her separation from Daniel, many men had approached her and asked her out on dates. Without wanting to hurt anyone's feelings, she would politely decline, stating she was in a relationship. Beth never lied, so she justified it in her mind as her relationship with Jesus. Beth had not been interested in dating since Daniel. Although she was lonely at times, she was still going through a grieving process.

Thanksgiving was wonderful. Beth really liked Doug and he was very good with Justin. They talked about college. Beth was impressed that Doug had graduated from MIT, which was regarded as the top technology school in the country. She had gone to Northeastern University, which was a good school, but MIT was the best. Running was a topic they had in common. Doug had run three marathons, including the Boston Marathon, which was a dream of Beth's. They talked about different local road races and good bike paths free from car exhaust fumes. Doug asked her what type of running shoes she felt most comfortable wearing and she asked him what his average running time was. The conversation moved back and forth naturally without pain or hesitation. After dinner Beth excused herself to assist Allison with the dishes. During the monotonous task of cleaning up, Allison quickly changed the subject and began prodding Beth about Doug. She relentlessly tried to convince Beth that it was time to think about dating again. Beth thought about it over dessert and came to the conclusion that maybe Allison was right.

It wasn't long afterward that Doug asked Beth if she would be interested in going for a run Sunday morning. Beth had declined, stating that she spent Sunday mornings at church. Allison intervened and said, "Beth, I'll watch Justin Saturday morning while you go running, if you like.?" Beth agreed that Saturday would be fine. The run went better than expected for both of them. It started as a six-mile run and they ended up walking another five. They had a long talk and Beth had found herself laughing and smiling more than she had in a long time. Doug was quick-witted and very funny. They stopped at a small café and Doug bought her a coffee and bagel. It was the best cup of coffee she had tasted in a long time.

Beth glanced down into her wine glass and it was empty. Justin had woken up from his nap and was standing at the door adding more prints to the pane. He was nearly two and a half years old and was getting around very well on his own. Beth took a gander into her garden, wondering where the past two years had gone. She went inside to the air conditioning.

Chapter 16

It was Sunday morning and already the temperature had reached eighty-four degrees. As usual, Beth had been scrambling to make breakfast and get Justin dressed. Justin loved Sundays because church was his favorite place. Religion was most important to Beth and she made sure they never missed service on Sunday. Afterwards, they would go to prayer meetings, then have snacks and mingle with the other parishioners. They prayed together at least three times a day. Before every meal they would bow their heads to give thanks to the Lord for their bounty. At night they would get on their knees with a rosary in hand and pray. They prayed for Daniel, that he had found peace in Heaven with the Lord. With their heads bowed, they asked God to bless their family and friends. They prayed for world peace and that the hungry be fed. Every day they said a special prayer for someone Beth had read about or they had heard about who had troubles. They didn't have to know the people they prayed for. As long as they needed help, it was a good cause.

During service, Justin would sit completely still and listen to the sermon. Beth felt blessed that Justin was so well behaved during service. Most of the kids his age wouldn't sit still for five minutes. After church, Justin would attend Bible readings while Beth met with her prayer group.

The prayer group had finished, and as usual Beth made her way to the bible-reading classroom where the kids were sitting in a semi-circle while the instructor read passages from the Bible. Beth stood by the door watching as class was in progress. The kids looked like little angels sitting side-by-side looking up and giving full attention as the teacher read a verse out loud. Ms. Brenner had been teaching Bible study for thirteen years. She loved kids and this class was her favorite. She enjoyed teaching the younger children because they were innocent and impressionable. She felt she could help mold them into something positive and set the pace for a life of good character and morality.

"This is a passage from Job." Brenner was sitting with perfect posture as she read. "As long as my breath is in me. And the breath of God in my nostrils." As she briefly hesitated, Justin stood up looking straight at her, and he began to speak.

"My lips will not speak wickedness. Nor my tongue utter deceit."

The room was completely silent and Beth stood there in awe. She felt her legs grow weak and she moved into the room to take a seat. She did not interrupt the class. She was at a loss for words. Ms. Brenner didn't say anything as Justin sat back down. Then she finally broke the silence and finished the passage.

"My lips will not speak wickedness. Nor my tongue utter deceit." She was looking directly at Justin. "That's it for today, children. Be good and love God."

Ms. Brenner could not wait for the class to exit. "Beth, can I speak with you for a minute?"

"Yes," Beth replied.

Beth knew what she was going to ask, but she didn't have an answer.

"Beth, you heard Justin quote Job's passage, didn't you?"

"Yes, I did"

"Have you gone over that passage with Justin at any length?"

"No I haven't, Carol. I was wondering if you had."

"No, we have never covered that passage. He is only two and a half years old, right?"

"Almost," Beth answered.

"I know Justin is very bright, and maybe even at a genius level, but how would he know the passage verbatim if he hasn't been taught it? The way he spoke was as if he knew it by heart."

"I can't answer that question, Carol. I will ask him tonight and let you know what I learn from him."

"Please do, Beth. I am curious."

Beth collected Justin as he was thumbing through a book on Noah's Ark.

"Beth," Ms. Brenner looked as if she had seen a ghost.

"Yes, Carol."

"Have a great day and God bless you and Justin."

"Thank you, Carol. God bless you as well."

Chapter 17

▼

The first thing Beth did when she arrived home was to call Nancy. Unlike most Sundays, they didn't stay for snacks and socializing. Word about what had occurred would spread like wildfire and Beth knew she would be confronted by the priest soon enough. She didn't want to deal with it until she had a chance to speak with her son and sort it out. She didn't have any answers to give.

Beth knew what she had to do, but wanted to hear what her mother had to say about the matter. She and her mother thought alike, and she figured her mother would suggest she ask Justin where he learned the passage in a gentle non-intrusive way. Justin was so far above children in his age group. He started walking when he was eleven months old, and he was putting sentences together before he was two years old, but this was way above the norm.

Nancy wasn't as surprised as Beth thought she would be. Her mother agreed she should ask Justin how he came about knowing the passage. She also said, "We are all children of God, but Justin is special. God has chosen him to do good things with his life, to spread the gospel and truth. That is how he knows the passage." When Beth hung up the phone she sat down and thought about what her mother had said. Could her mother be right? Was he a saint or an angel sent down to us from God, or was he just super smart with a retention level that was way off the charts? Maybe he heard the passage once and it stuck with him. Beth had to ask Justin. He was the only one who had the answers. But he was only a child.

Justin was watching Barney as Beth walked into the playroom. Beth didn't care for the overweight purple dinosaur with the obnoxious voice, but she tolerated him for Justin's sake.

"Hello, Sweetie," Beth sat down on the floor next to Justin.

"Hi Mommy." Beth put her arm around Justin and pulled him close.

"Can we turn Barney off for a few minutes so I can talk with you?"

"Okay."

"Sweetie, this morning at Bible class you stood up and said a passage from the Bible. How did you know it? Where did you learn the passage?"

"I don't know, Mommy. I just knew it."

"Have you heard it somewhere before?"

"Yes."

"Where, Sweetie, where have you heard it?"

"I don't know."

"Have you heard any other passages?"

"Yes." Justin answered with unusual confidence.

"Which one?"

"All of them."

Beth felt exhilarated as she put her arms around Justin. "Do you know how much I love you, Sweetie?"

"All the way to Heaven and back."

"Yes, Justin, all the way to Heaven and back."

Chapter 18

▼

The doorbell rang and Beth answered it dressed in her favorite black dress. Every woman has a favorite black dress, whether they own one or admire one in a store window. Beth always looked thinner in black. Doug had on a dark blue suit with pinstripes and black wing-tipped shoes. Beth thought he looked like a politician in a suit. She was glad he wasn't. Allison was watching Justin for the evening while Doug and Beth went out to Doug's favorite Italian restaurant. Beth had not said anything to Allison about what had happened. She wouldn't understand, or might think Beth was losing it. She had received a call from Monsignor London on Thursday evening and he asked her if they could meet after church service on Sunday to talk. Beth agreed they could talk over snacks after her prayer meeting.

Genarro's Restaurant was a nice little place, an old house that had been converted into an eating establishment in 1958. Doug was a regular customer and had called in ahead of time to get the most romantic table available. This was a special night for Doug and he wanted it to be perfect for Beth. They had been dating for ten months and he was head over heels in love with her. They had been seeing each other at least two days a week and every time they ended the night he couldn't wait until the next time he could gaze into her eyes and see her warm smile.

Doug treated Beth with the utmost respect and had accepted her rejections when he tried to make sexual advances toward her. They had engaged in romantic kissing and touching but when things began to heat up, Beth would douse the flame with ice water. They were seated at a corner table near a window overlooking the street where people were busy strolling around window shopping and enjoying the evening. The weather had finally broken and the heat wave had subsided. The restaurant was small and dimly lit. There was a candle set on the table and Doug couldn't help but stare into Beth's eyes as the candlelight lit them up like a Christmas tree.

"Doug, can I ask you something?"

"Sure, anything."

"Do you believe in angels?"

"Yes, I believe I'm sitting across the table from one right now."

"No, seriously."

"I am serious Beth. Let me ask you something. When was the last time you committed a sin?"

"I don't know," she played it off.

"I have never heard you swear. I have never even heard you say a bad word about anyone. So have you?"

"I try to lead a good life and raise Justin to be a good Christian."

"Can you ever think of a time when you stole something or lied or did anything you knew was wrong?"

Beth had to think for a moment. "No, I can't."

"As I said, I'm having dinner with an angel, and probably the prettiest one that ever flew into Boston."

Beth reached over and held Doug's hand. "Thanks Doug, you are so sweet."

It was then that Doug put a small case on the table in front of Beth.

"Open it," Doug anxiously requested.

Beth slowly opened the velvet box and inside was a beautiful one-carat diamond ring with two rubies on either side.

"Doug, it's beautiful." She felt a slight hot flash come over her.

"Beth," he took her hand into his. "Will you be my wife? I love you more than I have ever loved anyone in my entire life, and I want to spend the rest of my life with you."

Beth hesitated. She was totally caught by surprise.

"I'm sorry, Doug, but I can't. I do care for you, I really do, but the time is not right for me."

"Okay," he said. "Would next week be better?"

Beth laughed. "It's just that I'm not ready for this. Maybe in time I will be, but not right now."

"I understand," Doug said, obviously disappointed.

"I really do care about you Doug. You are a great guy."

"Does that mean there may be hope for us in the future?"

"Yes."

"Then I'll wait. You can still wear the ring."

"I love the ring, Doug, but I can't."

"I'll hold it for you then."

They finished dinner and Beth asked to be taken home. There was so much going on in her life that Doug didn't realize. She had never mentioned to him what had happened in Bible study. He didn't know about the divine visions she had experienced. She was still getting adjusted to her new house and neighborhood. Summer was coming to a finish and she was preparing to return to school for a new year of teaching. He had no idea that her heart still ached for Daniel, and how heavily it still weighed on her. No one did.

Sunday morning arrived and Beth was up earlier than normal. It was still dark out when she crawled out of bed. She had tossed and turned most of the night and watched the clock as it pushed toward a new day. She thought she may as well get up instead of lying in bed waiting for the sun to show its face. There were so many issues in her life that kept her mind racing throughout the night. Doug's proposal had totally taken her by surprise. Then there was the pending meeting with Monsignor London in the morning. What was happening with Justin? How did he know the passage? She needed a break, time to relax. Beth decided she needed some time away. She would take Justin to Cape Cod the following week for a few days before the new school year began.

Sunday service was the same as any other, except Beth noticed more people than normal watching her and Justin as they entered the church. Was it her imagination or was it reality? Was she paranoid, over-reacting? During prayer meeting and Justin's Bible study she realized it wasn't her imagination. People were acting differently toward them. Most people were looking at them as if they had just arrived from Mars. Beth could sense the whispering and subtle staring. She knew word had spread about Justin and she felt uncomfortable.

After Bible study Beth was holding Justin's hand as they entered the snack room. Monsignor London was right there to greet them.

"Hello, Justin, Beth."

"Hello, Monsignor."

Justin said, "Hi."

"Justin, I bet you would like milk and cookies?"

"Okay," Justin replied.

"Ms. Conway will get them for you while I speak with your mother."

"Go with Ms. Conway, Justin. Mommy will come and get you in a few minutes."

Ms. Conway was a large woman of fifty-six. She had short gray hair and always wore a skirt and blouse. She had never been married and had devoted most of her time to the church. She would organize fundraisers and church-related events. Monsignor London could always count on Ms. Conway to help with any tasks that needed attention. She was always delighted to help. She had nothing else to do. Except for the church, she was alone. Ms. Conway took Justin's hand and made off to the snack area. There was a table with doughnuts, pastries and cookies to eat. Hot coffee, juice and milk were situated on a small adjoining table. People were standing around chatting, nibbling their snacks and sipping their drinks. Monsignor London suggested they go into a conference room where they could talk in private. Monsignor opened the door and Beth entered the small room furnished with an oval table and six chairs. Monsignor pulled back a chair for Beth and she took a seat.

"Thank you," Beth said.

"You're quite welcome, Beth." There was a window overlooking a parking lot. The ceilings were twelve feet high and the walls were bare except for a long picture of the last supper that hung on the wall to the right of the window. On the other wall hung a large wooden crucifix.

"Beth, I have received a couple reports last week regarding Justin. I was informed that he stated the second half of a passage written in the book of Job verbatim. I was told that particular passage had not been covered in bible study at all. Is this true?"

"Yes, Monsignor."

"Have you gone over the passage with Justin before?"

"No, I haven't."

"How old is Justin?"

"Almost two and a half."

"So young. Can you explain this?" London looked puzzled.

"No, Monsignor, I can't."

"Children his age can barely understand passages from the bible, never mind cite them."

"Justin is different from other children. He has a gift," Beth said.

"Yes, I am told he is special. Has he cited any other verses?"

"No, not that I have heard."

"I would like to speak with Justin if you don't mind."

"For what purpose, Monsignor?"

"I would like to read some passages from the bible and see if he responds. To see if he is familiar with any of them."

"Monsignor, I don't mean to be disrespectful, but I would prefer that you not speak with Justin."

"Why not, Beth? I just want to get to the bottom of this. I am intrigued."

"Since last Sunday I have noticed that people in our parish have acted differently toward us. I don't want to be treated differently than anyone else. I don't want Justin treated differently than the other kids. I just want to continue living like we did before last week."

"Aren't you curious, Beth, how Justin could know the passage from the book of Job without ever learning it?"

"Well, yes, but I don't want Justin to be put on the spot. I don't want him to be some kind of religious experiment. He is just a baby."

"I understand, Beth and I promise it won't be like that. I will make him feel like it's just another Bible study."

"I would like time to think about it."

"Alright then, I'll wait for your call. You may be present when I speak to him."

"Of course, I would want to be there. I will let you know next Sunday. I am taking Justin to the shore this week for a few days."

"Enjoy your week then. God bless both of you." Monsignor made the sign of the cross. Beth found Justin playing in the recreation room and took him home.

Monday morning arrived and Beth woke up to Justin pawing her arm while she lay in bed. She had slept for nine hours, which was unusual compared to her normal six hours.

"Good morning, Sweetie." Beth reached over and pulled him up onto the bed and held him close to her.

"Good morning, Mommy."

"I am so excited that we are going to the beach today."

"Me too, mommy."

"We will have so much fun. We can make a sand castle, collect shells and beach stones, go swimming and have a picnic."

"Can we get ice cream?"

"Yes, Sweetie, we will eat lots of ice cream." Beth tickled him until she heard him break out in laughter. It didn't matter how bad her day was or how awful she felt. Hearing Justin laugh always made her feel better.

The good thing about traveling to Cape Cod on a Monday was the lack of traffic one encounters when compared to the weekend. It was a smooth ride all the way to Hyannisport where she checked into a motel at 11:20 AM. It was a small motel located right off the main drag with an in-ground pool and a hot tub. Beth could not wait to stretch out in the hot tub. The recent days that had passed had caused her shoulders to knot-up. After checking in, they had lunch at a local diner and returned to the room to pack up for the beach. The next two days were quiet and relaxing with perfect weather. There wasn't a cloud in the sky, and the recent heat wave had caused the water temperature to rise above normal. They spent time enjoying each other's company, and the serenity of the ocean helped Beth to unwind. Beth rented a fishing pole and they fished off the pier for whatever might be unlucky enough to run into their hook. It was a learning experience for both, and Beth was entertained by how much compassion Justin had for the worm. They didn't catch a thing but had a great time casting the line and pulling up clumps of seaweed. The week was flying by as it always did on vacation. Beth had forgotten about all her troubles in the past few days. They had done everything she had planned and more. They had stopped for ice cream every night and tested different flavors. Justin's personal favorite was cookie dough. Beth loved all of them, but was partial to pistachio.

Thursday morning arrived and Beth decided to stay another day. School was starting on Monday and she would be ready as long as she had the weekend to prepare. They had just arrived at the beach and decided to take a walk. The sun was warming their backs and Justin was entertaining himself by attempting to jump out of his shadow. The gulls were gliding above without expending much energy as the breeze off the ocean carried them along. It was low tide and the waves were non-existent, which made skimming stones a much easier task. As they were searching for flat stones, Beth looked over at Justin, who was kneeling down over a bird. As Beth approached, she noticed a small gray and white bird. It was apparent the bird was dead.

"Justin, Sweetie, the bird is dead, just leave it."

Justin didn't say anything. He looked up at his mother as if it were the first time he had seen a dead animal close up. While still kneeling on the sand, he picked up the bird and cupped it in both hands. He closed his eyes for a moment, and then stood up, and with a smooth, gentle, upward motion he released the bird. The bird took off in flight and soared into the sky, flapping its wings, full of life. Beth and Justin watched the bird fly away along the shore until it was out of sight. She looked at her son and he looked back with a smile on his face. Beth began to cry, for the miracle she had just seen reassured what she had suspected. Justin was an angel sent from God.

"Don't cry, Mommy. The birdie is free," Justin said as he walked toward his mother.

Beth got on her knees and held her son and together they prayed.

Chapter 19

In the distance they could hear the church bells chime. They sounded like they did every Sunday morning, but on this day they resonated a more beautiful tune. They meant more to Beth now. Everything meant more to her. She had often thought about what she had seen at the beach, and she was scared, yet enlightened. In her heart she had always known there was a higher power, but now she had seen a miracle with her own eyes. There wasn't any room for doubt. Beth had always been a highly spiritual person, but she experienced a whole new feeling of spirituality and serenity now. There truly was a God and she and Justin were safe. They were loved.

Monsignor London had been waiting all week for Sunday to arrive. Gossip had spread throughout the parish, and he wanted to find out for himself what was happening. He was a good man who believed in God, but like most priests, there was always doubt in his mind if He truly existed. He had never witnessed a miracle or had a divine experience. There were signs throughout his life and he chose to embrace them. Were they coincidences or real signs from Heaven? He wasn't exactly sure.

Service had ended, and Beth saw Monsignor waiting as she and Justin exited the church. She thought about telling Monsignor about the miracle on the beach but decided against it. She decided not to tell anyone. Who would believe her anyway? Monsignor London had decided they would talk in a less formal environment. Instead of the conference room they went to his quarters. Beth had decided to allow Monsignor to meet with Justin with her present in the room. They had agreed she would just listen and observe while Monsignor spoke with Justin. The living room had a hardwood floor with a large Persian area rug that lay in the middle. The ceiling was sixteen feet high and the trim work was beveled oak with huge circular doorframes. The room was decorated with antique furniture and Christian art. Justin took a seat on the couch next to Monsignor London and Beth sat in a chair a few feet away. Beth felt a little uneasy, mostly for Justin. She didn't sense he was feeling the same way and she was right.

"Justin, I have heard you are doing exceptionally well in Bible study, and your mother and I decided to do a special Bible study class alone with you, today."

"Why?" Justin asked, while toying with the dial on his florescent green watch.

"Well, we believe that you are so far ahead of your classmates that we can work together to find your full potential without interrupting the rest of the students. Do you understand?"

"I guess so."

Monsignor picked up a Bible. "I have heard from Ms. Brenner that you know some passages from the Bible and we all think that's great. You can be so proud of yourself for that, Justin, just as we are proud of you. I am going to read from the Bible and let's see if you can finish the verse, okay?"

"Alright," Justin replied.

Monsignor had his places marked in the book and began reading. "As long as my breath is in me. And the breath of God in my nostrils." He hesitated. Can you finish this passage?

Justin looked at him with confidence. "My lips will not speak wickedness. Nor my tongue utter deceit."

London looked at Beth, obviously impressed. "Very good, Justin. Let's do another."

"The words of his mouth are wickedness and deceit." Monsignor looked at Justin in anticipation.

"He has ceased to be wise and to do good."

"Would anyone like a glass of water?" Monsignor asked.

"Yes," Beth replied.

Monsignor got up and poured from a pitcher of water. He handed a glass to Beth and quickly took a drink himself. He thumbed through the Bible, found his place and began reading.

"The prudent man foresees evil and hides himself."

"The simple pass on and are punished." Justin blurted out with little thought.

"Okay, very good, Justin. How about one more?" He took another drink. He wished it were wine.

"Those who dwell under his shadow shall return." Justin reached over and placed his hand on the Bible and looked at his mother.

"They shall be revived like grain and grow like a vine."

Beth sat there with a smile, not only from her mouth but her eyes as well.

"Justin, Beth, let us pray together." Monsignor reached out to Beth, she got up and knelt next to them. They joined hands and he began with the Lord's Prayer.

The Monsignor saw them to the door and raced to the cabinet to an un-opened bottle of blue label scotch he had kept locked up for a special occasion. He opened the bottle and poured into a crystal glass and took a large gulp. Monsignor loved classical music and kept his albums in top condition. He never listened to CDs or tapes. The quality on a good turntable could not be matched. He placed the album on the record player and retreated to his thinking chair. He took another gulp of his scotch and placed it on the table. He picked up a pad and pen and began taking notes on what had just occurred while listening to Beethoven's Symphony Number Three. He would have to report what he had seen to the Cardinal and wanted to make sure it was exactly as it had happened. There would be many questions and he didn't have all the answers. No one did. Monsignor London had asked Justin before they left, where he had learned the passages. Justin answered, "I don't know, I just knew them." Monsignor couldn't figure it out. There were over seventeen hundred and fifty pages in his copy of the King James Bible. He had read the Bible hundreds of times throughout his religious life, and he didn't know all the passages by heart. How could a boy so young, who couldn't even read, memorize all the passages in the Bible? He poured down another large gulp of scotch.

Chapter 20

The school year had passed quickly. It was the end of April and Beth would soon enjoy summer vacation with Justin. Since the incident at Bible study, people at church had adjusted and it was business as usual. The word had spread that Justin had a gift, and though people were curious, they didn't make an issue out of it. Beth was pleased. Her relationship with Doug had flourished and she was loving him more every day. Doug, raised as a Lutheran, was a religious man, but he accepted the rumors of Justin as an intellectual gift rather than a religious one.

Cardinal Zupra had received a letter from Monsignor London in early autumn and decided to visit the church two weeks later. He attended Justin's Bible study where he sat and observed. This was the only class he attended, and everyone knew the reason, but no one spoke of it. He conveniently met with Beth and Justin afterward near the snack tables where he made small talk. Afterward, he instructed Monsignor to keep an eye on things and to keep a low profile on the matter. The next day the Pope learned of the boy and what had occurred.

The room was shaped like a big horseshoe. In the center was the support staff and administrators. The shoe itself consisted of rows of desks where reporters sat typing away or dialing phones when they weren't on the street. Frank Soto was sitting at his desk when the phone rang. It was an anonymous caller who stated there was a miracle child who attended Bible school at Saint Patrick's in Cambridge. The woman on the phone stated he was a three-year-old boy who memorized the entire Bible chapter and verse. She went on to say he could barely read and had no special schooling on the Bible. The last thing she said was, "his name is Justin," and the phone went dead.

The day was perfect for a birthday party. Sara Anderson lived five houses up the street from Justin and had turned four the day before. All the children from the neighborhood had been invited to the party. It was Saturday and the yard was set up with a piñata and pin-the-tail on the donkey. They would bob for apples and play many different games throughout the day. A few of the kids were playing with a ball and Rebecca Horsen, a four-year-old from the neighborhood, followed it as it rolled into the bushes. She reached in to retrieve the ball and hit a bee's nest with her right hand. Within seconds, yellow-jackets had swarmed over her, stinging her on the arms, face and neck. At first the attack went unnoticed until one of the parents heard her screaming. She was running and flailing about as a cloud of bees followed her. Rebecca's mother, while looking through the kitchen window, noticed her daughter running frantically and knew something was wrong. She quickly ran outside, picked her daughter up and brought her back inside. Everyone else hurried inside or ran around to the front yard where it was free from the swarm. Rebecca's mother realized her daughter had been stung many times, but didn't know she was allergic to bee stings. Rebecca, an adorable little blond girl with blue eyes, had her hair in a ponytail and was wearing blue jeans and a tee shirt. She had been stung seventeen times and her throat began to swell, inhibiting her ability to breathe. She was lying on the living room floor and it was obvious she was unable to take in air. She started sweating profusely and was making sucking sounds as she attempted to breath.

"Call an ambulance!" her mother frantically shouted.

Rebecca started turning blue. The guests were all standing around Rebecca as her throat completely closed up. She could no longer breath. Her mother was screaming for help. One parent suggested doing a tracheotomy. Rebecca just lay lifeless, as her mother was performing CPR. It was then that Justin broke through the people who were watching in horror and approached Mrs. Horsen.

"Please let me try?" Justin calmly asked.

Mrs. Horsen was not paying any attention, the room was spinning and she was crying hysterically attempting to blow air into her daughter's lungs. Beth grabbed Mrs. Horsen's arm.

"Connie, let Justin through. Let him try."

Mrs. Horsen fell back onto the floor sobbing in total agony. Justin slowly sat down and picked Rebecca's head up and covered his mouth over hers. He closed his eyes and began blowing air into her mouth. After one long breath he stopped and sat there holding her. He looked up at his mother and looking back into his eyes, she knew the little girl would be okay. Beth's heart, which had been pounding, began to calm. Everyone in the room was quiet as they watched in amazement. Mrs. Horsen, still crying uncontrollably, hadn't noticed what had occurred. Justin looked back down at Rebecca and her color was coming back. She began breathing again as her throat was opening up. Rebecca opened her eyes and Justin smiled down at her.

"She's alive!" Mrs. Johnson said.

"Oh, my God!" Mr. Harper said, as Rebecca started moving her arm.

Mrs. Horsen broke out of her hysterics and screamed, "My baby!" wrapping her arms around her daughter, holding her close.

"Thank God!" she said. "Thank God!"

"No, thank Justin," Mrs. Johnson said.

The ambulance arrived and the EMT suggested Rebecca be taken to the hospital to get checked out. Mrs. Horsen drove her daughter to the doctor who examined her and said she was fine. Beth decided to take Justin home. A few people stayed to break the piñata but nearly everyone had left. With the exception of Rebecca, everyone at the party had witnessed a miracle and needed time to reflect on what had occurred. It didn't take long for the word to get out and rumors to snowball. Beth knew she couldn't keep what had happened a secret but she had to protect Justin. She decided to see Monsignor London and tell him everything that had happened, her visions, the bird being brought back to life and Justin saving Rebecca's life. She had also decided to tell her mother everything as well. Even if Monsignor didn't believe her, she knew her mother would. Her mother had said time and time again that Justin had a gift. Beth needed to tell someone the whole story. She wasn't crazy. These occurrences happened. They were real.

The break room at the newspaper company was a large rectangular room with light blue painted walls and vending machines lined up along one side. There were three refrigerators and four microwave ovens, a large sink and dishwasher for those who spent more time there than they cared to. Tables were lined up throughout the room, mostly unclean. Frank Soto was sitting alone as usual reading the paper while eating a baloney sandwich. He was a tall thin man who always wore jackets with elbow patches, blue oxford shirts and khaki pants. His dark hair was bushy and usually uncombed. He had been a reporter for seventeen years and was one of the best. He was so good he didn't have a girl or any real friends. He knew almost everything that was going on in the city and if he didn't he would always find out.

Two women sitting at a table next to Soto were talking about a miracle that happened a couple of weeks ago in Arlington. Soto was a professional when it came to eavesdropping, and although they didn't realize it, he was listening to their every word while pretending to read. The woman telling the story could have been a narrator for a documentary. The woman listening was giving full attention and looked as if she was a kid sitting by a campfire.

"A little girl was stung to death by a swarm of bees, and a little boy appeared out of nowhere and brought her back to life by blowing one breath into her mouth. This happened after several adults attempted to give her CPR. A couple of minutes later she was running around playing ball. One woman said she saw a halo over the boy's head." Frank got up and walked out, leaving his sandwich on the table. He immediately drove to Saint Patrick's and began asking questions. After three days of snooping around, he ended up knocking at the front door of the Horsen's home. Connie Horsen answered the door.

"Yes, may I help you?"

"Mrs. Horsen?"

"Yes."

"My name is Frank Soto and I am a reporter with the Journal. May I speak with you for a few minutes please?"

"This is about my daughter?"

"Yes ma'am, it is."

"Come in," Mrs. Horsen stretched open the door.

"I have knowledge that your daughter was attacked and stung by a swarm of bees a few weeks ago, and she had an allergic reaction and suffered complications?"

"Yes, Rebecca was at a birthday party when she disturbed a bee's nest and was stung several times on her face, neck and arms."

Soto had a voice-activated tape recorder playing in his jacket pocket. "Can you tell me what happened?"

"It was a miracle. A three-year-old neighborhood boy saved my daughter's life. She had stopped breathing and had turned blue. I thought she was dead. I couldn't bring her back and Justin came over and blew air into her lungs and she was fine a few seconds later. It was amazing!"

"What is Justin's last name?"

"I don't think I should give out that information without his mother's permission."

"His mother's first name is?"

She reluctantly answered, "Beth."

Soto outstayed his welcome and left after he had all the information he needed. His article would make the front page and once again he would prove to the world he was the best investigative reporter that ever came down the pike. This would be the story that would give him the ammunition to ask for a raise. He drove back to the office and started writing. The next morning he drove to Beth's house after learning where she lived from one of the people at the local coffee shop. He spent an hour and a half sitting around the coffee bar making conversation and listening to the locals talking about the party and what they had heard through the grapevine. Soto stood on the front steps knocking on the door when Beth came walking around from the back of the house with Justin following her.

"Can I help you?"

"Yes. I am Frank Soto and you must be Beth." Her beauty took him aback.

"Yes."

"Is this Justin?"

"How can I help you, Mr. Soto?"

"I am from the Journal and I'd like to talk to you about the incident that occurred a few weeks ago at the birthday party for Rebecca Horsen."

"I'm sorry, Mr. Soto, we are not interested in speaking about that."

"I can assure you, Beth, it will be confidential." The recorder was running.

"I have nothing to say. Good day, Mr. Soto." Beth took Justin by the hand and walked into the house.

Frank Soto didn't say a word, he just stood there smiling. He had been in the business long enough to tell from the way she reacted that no other reporters had been by to see her. If he hadn't been the first, she most likely would have told the story again or simply stated that she already told the story to another reporter, which in her mind would have exonerated her from going over it again. Soto was an expert at reading people, and he could tell by the look on her face he had been the first one to approach her. To Soto, it was the look of money.

Chapter 21

The next morning, news stands were preparing to open and paper carriers were arriving at the docks. Soto had been sitting at his desk since three in the morning waiting to get a call from printing that the morning edition had been completed. The call came in at ten past three, and Soto ran to the elevator and took it to the bottom floor where his pal Jonesie was waiting with a stack of papers, grinning ear to ear. He snatched the top paper from the pile and patted Jonesie on the back.

"I owe you, Jonesie," Soto said as he walked away with his nose glued to the front page.

The headline read, **"IT'S A MIRACLE,"** and the caption below. **"Three year old boy brings dead girl back to life with a single breath."** Within a week every major newspaper in the country had reporters snooping around Arlington and Cambridge. Most of the parents who witnessed the miracle were selling their story to anyone with a price. People from tabloids, magazines and religious groups were asking questions. "Sixty Minutes" and talk show representatives were calling Beth's house for an interview. She was getting certified and priority mail from any organization that might profit from her story. To avoid the media, Allison offered to have Beth and Justin stay at her place until things calmed down. She gratefully accepted, packed up some things and locked up her house.

Beth never missed church, even when she was sick she would drag herself out of bed and go. This day would be a first. She didn't want to deal with the crowds and all the hype and confusion. She called Monsignor London and asked him if they could meet. She didn't realize it, but she had just beaten him to the call. He asked if it would be all right for the Cardinal to accompany him because the

Bishop was ill. Beth agreed. Allison stayed with Justin, and Beth drove to Monsignor London's rectory for the meeting. If she had to miss church, she could at least pray with the Cardinal, she thought.

They met for over two hours and Beth told them everything. She told them about the divine visions through her window. She went into detail about the resurrection of the bird and the most recent event regarding Rebecca Horsen. Monsignor saw with his own eyes how Justin cited passages from the bible. They asked her many different questions about Justin and his behavior. They opened up the truth about Daniel and his inability to produce children. She told them about her doctor's visit that her hymen was still intact after her pregnancy. Beth had broken down in tears while telling her story. When she was finished she felt as if a ton of bricks had been lifted off her shoulders. She had kept it all inside and carried the burden for so long. As she was driving home Beth wondered if they believed her. She put herself in their robes. Would she have believed her? She didn't have an answer.

An hour after Nancy hung up the phone with her daughter she had booked a flight to Boston. She had listened to Beth tell the entire story and didn't ask any questions. She just insisted she was flying up immediately and Beth didn't object.

A week had gone by and things were beginning to quiet down in the neighborhood. Beth and Justin thanked Allison and her family and went back home. Nancy was arriving the next morning and Beth was planning on meeting her at the airport. Doug had asked if he could come along and Beth said yes. Doug was curious as to what had been happening. Beth decided to tell him everything. He had read the paper and heard the news, but that's all he knew about Justin. He had not seen Beth and Justin in nearly two weeks and was becoming concerned. The flight into Logan was smooth. It was raining but it didn't concern Nancy. All three of them met her at the airport and took her back to Beth's house. There was very little conversation while driving home, just usual small talk about the flight and the weather. Beth was glad to have her mother there. Doug had made reservations to a French restaurant for that evening, and Nancy insisted they go out. She assured Beth they would catch up on things in the morning. It would give her time to be alone with Justin. Nancy felt in her heart she knew who Justin was and she wanted to be near him as much as possible.

Monsignor London called and asked if he, the Bishop, and Cardinal could meet with Justin. Beth responded, not at this time, she needed time to think about it and would get back to him. Justin had been through a lot with the episode at the party, followed by the media confusion and having to stay at Allison's for a week. Beth wanted him to be able to have a normal life for a while. She wondered if his life would ever be normal. She wasn't optimistic.

Dinner was going well and Beth decided it was time to fill Doug in on everything that had happened. She started from the beginning and when she was finished he just sat with a blank look on his face.

"Do you still want to marry me and spend the rest of your life with me?" Beth asked. He didn't answer right away.

"Yes, I do, more than ever"

"Well, where is the rock?" she asked smiling.

"Let's go to my place and get it right now." Doug was excited.

They walked out the door holding hands and laughing. It was still raining but it had lightened up. Across the street a man sat alone in a black Ford, watching them through the beaded rain on his windshield, as they left the restaurant.

Four days had passed since the engagement. It was early Monday morning and the streets were semi-dark and lifeless. The pavement was shining from the reflection of the streetlights on the morning dew. The lingering fog was slowly beginning to disappear. Doug had hit the street earlier than normal for his daily run. He had an early meeting, so he set his alarm clock an hour earlier than normal. He had just started out onto Massachusetts Avenue when he heard the sound of tires squealing behind him. Doug turned and saw the car approaching, but it was too late. Before he could react the car struck him just below the knees while traveling fifty miles an hour. The impact sent him airborne nearly ten feet until he landed on his head with a devastating thump. The car came to a halt and then the tires screamed again, this time while going in reverse. Traveling twenty-five miles per hour, the vehicle backed up over Doug leaving him lying in the middle of the street motionless.

Across the street in the doorway of an old building lay a homeless man covered with a blanket and piece of cardboard. He watched as the black Ford sped off. With many years of drinking and drugs, his body had deteriorated, but his eyesight was fine, he had twenty-twenty vision.

Chapter 22

▼

The cell phone rang and Horace looked at the clock next to his bed. The time displayed on his digital alarm clock was being blocked by a half empty bottle of Jack Daniels. He pushed the bottle aside and saw it was 6:10 AM. He wanted to ignore the phone, roll over and go back to sleep, but he couldn't. The number was lit up and it was the department calling. Horace was a homicide detective in Cambridge and he had a job to do. He pushed the answer button on the phone.

"Washington."

"Detective Washington?"

"Yes."

"Sergeant Combs with traffic. We have a hit and run on Mass. Ave. Doesn't look good."

"Where?"

"247 Mass. Ave"

"Give me twenty minutes." He hung up, took a swig from the bottle and hit his speed dial.

"Hello," said the voice on the other end, not sounding too thrilled.

"Ken, we have a hit and run on 247 Mass Ave. I'm leaving in five."

"Great, I'll see you there," he said sarcastically.

Horace pushed the end button and took another swig. He got out of bed and went into the bathroom. Horace Washington had been a cop for twenty-eight years and that's all he knew. His father had been custodian for the city of Boston for thirty-seven years and had died of heart failure in the hallway of John F. Kennedy Jr. High School with a mop in his hand. He had always wanted a better life for his son, and the day Horace graduated from the police academy he was smiling from ear to ear. There were seventeen cadets in uniform that day and Horace was the only black man to receive a badge. Thomas Washington was ashamed that he had wasted his life cleaning toilet bowls and emptying trash cans. His son wouldn't feel the shame that he had. He was determined that his son would do great things with his life.

Horace was proud of his father and loved him dearly. He grew up having very little, but he had his family and his father was always around. He knew he was lucky because most of his friends couldn't say that. As a child with four siblings, things were tight, but he made due with what he had. He always knew there was no replacement for love.

Horace worked in uniform walking the beat for six years until he was discovered after chasing down an armed robber, who had shot a liquor store clerk. He was transferred to radio car patrol on the graveyard shift and worked there for eight years until he made it to the day shift. He was a dedicated cop, which may have contributed to the demise of two marriages. Although Horace had no formal college education, he was street smart and became the best homicide detective the city of Cambridge had ever employed. Making detective was a dream come true. He had worked in uniform for sixteen years and all the long hours working the streets had finally paid off. He loved being a cop, but it came with a price. Over the years he had seen so many dead bodies. There were the young boys lying in the street with bullet holes torn through their gang colors, the wives found stabbed to death in their dingy apartments, hookers that had been sodomized, strangled and thrown into dumpsters. And worst of all, the children that had died by the hands of abusive parents. So many bodies, so much pain. The corpses would come to him at night while he slept. The faces of the dead would haunt him in his nightmares. As time passed he found refuge in the bottle. Drinking helped him to forget all the filth in the world. When he drank he seldom had dreams. Life wasn't so bad when he was drinking, until the next morning when he woke up.

As Horace approached the scene there were three cruisers already there. Two officers were roping off the crime scene with yellow ribbon. The street was cordoned off and people began gathering around the scene wondering what had happened. Ken had arrived on the scene four minutes earlier. Horace went through the barrier and walked right to the body where Ken was standing.

"What's it looking like?"

"Just got here. Lets take a look and see," Ken said as he snapped on surgical gloves.

"Sergeant Combs, would you clear everyone out of the area? We need to maintain the integrity of the crime scene. Let me know when the photographer arrives," Horace said. "From the position of the body it looks like he was struck about fifteen feet from the south and thrown here. There are no skid marks, which indicate the driver either didn't see him and didn't have time to brake or he saw him, and didn't want to break. The skid marks start about ten feet after impact and go for thirty-four feet." Horace had the measuring tape in hand. "This would put the vehicle speed about fifty to sixty miles an hour on impact."

"It appears there are double marks after impact," Ken said.

Horace kneeled down close to the body. "From the trauma on the knees it looks like he was hit in this area." He pointed with a pen just below the knees.

"Look at the tire marks on his thighs and neck," Ken said while looking at Horace.

"Not only did the bastard run him over, he backed up and ran him over again in reverse."

"Looks that way, partner, and he was moving pretty damned fast when he ran over his neck," Ken said.

"Yeah, and he was most likely still alive until he was hit the second time," Horace said as he stood up. "Whoever did this knew who he was running over and he made damned sure he finished the job."

"A guy can't even go out for a nice morning run to start out his day without getting whacked." Ken sounded agitated.

"Not this poor bastard, anyway," Horace replied. "Who reported the body?"

"The guy standing over there." Ken pointed to a man talking to a uniformed officer. "He was driving southbound when he saw the body in the street. I'll speak with him." Ken walked over to the man. The photographer had arrived on the scene.

"Hey, Dan, make sure you get some close-ups on this one and some good shots of the scene. Need to get the brake marks and can you take some shots from the south about a hundred feet and work in every twenty-five feet. Also do the same from the north."

"John," Horace said to a crime scene investigator from the traffic unit. "Can you fine comb the area for any debris that may have detached from the vehicle?"

"Sure, Horace."

"Forensics will go over the body once you're done. Has the coroner been notified?"

"Yes, he's on his way."

Ten minutes later, Ken finished interviewing Mr. Colletti and made his way back to Horace.

"Did our witness see anything?" Horace asked as he took out a handkerchief and blew his nose.

"He said the streets were empty except for one car he observed heading northbound just before he saw the body. It was a black sedan."

"Did he get a description of the driver or a plate?"

"Nothing, just the color of the car. He wasn't even sure what make."

"Alright, Ken, do you want to start on the east side or west?"

"I'll take the east."

"Okay, we need to find out if anyone saw anything before the impact, during or after. If anyone saw him running. Did anyone see the impact? If not, who looked out the window when they heard the tires wailing? Were there any suspicious vehicles seen in the area? Anything out of the ordinary. Someone saw something. This is Cambridge. Someone saw something."

"What's that over there?" Ken said, pointing to the doorway of a building.

They walked over and found a blanket and cardboard box torn open lying in the entrance of the building.

"Someone was here tonight," Horace concluded as he picked up a pack of peanut butter crackers with two remaining. He reached down and picked up a spent cigarette butt and slid both items into a plastic evidence bag. "Hopefully we can get a print off one of these."

"It looks like he may have left in a hurry, too. We need to find out who stays here. Whose blanket this is. Lets get to work."

Ken started knocking on doors on the east side, while Horace hit the west. They knocked on every door of every apartment that was in site of the scene. It took them most of the day. They didn't find anyone who saw anything that could help them. They spoke with several people who had seen a homeless man in that particular doorway on a few different occasions. The description was similar from all witnesses. He was a white male in his mid-to-late forties with a graying beard and long dark hair. He had a medium build and was about five nine to five ten. Horace figured somebody on the force knew who this guy was. He got on his radio and called for the uniformed officers who worked in the district to meet with him. A few minutes later a cruiser arrived and Horace was there to meet them.

"Good morning, fellas."

"Hey, Horace," said the driver who was the senior officer. "What happened this morning?"

"Looks like murder. We are looking for a bum who may have seen something. We think he was camped out in that doorway over there." Horace pointed. "You guys know who he might be? He is described as a white male mid-to-late forties, with a beard and long dark hair. Medium build about five ten."

"I've seen that guy around," the junior officer said.

"Yeah, I remember him too. I think I ran him a few weeks ago for a warrant check. Hang on while I check my notes." It took a couple minutes and the senior officer found a name in his note pad. "Michael Dobson. I'm pretty sure that's the guy. DOB 6/3/56, SS# 025-50-1670. No known address. He was clean, no tickets."

Horace wrote down the information. "Okay, guys, thanks. I need to talk with this guy, so keep your eyes open and spread the word."

"You got it, Horace." They drove off. Ken came walking over.

"Any luck?"

"Just on the homeless guy. I got a name and his information. We need to find this guy. Right now he is all we have to go on and he may not even have been here when it happened."

"We'll find him," Ken said. "We'll find him."

Ken was one that never gave up. He had been an athlete all his life. He was a hockey player ever since he was seven years old. He played Little League and was the king of the ice in high school. He received a scholarship for hockey and attended Boston College where he earned a Masters Degree in Criminology. Ken graduated top of his class and took the civil service test two months after graduation. He scored a ninety-nine, which put him in the first academy class. He worked in uniform patrol for two years until he made detective. He was labeled as a hot dog and was known to be a scrapper in the street. There had been several complaints lodged against him for excessive force but he managed to slip out of them. The name Ken McLaughlin was well known throughout law enforcement in Eastern, Massachusetts. This was because his father, Ken Senior, was a retired Deputy Chief of Police in Boston. This didn't hurt Ken in his efforts to become a homicide detective.

Married with a four-year-old boy, Ken was already preparing to get his son Colin into hockey. He purchased for Colin, his first set of skates when he was two, and he took him skating every week hoping one day he would play in the NHL.

The investigation into the murder of Douglas Brady was ongoing. Forensics had determined the cause of death was attributed to a broken neck. It had been determined Doug was hit directly below the knees and received two fractured legs and a fractured skull. The perpetrator then drove in reverse, running over his neck and legs, which had most likely killed him. There were traces of black paint taken off his upper shin, and a subsequent investigation determined it was automobile paint consistent with that of a Ford product. Horace and Ken directed their focus on his family, co-workers, friends and acquaintances. They wanted to know who Douglas Brady was, who wanted him dead and why.

Chapter 23

The classroom was your typical World History classroom. A map of the world was stretched out covering a large portion of one wall. A board with current events from around the globe and photos of world leaders and historical figures hung so that one couldn't mistake the class for anything other than World History. There were twenty-four students sitting in Beth's senior class. She felt teaching seniors was not as difficult as freshman and juniors. Seniors showed more interest and most of them realized college was approaching very soon.

"Alexander was loved by the men he commanded. I want you to write an essay stating why. Also, how was his relationship with his army similar to his relationship with Homer? One more thing, where was Alexander's army in the autumn of 327 BC and what was his purpose for marching there? That's it, have a nice day."

The bell rang and the class filed out. When the class had cleared out of the room, Beth saw Allison standing in the doorway.

"Allison, what are you doing here?" Beth looked into her eyes and knew something terrible had happened.

"It's Doug," Allison began to cry. Beth quickly found a chair. Her heart was beating faster.

"What is it, Allison?" Beth was hoping it wasn't too serious but she had a bad feeling.

"Doug was in an accident. He's dead."

Beth's head started spinning. She was numb and was hoping it was a bad joke or a mistake, but looking at Allison, she knew it was real. Allison, still weeping, put her arms around Beth and they held each other. Beth sat there unable to cry. Allison cried for both of them.

The funeral for Doug was held in Philadelphia where his family lived. They were planning on driving down to stay with Doug's sister over the holidays. Doug was excited about the trip and was looking forward to having Beth meet his father and two sisters. It never crossed her mind she would be meeting them alone. Beth decided she would fly down to pay her respects and meet his family. Doug would like that, she thought.

During the flight down, Beth was distraught with the anticipation of facing his family and seeing Doug lying lifeless in a box. The flight home was even worse because the reality had set in once she actually saw his corpse. It was on the plane home that Beth had shed her first tear for Doug and they continued to flow for two weeks. The sight of him lying in the coffin made her angry. Who could do this, and why?

Doug's family was cordial and tried to make conversation with her, but she knew they were just trying to be polite. They didn't know her and how she felt about Doug. She was just a pretty face, not family, not blood. The short conversations they had were civil, but generic. She sat in the plane looking out the window down to the lights below. She passed over them like the years of her life; gone in an instant, never to know why they were there and who turned them on and off.

Allison was with Justin at the airport when Beth arrived. She had not spoken with Justin about Doug's death. She decided to speak with him that night. The message light on her answering machine was blinking when she got home. There were several messages taped. She put Justin in the tub, took off her shoes and sat down to listen. Her mother had called, and in a concerned voice, pleaded for Beth to return the call right away. A couple of friends from work called checking in to see if she was all right. There was a message from Monsignor London who wanted an answer on scheduling a meeting with Justin. The unfamiliar voice of an agent representing a talk show and a Ms. Simsbury from the New York Post, both called in search of a story. The last message was from Detective Washington, who wanted to speak with Beth regarding the death of Doug Brady.

Justin was clean and in his pajamas. Beth was sitting on the edge of his bed after tucking him in.

"Sweetie, I want to talk with you about Doug."

"Okay."

"Doug had an accident last week and he was killed. We haven't had a chance to talk about it so I want to understand how you feel about it."

"He is in heaven with our father," Justin said very calmly.

"Yes, Sweetie, he is in heaven." Beth had to work hard to hold back her tears.

"I am going to miss him Mom, but I'll see him again in heaven. We both will."

Beth was amazed at how strong he was. "I will miss him too, Sweetie."

"He is at peace now Mom, and he's smiling down at us from up above." Justin's words made her feel better. He had such a tremendous vocabulary and he was so wise for such a young boy. She was a blessed woman, she thought, as she kissed him goodnight.

The bar was a dive on the west side of Boston. It had a four-foot high leprechaun holding a mug of beer at the entrance of the building. The floor was sticky and the long rows of bottles dusty. It was an establishment where many of the patrons were cops and firefighters and the people that weren't, wished they were. Horace and Ken were sitting at the end of the bar near the entrance, setting back a few. Horace had his usual JD on the rocks and Ken an imported draft beer.

"How are we doing on the list?" Horace lifted his glass.

"We have to talk with the girlfriend, two more co-workers and a tennis pro."

"We have messages into all of them, right?"

"Yeah, the tennis pro, we are meeting with at ten in the morning and we are waiting to hear back from the rest."

"We need to see the girlfriend as soon as possible," Horace said. "She flew down to the funeral in Philly. She should be back tonight."

"Okay, why don't we stop by first thing in the morning and have a chat with her?" Ken said.

"Good idea."

"You want to watch the Bruins?"

"I fucking hate hockey," Horace blurted out in a serious tone.

"Is it because there are maybe two black players in the entire league?"

"No, it's because I can't play."

"Get some skates. I'll teach you."

"So you can check my ass into the boards? Forget it. I'm history." Horace stood up and emptied his glass.

"See you at eight sharp," Ken said.

"Thanks for the warning," Horace replied as he walked out.

As partners, they worked well together and tolerated each other; but they both suspected the other to be a racist. But that was the way it was. Everyone got along, but deep down there was a feeling of prejudice on both sides. The black officers felt that most white officers targeted blacks on the street and the white officers didn't trust that the black officers would always back them up against their own. Ken stayed and watched the first period, and then he went home to his family.

The next morning Horace and Ken were knocking on Beth's door at 8:30. She had taken three days off from work and this would be her last. The door opened and Beth was wearing her running attire.

"Hello, may I help you?"

"Yes, I'm Detective Washington and this is Detective McLaughlin. I had called and left a message on your machine."

"Yes, I'm Beth, please come in." Beth opened the door. "Can I offer you some coffee or juice?"

"Coffee would be great," Ken replied.

"No thanks," Horace said.

"Why don't we sit in the kitchen while I make a fresh pot."

They sat down and Justin walked into the room.

"Sweetie, these men are detectives. Detective Washington and Mac."

"McLaughlin." Ken finished for her.

"This is my son, Justin."

"Hello, Justin," Horace said.

"Hey, sport," Ken said.

"Are you real policemen?"

"Yes we are," Ken said proudly.

"Your job is to help people when they need you the most, right?"

"That's right, Justin," Horace responded.

"One day you will be rewarded in the kingdom of our lord."

Horace looked at Ken and then at Beth. He was astonished by Justin's vocabulary.

"I hope you're right, Justin." He knew the boy was special.

"Justin, Sweetie, I need to talk with these gentlemen, so how about we find a book for you to read."

"Goodbye," Justin said. They both said goodbye to Justin and Beth took him into the other room.

"That is one bright kid," Ken said.

"Yeah, religious too," Horace added.

Beth came back into the room.

"You have a special boy there."

"Thank you, Detective Washington."

Horace started with the questioning. "Beth, as you know we are investigating the murder of Douglas Brady."

"Are you sure it was murder?"

"Yes."

"He was struck while running. Couldn't it have been an accident?"

"No, the driver hit him and then backed up over him again. It was murder."

"Oh my God!" The concern in her eyes was obvious. "How can I help?"

"We just want to ask you a few questions. Sometimes it's the most insignificant details that can close a case."

"Alright," Beth said.

"How long had you known Mr. Brady?"

Beth didn't like him asking the question in past tense.

"Nearly two years. We were engaged to be married a week ago."

"Where were you on the morning of the sixth about 5:15 AM when Mr. Brady was killed?"

"I was here sleeping."

"Were you alone?"

"Yes, of course. My son was here."

"How would you describe your relationship with Mr. Brady?"

"We loved each other."

"Any problems, any fighting going on?"

"No, we got along just fine."

"I know these questions may seem personal but I need to ask them in order to conduct a thorough investigation," Horace said.

"I understand."

Ken just sat sipping his coffee. He was glad Horace had this line of questioning.

"Would you describe your relationship with Mr. Brady as intimate?"

"We were waiting for marriage.

"Do you know anyone who had a grudge against Mr. Brady? Anyone he had an issue with at work or in his personal life, anyone at all?"

"No, Doug was well liked by everyone." She hesitated. "He was a good man."

"Did Mr. Brady use drugs of any sort?"

"No, he was against drugs. He didn't even like taking aspirin."

"Was Mr. Brady involved in gambling at all?"

"No, not that I'm aware of."

"Have you noticed anything suspicious lately? Anyone strange you may have seen on different occasions or anyone following you. Does anything unusual come to mind?"

"No, nothing."

"What kind of car do you drive?"

"A Nissan Maxima."

"What color?"

"Green."

"Do you or Mr. Brady have any acquaintances who own a black sedan?"

"Not that I can think of."

"You haven't seen anyone suspicious operating a black sedan, have you?"

She thought for a moment before responding. "No, not that I can recall."

"I think that's all for today. We really appreciate your time. We will keep you apprised if anything turns up. If we need to speak with you again, will that be okay with you?"

"Sure."

"We are sorry for your loss."

"Thank you."

Beth wanted them to leave.

"Thank you." Ken said.

Beth walked them to the door and saw them out. She checked in on Justin and then went straight to the bathroom where she took a hot shower. Her tears were hidden in the water.

There was a knock at the door and Beth didn't want to answer it. She didn't want to see anyone. She had just dried her hair and gotten dressed. She peeked through the window and saw it was Allison. She let her in.

"Aren't you going running this morning?"

"No not today. The police were just here. They asked me questions about Doug and our relationship."

"They spoke with Tom at work the other day too," Allison said.

"I don't know what it is Allison. Whenever I fall in love with a man he ends up dead. What did I do to deserve this?"

Allison didn't have an answer for her. Nobody did.

Sunday arrived and Beth had not returned Monsignor London's call. The agent for the talk show had stated there would be a significant sum of money to be paid for Justin to appear on their television show. Beth was not interested and didn't return her call either. The prayer meeting was over and Beth made her way down to Justin's bible study class. As usual she stood by the door looking in. She spied the room but didn't see her son. She immediately entered the classroom and interrupted Ms. Brenner.

"Where is Justin?"

"Hi, Beth, he's fine. Monsignor took him to the conference room. He said it would be all right with you."

"Well it's not! I don't want him leaving this class without my approval. Do you understand?"

"Yes, I'm sorry, Beth." Ms. Brenner was blushing with embarrassment.

Beth turned and walked away heading straight to the conference room where she found Justin sitting with Monsignor London, the Bishop and the Cardinal. On the table lay a Bible, a pad and pen.

"Excuse me, Monsignor. May I speak with you?" Beth interrupted.

"Yes, Beth. We were just about to come and get you." Beth backed out of the room and he followed.

"What are you doing taking my son out of class without asking me first?"

"Calm down, Beth. You didn't return my call and the Cardinal made a special trip out here to meet with you and Justin. He is a very important and busy man. I didn't think it would harm anyone to allow him to meet with Justin for a few minutes."

"Well, you thought wrong, Monsignor, and it is inappropriate. How long has he been in there?"

"Only about twenty minutes or so."

"This meeting is over," Beth insisted.

"Beth, wait a minute. Do you realize how gifted Justin is?"

"Of course I know. He is my son. I told you the things he has done."

"We think he may be sent from God. An angel or prophet. Do you know what this means, Beth?"

"Yes, it means if you ever speak with my son again without clearing it with me first, I will call a lawyer!"

Beth went back into the room. "I'm sorry, Your Eminence, but I need to take Justin home now." She took Justin by the hand and walked out without saying another word.

Beth was so angry she was trembling as she walked out of the building. Justin had a way of calming her down and he did so during the drive home. The three men continued their meeting without Justin present. They talked about Revelations, the second coming of Christ and what future plans they had in mind for Justin.

Chapter 24

Five months had passed since the murder of Doug Brady. The investigation had not turned up any evidence or leads that gave Horace and Ken any indication of who ran him over and why. A week after they interviewed Beth, they had met with her once again after they learned Justin was the miracle child that was being broadcast all over the news. They asked her why she didn't bother to mention to them who Justin was. Beth responded that she didn't feel it was pertinent to the case. They disagreed by stating there was a possibility that it could somehow be linked to the case. Beth quickly dismissed that theory and put it out of her mind.

Horace had pretty much given up on the case and had moved on to other homicides. However, Ken couldn't let it go. Horace didn't know if it was because Brady was nearly the same age as Ken or because he was an athlete in his prime just like Ken when he was murdered. He wasn't sure and didn't ask.

The call came in at 4:45 on Friday afternoon. Ken was ready to call it a day when Horace asked him to pick up the line.

"Detective McLaughlin."

"Yes, this is Detective Robbins with Boston PD narcotics."

"How are you doing?" Ken asked.

"Good, I have a guy you may want to talk to."

"Okay, who?"

"Michael Dobson," Robbins said.

"I'll be there in thirty minutes or less." Ken felt an adrenalin rush.

"Horace, they're holding the bum, Dobson in Boston lock-up. I'm going over there. You coming?"

"Yeah, let me use the john first."

Dobson had been arrested for buying a small amount of crack cocaine downtown and when the Narcotics officer threatened jail time he stated he had witnessed a hit-and-run in Cambridge. He agreed to talk if they would make him a deal. The interrogation room had light green walls that appeared almost white with the intense illumination reflecting off them. The chamber was empty except for a table and three chairs. A two-way mirror hung on the long wall near the entrance, but didn't fool anyone with half a brain. Dobson was already seated when Ken and Horace entered the room. They introduced themselves as the detectives who were investigating the murder of Douglas Brady. Dobson could have passed for the twin of Aqualung, Ken thought.

"We're told, you know something about the hit-and-run that occurred on Massachusetts Avenue in Cambridge about five months ago?"

"Yes."

Ken was asking the questions. "Okay, what can you tell us?"

"I was laying down trying to get some sleep in the doorway of a building on Mass. Ave. when I saw this guy jogging up the street. A black car came racing up the street and ran the guy over. Then he stopped, backed up, and ran him over again. Then he drove off."

"Did you get a look at the guy?" Ken asked in a very serious and intense manner.

"Not too clear, but I did see him."

"What did he look like?" Ken asked.

"He had short dark hair and must have been in his mid-twenties, maybe thirty."

"What kind of car was it?"

"It was a Ford, a Taurus I think."

"Why didn't you report it?" Ken continued to grill him.

"I was scared. This guy was crazy the way he ran over him the second time. I didn't want my ass run over like that dude, so I took off. I didn't know what to do. What if he saw me? I left Cambridge that day."

"I don't suppose you got a plate?"

"Yeah, I did."

"You got the plate number?" Ken asked in disbelief.

"Yeah, I remembered it because the numbers were like my birthday. 356. I was born on the 3rd day of June 1956, so I remembered the plate. I think it was ZZH356 or ZZT356. I'm not sure but I know the letters were ZZ."

"How do you know that?" Horace asked.

"Because I love ZZ Top. One of my favorite bands."

"I love them too," Ken said, excited about the discovery.

"Did my information help?"

"More than you know," Ken said. "I just wish you would have given it to us five months ago."

Ken and Horace went back to the station and Ken started running the plates. Horace had to leave. There was a bottle of Jack waiting for him. Ken stayed and kept searching. An hour later, after cross checking different letters that may have been mistaken for an H or T, he finally came up with the plate. It was ZZL356 registered to Felix Rent-A-Car in Burlington. At 7:30 the next morning, Ken was banging on Horace's apartment door. Horace had tossed quite a few back after leaving the station the night before, so he wasn't waking up too easily. Ken had been up since five, his mind racing. He wanted to find the driver and squeeze the cuffs on him until his hands turned blue. The door opened and Horace stood there looking like a zombie.

"What the fuck!" Horace said in an unhappy tone.

"Come on, partner, get your ass up. We have a bad guy to catch."

"The bad guy will still be there at nine."

"Come on, I'll buy you a coffee. Take a couple pills and drink some water. You'll be fine."

"I'll get dressed, give me a minute to clean up."

Ken looked around the apartment and began to feel bad for him. It must be a lonely existence, he thought. There were empty cartons of Chinese food that had been sitting out for a quite some time. Dirty glasses and dishes spread throughout the place. An empty bottle of booze was on the floor next to the couch where he had obviously spent the night. His furniture was old and dusty and the place smelled like a lockeroom. Horace chased three Tylenol down with a tall glass of water and was ready to go.

The rental agency was a small operation with about thirty-five cars. Most of them were Ford Escorts and Taurus's. They also had few Crown Victoria's for those who wanted to spend a little more. Dobson was right. The manager remembered the Taurus because it had been returned with damage to the hood and chrome near the front bumper. The color of the vehicle was actually dark green. Horace was impatient while they waited for the manager to produce the records that contained the information of the person who rented the car. His headache had not subsided and he felt nauseous. Had he been able to sleep a couple more hours, he would have been fine. Ten minutes later, the manager came out of the back room with a folder. They required a valid driver's license from anyone who rented vehicles from them, and they photocopied all licenses.

"Bingo!" Ken said, when he saw the photocopy of the license.

"Don't get too excited yet," Horace said.

"Did he have his own insurance to cover the damage?" Ken asked as he fumbled through the paperwork.

"No, he purchased it through us."

"Did he put it on his credit card?" Ken asked.

"Let me see."

Ken held open the folder for the manager.

"No, he paid cash and we took an imprint but didn't run it. He returned it a day early."

"So you remember this guy?" Ken asked.

"Yes, after looking at the picture on his license, I do. I had to record the damage to the car."

"It reads here the cause of the damage was a deer," Ken said, not appearing to be surprised.

"Yes, he said a deer darted in front of him and he couldn't avoid hitting it." The manager shook his head side to side.

"Did he say if the deer had died?" Horace asked sarcastically.

"I don't remember."

"Is there anything else you recall about this guy? The way he dressed or scars, a tattoo, maybe?

"No, he was well dressed, a suit, I believe. He was a foreigner though."

"A foreigner, like from what country, would you say? Ken asked with pen resting on his note pad.

"The middle east," the manager responded.

"That would make sense. The name on his license is Assad Madul. If you can think of anything else, please call me." Ken handed him his card.

On the way to the suspect's address, they ran the license and his date of birth through NCIC, the computer information system used by law enforcement. Ken was excited. He was getting close to bagging the perpetrator and he could taste it. Horace was sipping on his coffee as they were driving through the city. His headache was subsiding. The records check came back and Ken slammed on the brakes. Horace cursed as his coffee went flying out of the cup onto the dashboard. There was no record found for Assad Madul. There wasn't a record of anyone with the social security number printed on his license. They went to the address on the license and spoke with the apartment manager. He went through his records and he never had a tenant with the name Madul. They interviewed and showed his photograph to several people in the neighborhood and not one person recognized the photo. Assad Madul did not exist.

Chapter 25

Groundhog Day arrived and once again the furry little creature saw his shadow. Beth was hoping he wouldn't, she'd had enough of winter. It was a cold winter season and it snowed much too often, as far as Beth was concerned. Running on ice and snow made her daily jog far less enjoyable.

Since Doug's death, Beth tried to remain strong for Justin and for her own mental well being. She had decided to train hard and try and qualify for the Boston Marathon. This would keep her mind focused and her body fit.

She had also decided to attend church another day during the week. Saint Patrick's offered a service on Wednesday evenings and she and Justin were attending regularly. With these changes in her life, Beth rationalized it would be easier to cope with the loss of Doug. She had decided to open her heart up to the Lord, and by completely surrendering her soul to Him, she might turn her loneliness into a peaceful existence.

Race day was approaching and Beth was feeling confident. She knew she would have to train extra hard to make it to the finish line. Twenty-six miles was a long run for anyone and she had heard all the stories from Doug about Heartbreak Hill and hitting the wall. She was running eight to twelve miles a day and one long eighteen mile run a week. As race day closed in she was preparing for a twenty-two mile run. If she could make it twenty-two miles, her adrenalin should carry her the last four miles. At least that's the way she rationalized it. The most important feat for her was to cross the finish line. It was a goal she had always dreamed of and she was not going to fail.

During her free period, Beth sat in the faculty room reading a self-help book on coping with tragedy by moving on to live a spiritually content and happy life.

It was titled, "The Sun Will Rise." This was one of many self-help books Beth had read and they helped reassure her that better days were ahead. Most of the books had a religious theme. She was partial to those type of self-help books. In her spare time Beth spent much of her time reading. She rarely ever watched television except for the occasional Disney movie with Justin. She also enjoyed reading books about people who had survived the Holocaust and other tragedies of enormous proportion. She admired this type of people, and it made her problems seem less significant in the grand scheme of the world. Beth was reading a quote in her book that read, "One's measure of strength is not necessarily a physical strength, but a strength of character, that one can live through unbearable tragedy and devastation to move forward in life even stronger than before." As she was pondering this quote, her attention was drawn to a man who entered the room.

"Hello." He smiled at Beth.

"Hello," Beth replied.

He went to the kitchen area, poured a cup of coffee and returned.

"Would you mind if I sit here?"

"No, of course not," Beth turned back to her book pretending not to show interest.

"Thank you." He took a seat across from her. "I see you're reading Alexa Glassman?"

"Yes"

"The Sun Will Rise," he said.

"Have you read it?" She was surprised he knew the book.

"Yes, it helped me get through a very hard time in my life. It's a great book."

"So far it's wonderful," she said.

"My name is George."

"I'm Beth, nice to meet you."

"I'm a substitute teacher and this is my third time here. I'm still trying to find the bathroom."

"It's right over there." Beth pointed.

"Yes, that one I found."

"What subject are you subbing for?"

"It doesn't matter. I prefer Math."

"Math. Well, that's unusual to hear from a sub."

"My degree is in engineering. I was laid off recently so I decided to try subbing while searching for a job."

"How do you like it?" she asked.

"It's kind of like baby sitting."

"Welcome to the wonderful world of teaching, George." Beth stood up and shook his hand. "It was nice meeting you," she said.

"The pleasure is mine."

As she left the room, he sat with his coffee thinking how interesting she was. He would start subbing there more often. George Farkis was a tall, dark and very handsome man with a good build. He had short hair and a neatly trimmed mustache. He was very intelligent and well educated. Once George set his mind on something, he was relentless in pursuing it. He could do anything he wanted, or have anyone he wanted.

A few days later Beth was having lunch with a group of teachers and George sat with them. He was such a gentleman and had a very dry sense of humor. Beth was intrigued by his broad knowledge of every subject matter that came up in conversation. He didn't boast, but offered his opinion in a very humble sort of way. Beth was fond of him, but kept her thoughts to herself. A week later Beth entered the faculty room and George was reading a book during a free period. Beth sat with him and they talked. George told her he had never been married and fathered no children. He grew up and attended school in San Diego. He had a brother, two sisters and a mother who was confined to a wheelchair. Beth opened up to George, telling him that she was a widow and had a son named Justin. That she was an only child. Her mother was living in Florida and her father had passed away. Their conversation seemed to flow without apprehension and George had been waiting for the right moment to ask her out. His heart was pounding and just before the bell rang for the next class, he asked her if she would like to have dinner with him. Beth agreed.

Dinner with George was delightful. He had taken her to a Greek restaurant and it had a theme that replicated the Parthenon. The food was excellent and the conversation superb. They talked about their dreams and goals, some obstacles that had come along the way, and how they overcame them. They spoke briefly about religion and having faith in mankind. They touched on music, sports and the theater. He was such a well-cultured man, she thought. Beth needed male companionship, but wanted to keep it at a friendship level. She was not ready for romance, but George wouldn't settle for anything less. After dinner he drove her home, walked her to her door where he tried to kiss her goodnight, she simply turned her head and gave him a light hug and thanked him. Beth went inside and George walked back to his car and got in. He sat there for a few minutes thinking about the evening spent with Beth and how he was going to win her over.

Chapter 26

Justin had a sleepover at Allison's house so Beth could enjoy the night out with George. She was relieved she wouldn't have to wake Justin late at night to take him home. Justin had pleaded with Beth to have a sleepover so he could play with the kids and it made sense to do so. When Beth got home there was a message from Ken McLaughlin. He wanted to meet with her as soon as possible. The next morning Beth was up early and went for a long run. It was cold out but she dressed for it. While running, she couldn't help but think about George and it somehow made her feel guilty. Doug had only been gone for half a year. When she finished her run she checked her running time and was pleased. She had run twenty-two miles in two hours and twenty-three minutes. After taking a shower she went over to Allison's house and picked up Justin. Then she called Ken and they made plans to meet at her house at 1:00 pm that afternoon. It was Saturday and she had no plans other than grocery shopping. Two hours later Ken arrived and was knocking at her door. Horace had taken the day off and was nursing a hangover. Beth answered the door and offered him something to drink as they made their way into the kitchen.

"Beth, I am pressed for time so I'll make this fast. We found a witness a couple weeks ago who saw the murder of Douglas Brady. He gave us a plate and we ran it and came up with a Middle Eastern guy by the name of Assad Madul. Have you ever heard that name?"

"No." Beth wondered why it took so long.

"That doesn't surprise me because so far this guy doesn't exist, at least not on paper. I had a photo of his license cleaned and blown up and have been showing it around town. I followed up on a couple leads I thought were good, but they didn't amount to anything." Ken reached in his pocket and pulled out a sheet of paper.

"Have you ever seen this guy?"

Beth looked at the photo, then back up at Ken.

"Oh, my God!" she said, her face turning pale, her stomach knotting up.

Ken knew right away something was wrong. "What is it, Beth?"

"It's George!"

Chapter 27

While driving back to the police station Ken dialed Horace on his cell phone.

"What are you calling for? It's Saturday and I'm off." Horace had been sleeping.

"We got a break on the Brady case, partner." Ken felt like a teenager who had just won a championship.

"Do you know how many times I've heard you say that and we ended up with shit?"

"Not this time. Beth identified his photo. John Doe is a substitute teacher at her school. She had dinner with the fucking guy last night."

"Holy shit!" He got Horace's full attention. "You got an address?"

"Not yet. Meet me at the station. I'm calling the principal to get an address on this guy. Then we'll see the judge for a warrant."

"I'm on my way." Horace hung up.

Ken had gotten a phone number from Beth for the Principal and Vice Principal. All teachers had their contact information in case of an emergency and Beth assumed this qualified. Ken called the Principal but got his answering machine. So he called Mrs. Camp, the Vice Principal and she happened to be home. Ken asked her to meet them at the school right away, where the list of substitutes and their information was on file. Horace arrived at the station a few minutes later and they immediately drove to the school where Mrs. Camp was waiting. They went into the administrative office and she opened a file cabinet.

"What did Mr. Farkis do?" Camp figured it was serious.

"He is wanted for questioning in a murder case," Ken responded.

"Oh, my God!" She felt as if she had been violated. She had hired him.

"Do we know for sure this is his real address?" Ken asked cautiously.

"It's where we mail his paycheck."

"Please don't breathe a word about this to anyone. Do you understand?" Horace got her attention.

"Yes, not a word," she answered without hesitation.

Judge Cameron was at the gym when his cell phone rang. He was half way through his nautilus workout and was not going to stop until he was finished. Ken and Horace drove to the gym and found him in the steam room wrapped in a towel.

"Is Farkis his real name?" The judge was concerned.

"No record of him."

"Other than a photo ID you have no clue who this guy is?"

"That's right, Judge, but he has been getting close to the victim's girlfriend. They had dinner last night."

"Do you think she is implicated?"

"Absolutely not. You should have seen her. She was spooked by the whole thing."

"I've heard of chasing another guy's gal, but killing her boyfriend to get next to her, that's certainly the extreme."

"Yes, it is, Judge." Ken was anxious to get the signature.

The judge signed the warrant and Horace called for back-up while they drove to the suspect's residence. Ken was pumped up and couldn't wait to get into the apartment. They had a warrant to search his apartment. They had a witness who saw the murder and the license plate of the murder weapon, the car. They had a photograph of the suspect who had the car in his possession when it was used in the murder and the suspect had been concealing his real identification. They had a link between the victim's girlfriend and the suspect. Even with all the evidence against him Horace knew it wasn't enough unless Dobson could identify the suspect in a line-up. Neither of them were optimistic that he could. It was too dark for Dobson to get a clear view of the driver. They were hoping that something in his apartment would provide direct evidence. If not, they would have to try sweating him for a confession.

The street was busy with cars rolling and people walking about. Ken and Horace sat in front of the suspects apartment building waiting for back up to arrive, when Horace broke the silence.

"Is that our guy?"

The suspect had just walked out of the building and was heading east on foot.

"That's him," Ken said.

They didn't need Farkis present to execute the search warrant, but they wanted to question him about the murder and false identification. They needed to know who George Farkis really was. Horace said he thought the guy was CIA. He laughed, but didn't completely rule it out.

Both men exited the car and started up the street on foot. The suspect stopped to buy a newspaper, and that's when they made their move.

"Mr. Farkis." Ken approached from the front and Horace moved to his side. "I am Detective McLaughlin and this is Detective Washington with the Cambridge Police Department."

Ken flashed his badge. "We have a warrant to search your apartment."

He looked at them and immediately threw a right-handed palm strike to Horace's nose, knocking him to the ground. The suspect ran eastward down the sidewalk, pushing people aside. Ken started chasing after him. With blood pouring from his nose, Horace got on his radio and called for help. Ken was on his tail sprinting down the street. The suspect took a quick left into an alleyway and started fishing through his coat pocket while he was running. Ken observed what he was doing, so he drew his weapon.

"Stop! We just want to talk," Ken commanded.

The suspect darted into a doorway, stopped, and a few seconds later continued running to the end of the alley and took a right onto a main street. Skating three times a week was paying off and Ken was gaining on him. All of a sudden the suspect slowed down and began walking fast, staggering before collapsing on the sidewalk. Ken caught up to him and rolled him over. He was frothing from the mouth. Ken called for an ambulance as he kneeled over the suspect who began to go into cardiac arrest.

Ken and Horace stood in front of Judge Cameron in his chambers.

"Mr. Farkis or Mr. Madul or whomever he is had a heart attack while running up the street just after we served him with the warrant. He's dead," Ken said.

"We would still like to execute the warrant," Horace said in a low, soft voice.

"On what grounds? He's dead. Can't bring him to justice in a court of law. It looks like he found his justice," Judge Cameron said with conviction.

"Judge, this guy has no identity. We have no next of kin, no family." Ken thought for a moment. "Okay. What about a conspiracy?"

"Go on." Cameron said.

"What if this guy wasn't acting alone? What if there were other people involved? Wouldn't that give us cause to search his place?"

"Look, Ken, Horace. You won't need a warrant to search his place if you can't locate any family. Just go in with a uniformed officer and inventory his place. The place has got to be cleaned out, right?"

"Right," Ken said. Thinking he already knew that.

"Ken, was the guy that much out of shape?" Cameron asked.

"He certainly didn't look it, but I guess he was."

"You sure you didn't shoot him?" Judge Cameron smiled.

"I'm sure, Judge."

"Get out of here, you two."

They decided to wait until the next day to at least make it appear like they actually tried to find a family member of John Doe. They called for a uniform car to assist and they met with the super before going up. He lived on the 11th floor, had taken a year lease under the name George Farkis and had been living there for seven months. The uniformed officers arrived and all five of them entered the apartment and most weren't too surprised with what they found.

"I guess this guy didn't believe in the comfort of furniture," Ken said sarcastically.

The room was empty except for a desk and chair. There was a computer and papers scattered about. In the kitchen sat a small table with one chair. Ken opened the refrigerator and found it full of fresh vegetables, eggs, spring water and orange juice.

"Looks like John Doe was a vegetarian. No meat anywhere." Horace was impressed.

"How can a guy who eats like this have a heart attack while taking a little run up the street?" Ken asked.

In the bedroom there were two suitcases with clothes neatly folded inside. On the floor was a sleeping bag.

"Not even a pillow," Ken said.

In the closet hung shirts and pants neatly cleaned and pressed with plastic draped over them. There were a few suits, two overcoats and a ski jacket. After the initial look through his place they all gathered back into the living room. Horace observed something in the desk drawer.

"Ken," he said looking surprised. "Look at this."

He picked up a manila folder and threw it on the desk. Ken opened it up and read. He looked up at Horace and said, "Don't anyone touch anything."

He put on his surgical gloves and Horace did the same. He said to a uniformed officer, "Sam, can you call for fingerprints? We need to find out who this guy was."

The folder contained several newspaper articles from papers all over the country that covered the miracle child incident.

"He wasn't after the girl," Horace concluded.

"No, he was after the kid," Ken replied.

"But why kill the boyfriend?" Horace asked.

"Maybe he wanted to get to the kid, but thought Brady was in the way," Ken said, scratching his head.

"Okay, we need to book all this paperwork and everything in the desk into evidence after the print squad is finished, also the laptop. We need to check all the pockets in his clothes. Anything that looks like it may give us a clue we tag and bag," Horace said, as he blew his nose.

"Check this out," Ken said. He picked up an old wooden box about fourteen inches long that he found in the desk.

"Open it up." Horace was curious.

Ken opened the box and found an old dagger with a solid gold handle and a long double edge platinum blade. The top of the handle had an inscription of a serpent with seven snakeheads.

Except for the dagger, everything had been booked into evidence and the department computer nerd was going through John Doe's files. The fingerprints came back. "No match found." Two days later Ken received the coroner's report. John Doe had died of cyanide poisoning.

Chapter 28

The phone rang while Beth was making a turkey dinner. She hurried and cleaned off her hands and raced to the phone. It was Ken McLaughlin. He called to tell her that George Farkis had died of self-ingested cyanide poisoning. He also told her about the newspaper clippings and that they still didn't know who Farkis really was. There wasn't even a trace of history on him.

After she hung up the phone, Beth knew she had to talk to someone she could trust, so she called her mother. Beth was scared and really needed her mother to come and stay with her, but she had not been well and Beth didn't want her traveling right now. They talked on the phone twice a week and Beth looked forward to those conversations. But she needed someone to hold her, someone who wouldn't end up dead a few months later, she thought.

Her faith in the Lord was her real strength and she had decided long ago to put her fate in his hands. All the bad things that happened in her life in the past few years had put her faith to the test. It wasn't until she had witnessed Justin on the beach that she knew there truly was a God and she was put on this earth for a reason. She found herself praying the rosary twice a day and sometimes more. Justin was growing up fast and he was so full of love for everyone and everything. He was a very quiet boy and so well behaved. Whenever he talked he made sense. He never wasted words like most children. Everything he said had a meaning behind it. Beth knew there was no other child on earth like him and she knew there was a purpose for him being here. She just wasn't exactly sure what it was.

Ken sat at his desk totally bewildered. John Doe had six different passports from all over the world, two fake licenses and social security cards. He had two passports from the United States, one from France, Germany, Iran and Russia. Every one had a different name and date of birth. Ken knew John Doe was up to something big, but what was it? It puzzled Horace as well, but it ate at Ken. They weren't able to come up with anything on him. They checked his fingerprints, dental records and DNA. They checked all his aliases and ran his photo through Interpol and came up with nothing. The passports and fake IDs were nearly perfect forgeries. They knew it had something to do with Justin, but they couldn't pin it down. Ken left the office, went to the ice rink and put on his skates. Horace went home to his bottle.

Justin was tucked in for the night. Beth had read him a story and sung him a song. "Scarborough Fair" was his favorite song because it was hers. She had a hard time singing it without shedding a tear. For it was a song that brought her back to when she first met Daniel. It was a song she held very dear and kept close to her heart. She took a long, hot bath and sat down to her book. It was 11:00 at night when the phone rang. Who could be calling her this late, she wondered. Beth answered the phone.
"Hello."
The voice on the other end was the calmest, most beautiful voice she had ever heard. It sent chills down her spine. Beth just stood there listening.
"Beth, this is your Father. You must protect our son from those who would do him harm. For he will spread the word of the truth. And those who listen will be enlightened and shall be saved." The phone went dead.
Beth dropped the phone and slid down the wall to the floor crying. Her crying soon turned into praying. She prayed most of the night until she fell asleep.

Chapter 29

Pinehaven, a small town located in northern Vermont, is a spot carved out in the middle of acres and acres of woods. The closest town is Claironton, eighteen miles to its west. Denmore Logging Company employs many of the townspeople, and cutting down pine trees is their main source of income. The town, with a population of fourteen-hundred people, is a close-knit community. Just like any town, they have people who break the law, suffer from personal problems, and commit sins. There weren't many visitors in Pinehaven except hunters and fisherman who make their way up during the season and usually go home with a good catch and a smile. The town hall is the Sheriffs Department, Firehouse, Department of Public Works, Power Company, Post Office, Tax Department and the Town Manager's office, all nestled into one building. There is a grocery store, a gas station, a liquor store, a bank, a hardware store, a few restaurants and a bar. The town has a Congregational Church that was erected when the town was built just before the Civil War. The school is an old brick building that had been added onto over the years as the town grew. The nearest hospital is in Claironton, so Doctor Ruthiford takes care of the sick and injured people of Pinehaven who don't require serious treatment.

    Beth was ten years older. The years had come and gone without any problems since she up and moved from Arlington. Life had given her the peace she prayed for since she and Justin found Pinehaven. Beth remembered as a child seeing a sign for Pinehaven on her trip to Boston. The vision of the sign stayed with her because she remembered the area as having towering pine trees and thought it seemed so heavenly. Pinehaven read like Pine Heaven to her. This was the place the Lord had offered for her and Justin, and the first time she drove into town, she knew it was meant to be. Beth had changed her name and stopped using credit cards. She needed to disappear. George Farkis was sent to harm Justin, and she knew there would be others. Before she left Arlington she had the phone company check the incoming call records and there was no record of the call she received from the man who claimed to be the Lord. All the other calls were on record, the calls from her mother, Ken and Monsignor London. It all started to make sense to her. The immaculate conception, Justin's miracles and the phone call. A man without an identity murdered Doug in order to get close to her so he could kidnap or even kill Justin. The world had become a dangerous place. She realized who Justin was and that protecting him was her priority.

With the profit from the sale of her house, Beth was in a good position financially. She purchased an old farmhouse in Pinehaven for less than twenty-five percent of the cost of her house in Arlington. She was able to find a job teaching grammar school in Clarionton. She enjoyed teaching children and the kids loved her.. Life had become simple and she had finally found peace and serenity.

Her mother passed away a year after they moved to Vermont and Beth was sad because she hadn't seen her mother since she moved. She was planning on flying to Florida with Justin in early summer, but Nancy had passed away in the spring. Beth believed her mother was in heaven and at peace with God. There was a time when she would have mourned her mother's death, but she had come to believe dying was just the beginning. There was a better life to come after death. A place with no pain and hate, a place free from worry and hopelessness, a place where one would experience total peace and fulfillment.

Beth and Justin had an agreement. She asked him to keep a low profile for his own safety and protection. He was still young and would have a hard time connecting to people about the truth anyway. He agreed to stay quiet, observe, and learn until he became a man.

Time had passed quicker than Beth would have liked. It was spring and Justin was celebrating the day of his birth with his mother. He was sixteen and no longer a child. He asked Beth to take a walk to a brook that ran along the abutment of their property.

"Mother, the time has come for me to touch all within my reach. It is the time to spread the truth of my Father's kingdom and cleanse the souls of those who have sinned. The fish that swim in this brook signify the people in Pinehaven." He reached down and touched the water. "This brook runs into the Warren River which then flows into the lake. The fish that swim here now will soon be swimming far from here. Once the people learn what has taken place, they will share the events that occurred here with others outside of Pinehaven. The news will flow into the outside world and many people will come to learn for themselves what is happening."

"Yes, my son. You have grown into a wonderful young man. You must do what you have been sent here to do. The Lord will protect you now."

As her life in Arlington had been a memory, so had the loneliness she once felt. Beth had found a full life with Justin and the Lord, she no longer desired the comfort of a man.

Beth decided to talk with Pastor Sherman. It was time for Justin to start speaking out and Beth didn't want Pastor Sherman to be taken by surprise. He was a good man who devoted his life to helping the people in town as best he could. He had come to the understanding that God had blessed Justin, that he had been given a special gift. Soon he would know the whole truth.

Chapter 30

The surveillance camera had a microscopic lens and was fixed on the apartment building at 94 rue de Richelieu, Paris France. It was 6:15 pm. on Thursday and the sidewalks were busy with people walking about and the streets were infested with automobiles. It had stopped raining and the sidewalk cafes were back in business. James Adams sat in front of the camera wishing he were sitting at one of the cafes below sipping on red wine with a beautiful French woman. He hated the French, but he found their women to be sexy. The Bureau had sent him to France eight months earlier and he couldn't wait to get home. The people were arrogant and had a superiority complex and he couldn't understand why. Most of them were unpleasant and uneducated. The ones that weren't were transits, he thought. James Adams had been in the FBI for eleven years and had climbed up the ladder relatively fast. He had graduated from Columbia and was recruited right out of law school. He paid for his undergraduate degree with assistance from the government through the GI bill. He figured three years as an Airborne Ranger had earned him the right to a four-year degree with Uncle Sam footing the bill. He had been sitting in front of the camera for three weeks and he was getting antsy. Bill Fisher was one of three agents who were assigned to the surveillance post. Winston Cabbot was the third. Winston was on his eight-hour break. There were always two agents in the apartment during the surveillance to relieve the other agent so he could rest his eyes or catnap.

"I am so sick of France," Adams said while rubbing his eyes. "We bailed these bastards out of World War Two and again in Vietnam, and how do they show their appreciation? They fuck us every chance they get. Hell they wouldn't even allow us to fly over their air space when we put a missile up Kadafi's ass. If it were up to me, I'd drop a bomb right on Paris. It's probably going to happen sooner or later anyway. We might as well do it now before they completely fuck up the United Nations."

"Well you better learn to like it here, partner. You may retire on this one."

"Do you want to get shot? Don't ever say that. Come and take this for a while. My eyes are burning."

Fisher took his place and Adams began stretching.

"This, prick, better show up soon or I may have to abandon my post permanently. You know what's worse than a French terrorist?"

"No, what?" Fisher was being polite.

"A French terrorist who isn't punctual."

"You are a little more anxious for him to show than I am. The guy is an evil bastard. You know he won't go down easy. What do we really know about this Frog? Hell, we don't even know his real name."

"Rene De Lorme is his last known alias. The guy is like a ghost. He reminds me of Carlos the Jackal," Adams said.

"When we bag him, it will be worth it. That's why we chose counter-terrorism, to rid the world of these maggots," Fisher responded with one eye engaged to the eyepiece.

"Maybe you did. I joined to see Paris," Adams started laughing. So did Fisher.

"I really miss my wife. I never thought I'd say that. I miss the way she smells. The way she laughs at my dry humor. It's the little things that I love about her. I am blessed to have found her. You know where I met her?"

"Alcoholics Anonymous?" replied a smirking Adams.

"No stupid, a tag sale, fifteen years ago."

"Is that where you got those shoes?"

"Fuck you, these shoes cost more than your car."

"They would be worth more if you put the pennies back in them."

"I've had enough of your shit. I'm opening up to you as a friend and what do you do? You bust my nuts."

"Sorry, Fish, I'm just bored. My mouth always gets me in trouble when I'm bored. Go on, tell me your story."

"Forget it, now. You ruined the moment."

"Moment. What is this, group therapy? Just tell me."

"Okay, I went to this tag sale and I was just walking around by myself looking for anything that caught my eye. I saw this coffee table. It looked like a stack of four books. They weren't real books, they just resembled them. The table was made of hard leather and the top opened up to a storage area inside. I was asking the lady how much she wanted for it when Carrie came over with her checkbook in hand, stating she was going to buy the table. She said she had run to her car to get her checkbook. I looked at her and I knew right away she was the woman I wanted. Do you believe in love at first sight?"

"Of course I do," Adams responded. "Do you see the girl sitting outside the café wearing the red leather boots and black dress?" Fisher looked through the scope.

"Yes"

"I loved her the first time I saw her."

"You just want to fuck her."

"Maybe you're right. Are you telling me you didn't want to fuck Carrie?"

"Yes, I'm telling you that. I just wanted to kiss her, hold her."

"So what happened?"

"I insisted that I had inquired about the table first, but I agreed to split the cost with her if I could come by her place and look at it once in a while. We were married a year later. The table sits in our library."

"That is a good story," Adams said looking real serious.

"Tell me, why haven't you married?"

"I don't know. I guess it's because I'm not in one place very long."

"Wouldn't you want to have someone to care for, to go home to at night?"

"Yes, I suppose, but I'm not about to settle for just anyone so I can have someone to iron my socks."

"Adams, nobody irons socks anymore."

"You know what I mean. I want to find a woman who is my best friend and lover, someone who will stimulate me intellectually and emotionally, a genuinely good-hearted person, with nice tits."

"For a minute I thought you had a heart in that chest of yours, and you went and ruined it with vulgarity."

"Fish, don't you know me by now? I was kidding. But nice tits wouldn't hurt."

"Do you think we'll be able to spot this guy?"

"I'll know him when I see him," Adams said with confidence.

There was a knock at the door and Adams went to answer. "Who is it?"

"It's me. Winston."

Adams opened the door a crack to make sure he was alone. His other hand was on his weapon, a Glock nine-millimeter handgun. Once he knew it was safe, he opened the door.

"Why don't we use a password, so we don't subject ourselves to being accidentally shot?" Winston asked.

"Okay," Adams replied. "Your password will be homosexual."

Fisher started laughing.

"Kiss my ass, James," Winston said.

"I'm outta here," Fisher said. It was his turn for a break. He walked out and Adams followed behind him to secure the door.

"I'll take the camera," Adams said.

"Why are you such a homophobic?" Winston asked.

"I'm not, I just can't figure out how any man could look at another guy's hairy ass and think, 'Hmmm, I gotta get me some of that.'"

"It's not just about sex." Winston said.

"To be honest with you, Winston, I really don't give a shit. If you want to bang some chap in the fart locker, that's your business. I certainly don't want you doing it on my watch, though."

"That's what I like about you James, you're so sensitive."

Just then Adams said, "Hold on. Take a look at this guy. See the two guys about ten yards behind him?"

"Yes, I do."

Walking toward the building was a guy dressed in a long black trench coat with a wide brim hat and dark sunglasses.

"That's him! That's the bastard!"

"How do you know?" Winston asked. "The guy's wrapped up like a Christmas present."

"I know because he tugged on his left ear. Five years ago someone pulled a Van Gogh on him and he is known to tug on it from time to time."

"For what?" Winston asked.

"To make sure its still there, I guess. He must have lost feeling in it after they reattached it. That's him. Get ready."

The man in black entered the building and the two guys behind him followed. Adams got on his radio. "Pappa has come home with two packages. I say again, Pappa has come home with two packages."

The building they had been watching housed two known terrorists, Pierre Rousseau and Maurice Laurent, both known to associate with De Lorme. Adams had received intelligence a month earlier and had decided to sit on their place hoping De Lorme would show up. The organization had ties to Alherita, which was responsible for several bombings throughout Europe and the Middle East. De Lorme was wanted for murder in the United States and Great Britain. He was also wanted for questioning by authorities in three other countries for terrorist related crimes.

Adams called Fisher and three other agents to assist in the arrest. He also called Alphonse Bovie, his contact with the Direction Centrale Police Judiciaire. Bovie was in charge of the French counter-terrorism unit, and he made sure Adams knew he was in charge. Bovie had two stakeouts of his own, one fixed on 94 rue de Richelieu and the other on the apartment where Adams was set up. Adams knew from the moment he met him, he was going to be a pain in the ass. Bovie had an irritating and condescending way about him that rubbed Adams the wrong way.

"Get your gear on and make sure you put the side wraps on for this one." Adams had a serious look on his face, and it concerned Winston, who was strapping on his Kevlar vest. The FBI provided the counter-terrorism unit with state of the art equipment. The lightweight Kevlar would stop most projectiles except high velocity rounds and Teflon bullets. Kevlar, an aromatic polyamide or aramid fiber, had been introduced in 1972. The chemical composition of Kevlar is poly para-phenyleneterephthalamide (PPD-T). It is made from a condensation reaction of para-phenylene diamine and terephthaloyl chloride. The Bureau offered soft Kevlar, which protected the groin area up to the throat. The vital areas had extra Kevlar padding coverage. The agents wore bulletproof helmets and a face shield. Fifty-two percent of law enforcement officers are shot in the head and sixteen percent are killed from being shot in the side. These areas are usually not protected by most law enforcement officers. Adams was very serious about his men protecting those areas.

They entered the building with M16 automatic weapons and 40 caliber handguns strapped on their hips. Fisher was point man with Adams and Winston following. The three back-up agents entered through the rear of the building. Adams looked over and noticed Winston was trembling.

"Winston, take it easy, I'll be watching your back."

"That's what worries me," Winston said.

Adams was excited and his adrenalin was flowing. This was the moment he was waiting for. He would take down these crumbs and go home. He and his team had their weapons held tight against their shoulders and were moving tactically towards the stairs. The apartment was located on the second floor, about halfway down the hall on the left.

"We got trouble." Adams was listening to the communication device attached to his helmet.

"What's the matter?" Adams responded to the agent entering through the rear.

"It's the French. It's that asshole, Bovie. He's pulling rank and moving through with his guys."

"God damn him!" Adams said shaking his weapon in frustration.

It was then that the shots rang out. Bovie and his men rushed toward the apartment and had not seen De Lorme's man at the other end of the hall. Bovie and his team took automatic fire from the man positioned in the hall. Two rounds ripped into one of his men, hitting him in the femoral artery in his left leg and right kneecap, dropping him immediately. They hit the ground and began to return fire but the attacker had ducked into a utility closet. He popped out and fired another three round burst, hitting another French officer in the jaw. The apartment door swung open and De Lorme tossed out a fragmentation grenade. It rolled down the hallway like a candlepin bowling ball, and when it reach its destination, it detonated, killing three men, one of them FBI agent Scott Marion. The grenade was followed by automatic fire from De Lorme, who was in a prone position using the doorway for cover, and Laurent, who was standing above him firing a Russian made AK-47. Adams and the two agents made their way to the top of the stairs on the other end of the hall. The smoke was thick from the grenade and automatic fire, and he could hear the screams from the wounded. They took the corner with Fisher on point.

"Watch out!" Fisher yelled as he dropped to his belly.

The man in the closet spun around and fired two shots. One hit Winston in the throat, piercing his esophagus before hitting his spinal column. He dropped and fell to his knees. Winston grabbed onto his throat and looked up at Adams. Blood was pouring out between his fingers and he was making gurgling sounds. Adams was pissed.

"Hold on, Winston. Agent down!" Adams screamed into his mouthpiece.

Adams nearly took the second bullet in the head. Both Adams and Fisher returned fire, and the terrorist ducked back into the closet.

"Hang on, Winston, help is on the way!" Adams yelled.

Adams gave a hand signal to Fisher and Fisher hit the ground in a prone position and began firing at the doorway to the apartment while Adams ran down the hall. He stopped in front of the utility closet and began firing through the door.

"Take this, you mother fucker!" Adams was on one knee and he nearly emptied a full magazine into the closet before retreating back down the hall. The door to the utility room slowly opened and the man fell out into the hallway face first, riddled with bullets.

"Dan, are you OK?" Adams was yelling into his mouthpiece for the agent at the other end.

"Yeah, but Scott's been blown to shit."

"What about Reggie?"

"He's with me. He's okay."

"We are going in. Use those French bastards as shields if you have to. Get in position."

"Are you ready?" The sweat was beading up on Adam's forehead and began rolling into his eyes.

"Ready." Dan responded from the other end of the hallway.

"Okay, on three, give these pricks everything you got. Watch the crossfire."

"One, two, three."

Dan and Reggie began moving toward the apartment with three French officers following behind them. Reggie had a twelve-gauge shotgun and was pumping rounds at the doorway while Dan and the others were firing with full automatic bursts. Laurent popped out to return fire and was hit in the chest with twelve-gauge buckshot. Adams was crawling up the hallway on the floor in a prone position on the opposite side of the apartment. As he got closer he spotted De Lorme, who popped out to fire at the other agents. Adams fired several shots which hit De Lorme in the groin and thigh. He fell to his knees and pulled the pin from another grenade and tossed it at Adams.

"Hold your fire!" Adams yelled as he picked up the grenade and ran toward the apartment. Rounds were flying everywhere and he wasn't sure he would make it. As he moved toward the apartment doorway he could barely hear. The ringing in his ears had dulled the sound of the gunfire and it grew louder as he moved down the hall. Adams took a round in the abdomen as he moved toward the door. He knew he didn't have much time and he couldn't allow himself to be delayed or he would be blown to pieces. He threw the grenade into the apartment and fell back onto the floor as it detonated, killing De Lorme, Rousseau and one of De Lorme's men inside.

"James, are you okay?" Dan asked from the other end.

"Yeah, the vest stopped the round." Adams was in pain.

"The French officers burst into the apartment, only to find the remains of four men.

Fisher, who had been right behind Adams, covering him, offered to help him off with his vest.

"Is it bad?" Fisher asked.

"I'll live." He hadn't noticed the pain until now.

Fisher helped Adams onto his feet. Bovie came strolling over with a smug look on his face.

"Good work, Rambo," he said.

Adams reached from deep within and found the strength to swing his M16 with both hands, hitting Bovie with a butt strike in the lower abdomen, knocking him to his knees. Then he followed with a kick to Bovie's face, fracturing his nose.

"That's for getting my men shot, you fucking French fry!"

Fisher and Reggie had to stop one of Bovie's men from going after Adams. The rest of them just stood watching and did nothing. Winston and Scott Marion died on the scene. Adams had a severe bruise on his stomach, but was lucky the round hit an area that had extra padding. The bullet did not penetrate the Kevlar.

Within minutes the scene was chaotic. There were French police everywhere. The sound of sirens in the distance was unable to drown out the screaming that could be heard from inside the building. Fire trucks and ambulances were arriving on the scene. Several more FBI agents had arrived on scene, securing the parameter and tattered apartment. Adams could hear the agents arguing with the French police officers about jurisdiction.

"Fish, get in there and make sure nothing slips through our grasp. I don't trust these French bastards. They would probably side with the terrorists over us just because they're French and we're Americans. See what you can find in their pockets and anything else that may give us a clue as to what they were up to. If they had a computer in there, and it's not blown to shit, we need to keep it in our sight at all times until all information is extracted from the hard drive. Put Reggie on that."

"Okay, I'm on it."

Two ambulance attendants were wheeling Winston out on a stretcher. The sheet covering his body was soaked with blood. Adams was sitting on the stoop with his hand on his forehead. All he could think about was how he told Winston he would watch his back. Bovie was holding a bloody handkerchief against his nose as he came walking over with a well-dressed man beside him. Adams wanted to kick Bovie in the face again.

"You will have to answer for this, Mr. Adams." The man pointed to Bovie.

"Yeah, and who the fuck are you?" Adams barked out.

"This is Mr. Revelon, the Police Commissioner," Bovie mumbled.

"Well, Mr. Revelon. He is lucky all he got was a bloody nose." Adams got up and walked over to where Winston was lying.

"You see this man?" Adams pulled down the sheet exposing his face and throat.

"This was my man. Take a good look at him. Scott Marion is another one of my men and they're upstairs putting him together like a puzzle so they can bring him out. They are dead because Mr. Bovie here had to be a hero and jump the gun. He alerted those assholes up there and they got the jump on us. He is responsible for all these deaths. So you make sure you put that in your report, because someone has to answer for that, Mister."

Adams snapped the sheet back up, covering Winston, and he walked away.

Chapter 31

The office space supplied by the French consulate for the FBI field office was an old rundown building that used to house an office for the French Department of Agriculture. They occupied the entire first floor of a three-story building. The upper two floors were vacant. Adams strategically placed buckets to catch the water as it leaked through the ceiling when it rained. There were two windows at either end of the brick building and they looked as if the outside pane hadn't been cleaned since the war. Adams sat leaning back in his chair with his feet on his desk, thinking about what had happened less than two hours earlier. He mustered up a bottle of Grande Mariner from his desk and filled a rocks glass to the top. Adams was in good physical condition and knew the hard stomach he packed may have prevented internal injury. He was in pain but wasn't ready to go to a hospital. He drank down half the glass and picked up the phone. The door opened and Fisher walked in. Adams put down the phone.

"How do you feel?"

"I've felt better." He finished the glass.

"You want one?"

"No, I need one." Fisher's nerves had been put to the test.

Adams poured two glasses and handed one to Fisher.

"What happened up there, James?"

"The French! That's what happened. Leave it to the French and they will fuck it up. They would fuck up a free lunch."

"What about notification?"

"I was just about to call when you walked in. I needed a drink first. How do you tell a woman who is sitting at home with three kids that her husband is in pieces?"

"I don't know, but I need a drink just thinking about it. On a finer note I have some good news."

"What's that?"

"I went through De Lorme's pockets and came up with an ID and keys, which may be to his current place of abode. The ID reads he is one Jean La Flem and resides at 224 St Jacques."

"Where is Reggie?"

"He is with the PC. Rousseau had a laptop and Reggie's not letting it out of his sight. He said the French police gave him a load of shit about national security and patriotism. Reggie is playing the game and said he is following the laptop wherever it goes."

"Let me make a couple calls and we'll go." Adams finished his glass. The pain was subsiding.

The second key Adams tried, opened the door to La Flem's apartment. They weren't sure what his real name was but they were determined to find out.

"I'm going to keep calling him, De Lorme." Adams said. "Until we find out his real name."

"If we find out." Fisher responded. "Do you think we should have notified the DCPJ that we are entering his apartment?"

"What are you, fucking crazy? You saw how they botched the raid. These people are morons. They would just screw this up too." Adams was determined to leave the French in the dark from now on.

They went through the apartment and found nothing that would implicate him to any crimes or terrorist activity. The apartment was well furnished and had some exquisite artwork hung on the walls.

"Mr. De Lorme had an eye for art," Adams said, as he picked up a large painting that sat over the sofa. Concealed behind the painting was a wall safe.

"Well, look what I found."

"Holy shit!" Fisher said.

"I wonder what he has inside?" Adams eyes began to sparkle.

"You're not thinking of blowing the safe?" Fisher asked.

"Blowing it? No. I have experienced enough explosions for one day. That is too noisy. I have a better idea."

"What's that?" Fisher blurted out like a curious schoolboy.

"We're going to take it with us. You stay here. I'm going to find a hardware store."

Sixty-five minutes later Adams returned with a chainsaw, a sledgehammer, bolt cutters, a hack saw, a boom box and a dolly. It took them thirty-five minutes to cut the safe free. With AC/DC blasting on the boom box they sawed and hammered until they were finished. They loaded it onto the dolly and wheeled it to the car and drove back to the office. For a few minutes Adams realized the excitement that thieves felt after a successful caper. It was almost addicting.

The safe was a small combination-locked, Gardall B1307 series. It was three feet high by three and a half feet wide. After wheeling it into the office, Adams and Fisher sat down and Adams poured two drinks.

"So, what do you think?" Adams asked while rubbing his forehead.

"Well, we could blow it up, but that may draw attention. We could find a locksmith but that could also draw unwanted attention. Or we could try and break into it ourselves," Fisher said.

"I have an informant back home who used to be a safe cracker. He may still be, for all I know. I'll give him a call and see what he says." Adams picked up the phone and managed to track him down ten minutes later. Richie Bolder had spent half his life behind bars and at fifty-nine he had decided to retire to a life of boozing and fishing. His last hitch was spent in the federal penitentiary at Leavenworth. He had been sentenced to fifteen years for an armored car robbery. After serving ten years he was released on parole. The two and a half million dollars stolen had never been recovered, and all three of the thieves had refused to disclose the whereabouts of the money. The FBI had followed them for fourteen months after being released, but they all resisted the nagging temptation of digging up the loot and going on a spending spree.

Bolder had a talk with Smiley and Tork, and insisted they wait until the time was right or they would jeopardize losing the money. They all agreed that they didn't want the time they spent in the joint to be for nothing. Fourteen months after they were released the Bureau could no longer justify the man-hours following them around, so the agents were ordered off the case. One of the agents, Eric Fortier, had gone through the academy with Adams and they had kept in close contact. After being taken off the case, Fortier had called Adams and told him the whole story.

Three guys hit an armored car in broad daylight and made off with 2.6 million dollars in unmarked bills, denominations of ten, twenty and fifty dollar bills. It was an inside job that was nearly a perfect crime, except that one thing went wrong. Smiley had taken a job as a guard and was working with his partner, Jeff

Smith, when the robbery went down. Smiley was the driver and Smith was riding shotgun. Bolder and Tork got the jump on Smith outside of the truck by putting a gun into his ribs. Protocol states the driver is not supposed to open the door for anyone during a robbery, not even police officers in uniform. Smiley didn't follow Protocol. He opened the door and Bolder got in the passenger side with Tork holding Smith at gunpoint in the back of the truck. They drove to a secluded wooded area where they had a car waiting. When they finished unloading the bags of money they left Smiley and Smith locked in the back. The plan was to wait eight hours and then call it in, so Smiley would only be trapped long enough for them to hide the cash and ditch the car. Smiley had been grilled by the feds on the robbery but kept his cool and stuck to his story. The polygraph exam performed on Smiley was inconclusive. Both Bolder and Tork had worn ski masks during the robbery to avoid recognition. However, during the robbery Smith had noticed a distinct familiar type of walk and build on Bolder. He was extremely bow-legged and Smith remembered seeing him one night in a bar downtown with Smiley. He never approached Smiley; he didn't want company that night. He just watched from a distant table. Smiley was his new partner and he hadn't known him very well at that point. Smith was able to pick Bolder out in a criminal photograph array book at the police station. The local police, in conjunction with the FBI, hit Bolder's place. Bolder and Tork were arrested after the police found the ski masks, leather gloves and weapons they used in the crime. Smiley was also arrested as an inside accomplice and they were all convicted for the offense.

Bolder had planned the robbery down to the most intricate detail. How could it have gone wrong? Just bad luck, he thought. What were the chances, he thought. The one night he and Smiley had gone out for a beer, Smith happened to be at the same bar and recognized the way Bolder walked.

Bolder decided to keep the money hidden until it was safe to retrieve. Then he would enjoy the rest of his life in retirement with $867,000 in cash.

The restaurant was busy when Adams approached Bolder, who was sitting alone in a booth chasing a cheeseburger down with a beer. This was the start of a relationship that would last for many years. Adams had identified himself and told Bolder that he knew they were going to dig up the money sooner or later. Adams made it clear he would be watching real close until that day came. That's when he would move in. The other option was a better one, Bolder thought. In exchange for his freedom to live without Adams on his ass, Bolder agreed to give Adams information, disclose upcoming robberies and information on perpetrators of robberies under investigation. Bolder decided he wouldn't give up anyone he knew personally or liked. But there would always be a cowboy in town stirring things up, and Bolder didn't have a problem ratting on them.

The instructions Adams got from Bolder were right on the money. He had bought the drill he was instructed to get, along with several picking tools and in no time they had the safe open.

They just sat for a minute admiring their work, wondering what they might find inside.

"Now I know what Geraldo felt like."

"What the hell are you talking about, Fish?"

"Geraldo Rivera, the reporter. Remember about fifteen or twenty years ago he found Al Capone's hidden vault?"

"No, I don't. What was inside?"

"Nothing, an empty bottle of wine or something."

"Well, that's reassuring, Fish, thanks."

"Lets hope this is not a re-run," Fisher said.

Inside the safe they found several passports from various countries. Nearly two-hundred thousand in francs, pounds and dollars, two nine-millimeter handguns, a Beretta and a Walther PPK lying next to a silencer. There was a stack of papers piled neatly at the bottom of all the scattered items that appeared to be written in some sort of code. Wrapped in a red velvet cloth was an old dagger with a solid gold handle with a double-edged blade and an inscription at the top of the handle of a serpent with seven snakeheads.

Chapter 32

John Lewis grew up in an environment that glorified alcohol abuse. His father, Burt, was a rugged man who made his living as a logger. Growing up, John remembered his father as being detached from his family. Burt regarded the patrons of Lucky's Tavern his family. Every day after work he would retreat to the bar and drink with co-workers and other local boozers.

Usually around eight o'clock, he would stumble home expecting a hot meal to be sitting at the table awaiting his consumption. After his fill, Burt would pass out to awake the next morning just to do it all over again. His lifestyle allowed for very little time to be spent with his family.

When the weekend arrived, Burt usually worked half a day on Saturday and headed to the bar early. Sunday was a day spent watching sports and drinking, usually at Lucky's, but occasionally he would sit home ignoring the rest of the family while taking control of the television. Burt was hard working and never missed a day's work. He justified his abuse of alcohol by using the hard-working-man theory.

As the years passed, John desperately missed having a father to spend time with. Having an absent father had left a scar deep inside that left him with an emptiness that could only be filled by looking up at the bottom of a bottle. John's mother, Kate was an enabler who spent most of her life with a sad feeling of loneliness. The most exciting thing in Kate's life was the Sunday crossword puzzle and once a year when Christmas arrived. She was thrilled Lucky's was closed and she had her family all together for a day of peace and quiet. This was one day that Burt tried not to over drink. Christmas was John's favorite day of the year.

John, a thin man thirty-two years old, had been employed with Denmar Logging Company for nine years. Just like his father before him, John never missed a day's work. And just like his father, John spent his life looking at the inner walls of Lucky's tavern. Leaving every night around eight O'clock with most of his paycheck behind, John would head home to a one bedroom apartment at the edge of town.

The bar was open for business at 9:00 AM, and like most Saturdays, John was one of the first to swing open the door for a hair of the dog. Justin was standing on the sidewalk as John strolled by on his way to Lucky's. John barely noticing the average looking young man standing erect wearing blue jeans and a plaid flannel shirt nearly stretching down to his knees. Justin was thin, yet well built from years of healthy eating and hard work keeping up the house and garden. His long, dark hair was kept neat bringing out the light in his blue eyes. He had his mother's eyes.

"Good morning."

"Morning," John replied.

"May I ask you something?"

"Yes." John stopped, hoping it would be fast.

"I see you are going into the bar."

"That's right."

"Could I buy you a cup of tea at the diner? I have something important to discuss with you."

"No, I don't think so, buddy."

"Please, just one cup of tea."

"I am busy right now."

"Are you too busy to save your life, John?"

"How do you know my name?"

"John, if I assured you this one cup of tea would save your life, would you come with me?"

"Of course I would."

"Then please come with me now."

"Okay, just one quick cup."

"Let's walk then." Justin smiled at John. John was wondering if Justin was gay.

"It's a beautiful morning, John."

"Yes, how do you know who I am?"

"I have seen you go into the bar every day. Let me ask you. Where is your father?"

"He lives in Clarionton."

"How is his life?"

"I don't know. Okay I guess."

"Do you think he is happy?"

"No"

Justin opened the door to the diner and they took a booth. The waitress came right over.

"Two cups of tea please." Justin ordered the drinks.

"Your father is all alone, John?"

"Yes"

"And your mother?"

"They are divorced. She moved away."

The waitress brought over the tea.

"Life is too precious to miss the beautiful things it has to offer by being trapped in the bottom of a bottle, John. When was the last time you sat and watched the sun rise or took a walk through the forest on your day off, sober?"

"I can't remember."

"These are the wonderful gifts that the Lord has given you. These are the most simple, yet best things life has to offer. These are the things your father has missed."

Justin and John picked up their cups.

"Drink this tea with me today and you will not crave alcohol any longer. Every new day that arrives you will start out with a new look on life. When you awaken, sit and drink your tea and enjoy the life that the Lord my Father has given you. You will be sober and will see life in a different light with all the glory and beauty every soul truly desires.

John took a drink of his tea and felt an overwhelming feeling of spiritual enlightenment that he never could have imagined. His body tingled as if he could feel his blood flowing strong and clean. His thinking became clear and precise. He felt like a new man. John looked into Justin's eyes and knew he had been saved. He took Justin by the hand and kissed the back of his palm.

"Thank you for saving my life."

"Enjoy your tea, John, and spread the word of our Father."

"What word?"

"That all who confesses his sins to the Lord and sin no longer will be saved. And shall dwell in the kingdom of my Father."

Justin walked out and John sat there with tears in his eyes. John finished his tea and went straight to the chapel to confess his sins. Never to drink alcohol again.

Chapter 33

▼

It was pouring rain as Adams pulled into the parking garage at the federal building in Washington DC. He had been home for a week, and had taken that time to relax and catch up on some reading he had been putting off on intelligence reports regarding past and current operations of Alherita. He also spent several hours studying the documents, which had been retrieved from De Lorme's computer in Paris. Reggie had made sure he was allowed to copy the information onto a disk. It was booked into evidence in Washington but he had printed a copy for Adams. The documents were written in code and Adams wasn't able to make anything out of it. It was strange, he thought. He never saw anything like it. He was totally lost. He had extensive training in decoding messages but had never seen such code. It wasn't written in any language foreign or domestic. Nor was it written in any information system technology language he had ever seen. The documents were sent to the decoding lab to be deciphered but he had a plan of his own.

Adams received a call from his supervisor, Leonard Book, shortly after returning from France. Adams could tell by his tone over the phone that Book wasn't too thrilled about what went down with De Lorme and his cell. Adams was on his way to a meeting with Book and he knew it wouldn't be a welcome home party. Adams hung up his coat and entered the main office area.

"James, welcome home. I heard about the gunfight at the OK Corral."

"How's it going, Simms?"

"Quiet, it's been quiet here since you left. I hear you can still throw a grenade pretty fast under pressure."

Adams smiled and kept walking. "It's all part of the job, Simms."

The meeting was scheduled for 9:00 AM. Adams entered the room at 9:05.

"You're late, Agent Adams," Book sounded out.

Adams looked at his watch. "Well, I apologize. There was some unexpected traffic due to the weather."

Adams took a seat and said, "Good morning."

There were five people in the room: Book, who was the Agent in Charge of the District of Columbia field office and Fisher, who was wearing his finest suit, two attorneys, one who represented field agents and the other who represented supervisors. There was also a well-dressed man whom Adams had not recognized sitting across from him.

"Agent Adams, you obviously recognize council for field agents, as they are present at most of your meetings." Book was being sarcastic as usual.

"Yes I do. How are you today, gentlemen?"

They both responded with greetings.

"This is Mr. Gerard from the French Embassy."

Adams nodded his head.

Book continued, "Mr. Gerard, this is the Agent in Charge, Adams and one of his men, Agent Fisher."

Gerard didn't look too amused.

"We have some questions gentlemen, regarding your conduct in Paris two weeks ago. There are allegations from the French government that Agent Adams assaulted DCPJ Commander Bovie with his M16 and shod foot, causing Mr. Bovie to receive a broken nose."

"Mr. Book, we would ask for a few minutes with agents Adams and Fisher," said Attorney Johnson, who represented Adams.

"Alright, make it fast."

The four of them exited the room and returned five minutes later.

"So what happened, gentleman?" Book was anxious.

"It was self-defense," Adams said in a non-convincing tone.

"Self defense?" Book raised his voice in disbelief.

"That's right, boss. After the firefight, this asshole Bovie came charging at me, frothing at the mouth and stammering in some French gibberish I couldn't make out. As he attacked me, I had my weapon in hand, and just put it forward, blocking his advance."

"What about the kick in the face?"

"I don't know about any kick in the face. He may have gotten a bloody nose during the struggle. Has anyone bothered to look into the fact that he botched the operation, causing the deaths of two of our agents? It seems to me this is a tad more important than a bloody nose."

"We are looking into that, Agent Adams."

"Well, that's good, Leonard, because I'm the one who had to watch my men being carried out on stretchers and I'm the one who had to call their loved ones to inform them of their deaths."

"So your statement today is that the incident which caused the injury to Mr. Bovie was self-defense?"

"That's right." Adams was getting pissed off.

"What do you have to say, Agent Fisher?"

"I was right there and saw the whole thing; what James said is just the way it happened, and there were two other agents present who saw the same thing."

"Yes, we have spoken to those agents already. It seems you all have the same story. Are you both willing to testify in front of a grand jury to this effect?"

"Absolutely," Fisher said. Adams nodded and raised his palm.

"Monsieur Adams, there was a safe stolen from the apartment of the suspect, Mr. De Lorme. What do you know about that?" Adams knew it was just a matter of time before the Frenchman would open his trap.

"I don't know what you're talking about." Adams was thinking about the items they took from the safe. They were sitting in his library desk at home. He was supposed to move them to a safety deposit box last week but had put it off.

"Someone went into his apartment, cut a safe out of the wall and took it with them," Gerard said.

"Sounds to me like it was one of his guys trying to avoid getting terrorist-related documents into the hands of your security forces."

"Well, that is very presumptuous of you, Monsieur Adams, but we have a witness that saw two men leaving the building wheeling a large item out on a dolly. Oddly enough, the two men that were seen, appear to fit the description of you and Monsieur Fisher."

"Did they see a safe?" Adams asked.

"No, it was covered with a blanket."

"How big is the apartment building, Mr. Gerard?" Adams continued quizzing him.

"Four hundred and fifty apartments, give or take."

"Four hundred and fifty apartments. How many people would you say move in and out of an apartment building that size every week? Adams asked.

"I was told there were three tenants moving that day."

"Well, there you have it, Mr. Gerard. It could have been tenants moving boxes."

"We will continue to investigate, Monsieur Adams. You will be notified if anything further is disclosed." Gerard said looking beaten.

"That's great, Mr. Gerard, and I'm sure you will notify me when Mr. Bovie has been disciplined for his role in the deaths of two federal agents."

"That is not your concern, Adams," Book roared.

"Are we finished here?" Adams asked.

"Yes, that's all for now. Adams, you stay put. I need to speak with you."

The room cleared out and Book and Adams remained.

"If I find out you had something to do with the robbery of that safe, I'll have your shield."

"Book, whose side are you on, anyway? Those French bastards jumped in front of us when we were moving in and caused two of our people to lose their lives. Doesn't that mean anything to you, or are you so bent on becoming a politician that you forgot what brotherhood in the agency means?"

"Adams, you are a fucking cowboy, and it's agents like you that give the rest of us a bad name."

"Well, the next time you are dodging bullets instead of paperclips, I'll consider taking that as an insult. Right now I have a job to do out there, on the street." Adams pointed to the window.

"That's right, Adams, you do, and it will be with a new partner."

"What are you talking about?"

"You have been immediately assigned to the southwest border to investigate a terrorist cell and your new partner is Agent Kimball."

Book picked up the phone. "Send Agent Kimball in, please."

A few seconds later the door opened and Agent Kimball entered the room.

"Agent Adams, say hello to Agent Kimball." Adams looked at Kimball and back at Book with a look of hate in his eyes. Book was smirking like a kid who had just pulled a fast one on his grammar school teacher.

Sara Kimball was an attractive woman in her early thirties. She had long hair that she kept concealed at work by keeping it neatly pinned up. She looked astounding, with her maple brown suit and matching hair and eyes, Adams thought. She was in very good condition from practicing yoga three to four times a week. It helped keep her physically and mentally fit.

"Agent Kimball has been investigating one Rojas Fuentes and some of his comrades for nearly a year. You will be working together on this investigation along with two other agents assigned to the case. Adams, being the Senior Agent, you will be held responsible for anything that happens during this investigation. Do I make myself clear?" Book firmly stated.

"Crystal," Adams said while looking at Kimball with a half smile.

"Agent Toomey, along with Kimball, will brief you at thirteen-hundred hours in suite 201."

"Alright then. Is that all?" Adams asked.

"Yes."

Adams started walking out. "Adams, I'll be watching you real closely," Book threatened with a frown on his face.

"Of course you will, boss. What else do you have to do?"

Kimball followed Adams out of the room. Book wasn't very pleased with Adams's sarcasm. Adams didn't care.

Chapter 34

Louis Siano had little ambition and no money other than what he was fortunate enough to hustle on the street or win by chance. He came from a family of gamblers and grew up with parents that lived week by week. He was never sure if there would be food on the table when he came home at night. Formal education to Louis was seven card stud and how best to bet the over and under on a football game. He never felt love and comfort from his family and his only excitement was the thrill of the game.

Five guys huddled in the alleyway throwing dice for dollars. Louis was the youngest of the bunch. Justin stood watching from the sidewalk. When the game ended, Louis, who was a winner that day, came walking out from the alleyway counting his money.

"Excuse me." Justin got Louis's attention.

"Yeah."

"I see you are a winner today."

"That's right, man. I cleaned house," Louis responded.

"What will you do with your winnings?"

"I don't know, man. What are you, selling something?"

"No, I would like to help you become a man with the greatest wealth that any person would desire."

"And how will you do that?" Louis asked with a snicker.

"Walk with me to the pond and we will talk."

At first Louis was apprehensive, but after sizing Justin up, he knew there was no threat present. When it came to making easy money, Louis would always listen, and he agreed to walk with Justin. They arrived at the pond, walked down a short dock that overlooked the water and stopped at the end.

"Look into the water," Justin requested.

Louis looked down to see his reflection, but noticed there wasn't a reflection of Justin standing next to him. He looked at Justin and then again he looked down to the water. This time, the reflection he saw was that of himself ten years later. He was alone and dressed in raggedy clothes putting his last quarter into a slot machine.

"The excitement you feel from winning will always be outweighed by the depression you will feel from losing. In the end, you will lose everything and will live a life full of despair and financial ruin. When you are fortunate enough to win, you will cause the people who lost, the same depression and despair that you will feel when you lose. Louis, in the end there are no winners."

Louis looked at Justin, unable to speak. *Where did the reflection come from, he thought.*

Justin picked up a stone and handed it to Louis.

"Take this stone and drop it into the water."

Louis took the stone and did as he asked. When the ripples in the pond cleared, there was a new reflection. It was Louis ten years later in the backyard of his home playing touch football with his beautiful wife and three children. They were laughing and having fun as a happy family.

"Which life do you choose to live?"

"This one," Louis offered without hesitation.

"Then let the stone signify the last dye you throw."

"Who are you?" Louis asked.

"I am your savior. Confess your sins to our Father, and live free from sin furthermore."

Justin walked away leaving Louis sitting on the dock, staring into the water. Louis began to pray.

Chapter 35

The FBI field office for the southwest territory, located in San Diego, CA, was a huge step up from the shit hole in Paris, Adams thought. He found his office and was arranging it when Sara Kimball knocked on the door.

"Come in."

"Hello, Agent Adams. How was your flight out?"

"It was as smooth as a baby's ass."

"Okay. Well, that's great," she replied.

"Why don't you call me Adams? If were going to be partners, we might as well get to know each other on a more personal level."

"Alright, Adams, you should know that I'm a married woman and you are my boss, so it won't get too personal."

"Married, huh? Why is it that all the special women seem to be married?"

"What makes you think I'm special?"

"Your perfume."

"My perfume?"

"White Diamonds, right?"

"Yes it is. Are you some kind of fragrance expert?"

"No, I just knew a very special lady once who wore that same perfume."

"Is this where you'll go into how you were in love with a special lady who broke your heart and now you spend your weekends roaming the local malls, smelling White Diamonds in a desperate attempt to relive the memory of a love lost forever?"

"No, actually, my mother wore it."

Sara started to laugh. She knew from the moment she met Adams, she was attracted to him and that attraction was growing by the second. Sara had always been attracted to the rough and tumble type, but she settled for a nerd. Her husband, Scott, offered her a sense of security and she had decided he was more the type that would make a better husband and father. He was an investment banker who had graduated from Harvard in finance and went on to earn an MBA.

"Have you ever been married?" Sara asked.

"Not yet. Do you have kids?"

"Yes, a boy eight and a girl five."

"What are their names?"

"Edward and Monica." Sara responded with a certain sense of noticeable pride.

"Nice names. So are the others here yet?" Adams quickly changed the subject.

"Yes. I saw them on my way in."

"Can you ask them to meet here in thirty minutes so we can go over the case?"

"Sure." Sara replied, while glancing around his office in admiration.

Adams was subtly checking out Sara's ass as she walked out of his office. It was very round and firm for a woman who had borne two children, he thought.

The office was large enough for his needs. It had a hardwood table with six chairs and a matching desk, with a tall maroon leather chair behind it. On the wall behind his desk hung a large symmetrical United States Department of Justice seal. There was a large globe sitting on a swivel stand. On another wall Adams hung his FBI Academy and college diplomas, and several achievement awards and plaques. On the opposite wall, hung various personal framed photographs of him and his friends golfing, scuba diving, skydiving, bungee cord jumping and sailing. There were also pictures of him and his co-workers in full counter-terror uniforms, and several photographs of his Airborne Ranger Unit, lined up below his honorable discharge.

Adams was glaring out his window in deep thought when he was disrupted by a knock on his door.

"Come in." Adams stood up.

"James Adams, this is Marty Shepard and Bobby White." They shook hands.

"Thanks, Sara. Have a seat." Adams motioned to the table.

"I've heard a lot about you," White said, "and I just want you to know it's a pleasure having you as a boss."

"Thanks, Bobby. I'm glad to be here. Anywhere other than France actually."

"I heard you had a war over there," Marty said.

"Yeah, it got pretty hairy. I'll tell you about it another time. I want you guys to call me by my last name, okay? I don't like being called James."

They all agreed.

"Let's get started. I have been briefed in Washington, but I want to hear from you guys what this case involves and how far you have gotten."

"Rojas Fuentes is very powerful in Mexico. He has many politicians in his pocket and his pockets run deep." Sara was pulling out a folder while speaking.

"He owns a company, Albatross Corporation. It is a textile importing company, which imports textiles mainly from China. It is a huge multi-million dollar business that has taken off ten-fold since the induction of China into the World Trade Organization in 2001. China exports in excess of 6.5 billion dollars in goods each year and much of it is textiles. We believe he is importing more than textiles."

"What do you think he's up too?" Adams asked.

"Arms. He has links to Iran and Saudi Arabia, as well," Sara answered.

Adams was rubbing his forehead. "Has he ever been arrested, anywhere?"

"No, he's clean. Make no mistake; he is well educated and very clever. He enjoys the protection of the Mexican government, which makes it difficult to get next to him," Sara said.

"How have they cooperated with you in the past?"

"They are real good at playing the game, but they spend more time watching us. I'm sure he's alerted whenever we cross the border," Sara offered.

"Sounds like we need to get enough on him so our side will put some pressure on the Mexicans, and maybe then we will gain some real progress. How is he linked to terror?"

"We have these photos that were taken by one of our undercover CIA agents who has been weathering the sand storms in Saudi Arabia and Iran for three years. He knows many of the players, and this guy walking with Rojas is one of them." Sara dropped several 8x10 photographs on the table. "His name is Forouq Manah Nahad, a native of Iran. He is also in the import-export business. He and Fuentes have been seen together in both Saudi Arabia and Iran. Here are some photos of Nahad with a known Alherta leader, Mateen Vairya Kamali. They are often seen together by our agents, mostly in Iran. But they have also been seen together in Saudi Arabia and France."

"Here we go again with the French. I hate the French," Adams said, smirking.

"So what do you think he's smuggling in?"

"We aren't sure, but this is what really bothers me." Sara set down three additional photos on the table.

"Fuentes has been seen with this guy in Ji'an China, which is right on the border of North Korea."

"What's his name?" Adams asked.

"His name is Boon-Lai-Deng."

"Sounds like something I ate last week at Bennie Hanna's. Go on."

Sara wasn't amused. "Deng has been linked to North Korean Military personnel. And I don't mean low ranking privates."

"What is his claim to fame?" Adams asked.

"Import,export business."

"Is this guy Deng a North Korean?"

"No, he is Chinese."

"I gotta hand it to our people over there. You know how hard it is to get around in China? Never mind right on the border of North Korea. You look up the word recluse in the dictionary and you get two things, a spider and North Korea."

Adams stood up and walked over to his window. "This guy Fuentes has some very interesting friends in the exporting business," he spoke with his back to them. "We need to get a money trail. We need to find out how the goods are coming in and where. We need to find out where the original ports of departures are. We need to find out who Deng and Nahad associate and do business with. This smells like shit," Adams said.

"He has a ship," Marty said.

Adams turned around. "Where?"

"We don't know where it is right now but it docks every four months or so in Mazatlan Mexico."

"Have you seen it?" Adams asked.

"No, this is new intelligence," Marty responded.

"Your job, Marty, is to find out about this boat. I want to know what months it is in port and for how long? What is it called? How big is it and what is the typical cargo? How many crew members, and who is the captain? Also, how long has this boat been in business? Most of that information can be found through the North American Free trade Agreement (NAFTA) records. Check into the (HS) system. That is the Harmonized System administered by the World Customs Organization. Find out the (HS) classification number for textiles in Mexico and crosscheck it with Albatross Corporation. If they are not abiding by the laws of NAFTA, we will have more ammunition to shoot for better cooperation with the Mexican government."

"You got it, chief." Marty was impressed with Adam's knowledge of the import-export laws and his ability to put together a quick investigative game plan.

"Bobby, I want you to work on the money trail. Check the accounts receivable records of Albatross Company. You can get these through the tax records at the Mexican Revenue Department. Let me know if you run into any obstacles. I have a friend in Mexico. Also, let's find out about Mr. Fuentes' personal banking practices. We need to link Fuentes with Deng and Nahad financially. See what we can come up with on those two. I want to know the names of their companies and any financial records you can find on their companies and them personally."

"Okay," Bobby responded.

"Sara, have you crossed over the border recently?"

"No, I did about five months back to do a surveillance on Ernesto Diaz. He led us to Fuentes."

"Okay. The Mexican government shouldn't recognize you with a different identity and change of appearance, especially, if you're posing as my wife. They don't know me at all. I'll work on getting some fake passports and we will learn more about Rojas Fuentes. I have a friend in the CIA. I need to call him for a favor anyway so I may as well get two for the price of one. I'll check and see if he can contact our operatives in China and Iran and learn what they can find out about Nahad and Deng. One more thing, let's keep a tight lid on this one. These guys are big players with long arms."

Chapter 36

The phone rang at the desk of CIA Agent Ryan Wysocki in Langley, Virginia. He sat at his desk looking at the phone while it rang. After five rings, he picked up.

"Yes."

"Ryan?"

"Yes."

"It's me, Hammerhead," Adams shouted.

"I was going to call you but I figured you were in jail or something," Ryan responded.

"Jail, what do you mean?"

"Yeah, I heard about D Day in Paris," Ryan said.

"Ryan, you, above all people should know to believe half of what you see and none of what you hear."

"I know you, pal. I have gotten drunk with you. Remember that night in Bangkok?"

"Actually I'm still trying to forget," Adams said.

"What's up, amigo?"

"I need a favor. Actually, I need two favors," Adams said.

"Are they going to get me killed or put in prison for life?"

"Probably."

"Okay. Let's cover the biggest one first," Ryan suggested.

"This has to be kept completely confidential. I am talking me, you, and your guy."

"Okay, what guy?" Ryan asked.

"You remember in DC, we were having dinner at that restaurant with the gay waiter who tried to grab your package while brushing crumbs off your lap?"

"Actually, I'm still trying to forget that." Ryan offered with a chuckle.

"You were telling me about your friend in Langley, who you said was the best decoder on the planet?"

"Yeah, John Goldstein."

"Yeah, that's him. I have some documents written in code that I can't figure out. I need him to read them."

"Alright."

"Will he do it?" Adams asked.

"I think so. It may take a while."

"That's okay. I'll send a hard copy by UPS to your house. Do not make copies and he is not to make copies. I want the same documents returned to me in order with the deciphered code. Can he be trusted?" Adams asked.

"This guy is as solid as a diamond."

"Good." Adams wasn't very relieved.

"What is the other gift to you, Master?" Ryan asked.

"Can you get in touch with your operatives in China and get all the info you can on one Boon-Lai Deng? He is known to associate with North Korean military types in the Ji'an area.

"Ji'an? That's a nasty place," Ryan said.

"Yeah, he is in the import-export business," Adams said.

"Is that it?" Ryan asked.

"No, also, have your guys in Iran look into another import export guy, Forouq Manah Nahad. They may find him in Tehran hanging with Mateen Vairya Kamali."

"The terrorist?" Ryan asked.

"That's him."

"Anything else? Would you like me to find out who killed Jack Kennedy?"

"No, I already know who did that." Adams said.

"Oh yeah, who?"

"Take a good look around you," Adams said.

"Goodbye, James."

"Don't call me James."

The phone went dead and Adams started laughing.

The next morning on his way to the office, Adams stopped at the post office and sent a package to Ryan in Virginia. He figured it was the safest way to send it.

Electronically would be too risky and he didn't have time to fly and deliver it in person. He was anxious to find out what diabolical scheme De Lorme was involved in. He knew the FBI was working on decoding the documents but they hadn't gained any ground. He needed the best on this one and Ryan swore by his guy. The CIA had the best decoders in the world, and if this guy is the best in the CIA, then Adams knew he was the man who could get the job done in a reasonable amount of time.

Adams stopped by Sara's office on the way in. She was scanning some files on her PC, when he knocked on her door.

"Good morning," Adams said smiling ear to ear.

"Hi." Sara looked up.

"I was wondering, if we could talk over lunch?" Adams asked.

"Actually, I want to talk with you about something you said in the meeting."

"Alright, what is it?" Adams asked.

"You said something to the effect of me changing my appearance?"

"Well, I'm not asking you to have plastic surgery performed."

"What are you asking, James? Sorry, I meant Adams."

"Well, I thought maybe you could change your hair style and color. Wear fake glasses and I could buy you a nice hat." His smile was fixed.

"Okay. And I'm supposed to be your wife?" Sara asked with a concerned look.

"Well, we won't have to sleep together, if you don't want to."

Sara put her hands on her hips. "I don't, I'm married, remember?"

"How could I forget?" Adams asked.

"When were you planning on leaving?" Sara asked.

"We should have the passports tomorrow. I'll brief you during lunch and then again, tomorrow, and I figure we can take the weekend to study the investigation plans and fly down Monday afternoon. How's that sound?" Adams asked.

"Sounds like my husband, is going to be pissed."

"Pissed at what?"

"That I'm leaving him alone with the kids again."

"Well, Sara, you need to have a talk with him and explain that you are on a case that is going to keep you away from home for several days at a time every now and then."

"How many days on this trip?" she asked.

"We should be back by the weekend."

"He is not going to be happy."

"Tell him you're in good hands with me," Adams said.

"I'm not telling him about you."

"Why not?" Adams asked.

"Because people have a habit of getting killed around you, that's why."

"We will just be a happy couple on vacation at one of the most beautiful resort areas in Mexico, and the best part is, Uncle Sam will pick up the tab," Adams said.

"I guess I could use a vacation." Sara was rationalizing.

"We will be working, but why not have a little fun while were there?" Adams asked.

"So I guess I'll see you at lunch?" Sara asked.

"I'll drop by and get you at noon."

"See you then." Sara was now the one smiling from ear to ear.

Chapter 37

For most people, life in Pinehaven had changed. Beth was teaching Sunday school and it was standing room only. Justin would speak every Saturday for ten minutes at the Congregational church and every word had a deep spiritual meaning. People began to come from all around the state to hear his words. Beth now understood why she had been put on earth. She had a message for the people and her message was the same as Justin's. The love she and Justin shared was beyond compare. Beth knew Justin was the Son of God and she had brought him into this world for a reason. Life for Beth was now a wonderful, peaceful existence. The love she had in her heart was dispersed among the hundreds of people in Pinehaven and didn't stop there. Like her mother, Nancy, Beth was a pure giving soul. Beth often thought about her father and mother, believing they would be proud of what she was doing with her life. She thought about what her mother had said about Justin, and it was comforting to her that her mother had died knowing who he was and why he was here.

Every day Marsha Brosner lived in fear. If suicide weren't a sin she would have taken that option years ago. The pain she felt was far beyond physical, and healing was almost out of the question for her. Her husband of seventeen years had been brought up in a life filled with hatred and abuse. He was a logger at Denmore Corporation for his entire adult life and his calloused and scarred hands confirmed it.

Marsha entered the church looking for an answer. Hoping to find spiritual comfort, she knelt down in the pew. Her eye was blackened by the hand of her husband. Her solo trips to the church had increased with time. The bruises she could once hide had turned into obvious fractures and lacerations. As Marsha lowered her head to pray, she was oblivious to her surroundings. This was the one place she felt safe. Marsha had always wanted a child, but she was unable to conceive, and there wasn't a day that went by that Jack Brosner didn't remind her of it. The emotional pain she endured was far worse than the physical pain. Her prayers were always the same. She asked the Lord to forgive her husband and to show him the wrong he is doing so that he might learn to love her and stop the abuse. When her prayers were finished, she walked out of the church with little hope. Justin was standing outside.

"It's a beautiful day," Justin said.

Marsha stopped and looked into his eyes. She saw love and compassion.

"Yes it is," she responded.

"My name is Justin, and I'm glad you have once again come to pray and worship our Father. Your prayers will soon be answered."

Marsha started to cry. A powerful feeling of hope and contentment overcame her as she looked into Justin's eyes and heard his words. He was an angel sent from God, she thought. She did not have to tell Justin what she had endured. He already knew. He saw it in her tears of hopelessness.

"Come and walk with me for a while." Justin offered his hand and she took it.

Jack Brosner had just sat down to eat his lunch. Like most days, he ate alone. He had an anger embedded inside that came from years of emotional and physical abuse at the hands of his father. Like a bad seed, it had been passed down from generation to generation. He sat on a pine tree that had lost its life earlier that morning.

"Jack, may I speak with you for a few minutes?" Justin stood looking down at him.

"Who are you?" He grunted.

"I am Justin. I just left Marsha, your wife. We prayed at the same church."

"What do you want?" Jack was a large man with a beard, wearing a wool plaid shirt, blue jeans and steel toed timberland boots.

"I know you have been abusing your wife."

"She told you that? That bitch is a liar. And it's none of your business anyway."

Jack stood up with his fists clenched. Justin reached out and grabbed both of his wrists. In an instant, Jack's arms felt as if they had turned into lifeless rubber. His facial expression had quickly turned from anger to fear. Now, he was the helpless and vulnerable one. He was unable to raise his arms or move his fingers.

"You were given these hands to serve as the tools of your labor, not to raise them against your wife. Go home and love your wife and ask the Lord for forgiveness and sin no more."

Jack looked into Justin's eyes and felt his heart open up. The pain that had plagued him his entire life had fled from his soul in a single moment. He fell to his knees weeping like a child.

"I'm sorry," he said. "I will be a good husband. I'm so sorry."

"Go home and tell Marsha and love her as a husband should."

As Justin walked away, he looked up into the sky as the sun was peaking through the pine trees. What a glorious day it was, he thought.

Chapter 38

▼

Mazatlan Airport was fairly quiet when Mr. and Mrs. Henry Levington arrived. They checked through customs without a problem and found a taxi waiting outside the airport.

The ride to the hotel was about fifteen miles and they were performing spectacularly as husband and wife. Adams made sure he held her hand, opened the car door and handled her bags when necessary. Sara had not had this type of treatment since she first started dating her husband, and she loved every minute of it. About twenty-five minutes later they arrived at the Hotel Playa Mazatlan located on Puerto Viejo Bay. The room was waterfront and Sara was in awe of the view. Adams had made sure they secured a room with a view of the bay. There were two queen beds, a desk and a sitting area. A portable bar was fully stocked with all the liquor they would need. Adams walked out onto the balcony.

"You certainly know how to spend Uncle Sam's money."

"Look at it like a bonus." Adams said.

"I'll take the bed closest to the window."

"You got it." Adams put his bag on the other bed. "It's dinner time. Why don't we clean up and grab something to eat?"

"Alright. I'll be ready in ten minutes," Sara said.

Adams had made sure Sara understood they were not to discuss the case in the hotel room. He decided not to bring bug detection equipment along just in case customs did a complete search of their baggage. He didn't believe the room was bugged but he didn't want to take any chances. Any conversation they had regarding the case had to be outside the room. They found a restaurant within walking distance from the hotel and sat down at a table overlooking the bay. The scenery was spectacular and sound filled the air with three musicians playing guitar and singing a salsa.

"Tomorrow we will rent a boat and spend the day sailing south along the bay." Adams was an avid sailor.

"That sounds more like fun than work," Sara said.

"It will be both. Fuentes's villa is located right on the water off of Paseo Claussen Ave. We need to get some shots from the water tomorrow. We can take some photos later in the week from the street. He is known to frequent a place called Gringo Lingo. It's a nightclub he likes to dance at a couple times a week from what I've been told. We can go dancing and maybe we'll get lucky and spot him. I'd like to find out who his acquaintances are."

"Okay, sounds good to me. Are you sure you know how to sail?"

"Don't worry, Sara. You're in good hands. It will be a great day."

They finished dinner and made their way back to the room. Sara was tired and wanted to call her kids and say goodnight.

The alarm went off at 7:00 AM. Adams was already awake and standing on the balcony when Sara woke up.

"Good Morning. Did you sleep well?" Adams asked.

"Yes, do you know you talk in your sleep?"

"I hope I didn't say anything to offend you?" Adams said.

"No, I couldn't make it out. You were mumbling."

"Good."

"As soon as you're ready we'll have breakfast and set sail."

"Alright, do you have the camera?" Sara asked.

"All set."

"Let me take a shower and I'll be ready to go." Sara said.

Adams was listening to the running water. He thought about the hot water pounding off her naked body. He fantasized about taking off his clothes and climbing in with her. He began to get aroused so he took a cold drink of water from a bottle and defiantly changed his thoughts to what was on the menu.

After breakfast they rented a small sailboat and began their day sailing along the shore. It was a perfect day for sailing, with the wind at eight knots and not a cloud in sight. Adams spent the day teaching Sara sailing terminology and how to maneuver the vessel. As they sailed near Fuentes's villa, Adams drifted as close to shore as possible while Sara took pictures. It was a magnificent compound with a stone wall surrounding it. There appeared to be a main house and a maid's quarters to the south. There was an iron gate that opened to a private beach. They could see two large dogs that appeared to be Doberman Pinchers roaming near the gate. The villa was like a fortress, Adam's thought. What was he hiding?

They started to set sail back to the hotel. Adams popped open a bottle of wine and brandished two glasses. After pouring a second glass he leaned over to kiss Sara and she turned away.

"Adams, I can't."

"I'm sorry. I'm really attracted to you. I shouldn't have done that." He got up and stood holding the mast, looking out into the open bay. Sara got up and moved next to him. She had to have him. She knew it was wrong but she couldn't control her feelings. She had never felt this way before. The setting was so romantic and he was such a gentleman with a handsome face and a strong, hard body.

He turned to face her and she kissed him. They fell into a long passionate kiss that felt as if it were choreographed perfectly. He ran his hands along her outer thighs working his way down to her buttocks while their lips and tongues explored each other. Sara started unbuttoning his shirt while he kissed her neck and ran his hands over her firm breasts.

She helped him off with his shirt and began kissing his chest. She began to pull his shorts down and he stopped her. He laid her down onto the floor of the boat and took off her blouse. She was perfect, he thought, as he began kissing and sucking her breasts. Adams slid his hand down her shorts touching her between the legs. She was moaning with pleasure and he was growing hard.

"Make love to me," she commanded.

Adam's slid her shorts and panties off until she lay completely naked before him. He kissed her lips and neck working his way down without neglecting any part of her body until he found himself between her legs. Sara had never felt so much pleasure before. After a few minutes she pulled him forward and tore his shorts off in a frenzy and guided him inside her. They made love until they both climaxed together in a complete moment of ecstasy.

As they sailed back to the hotel there was very little dialogue. He held her close and could sense something disturbed her. He asked her if she was okay. She said yes, even though deep down in the pit of her stomach she felt guilty. They spent the next three days taking more pictures of the villa and went to the nightclub hoping to find Fuentes, but he never showed. The rest of the time they went diving, rented jet skis and went parasailing. The rest of the week they slept in the same bed.

Three weeks had passed since they returned from Mexico. The weeks that followed had been a combination of investigating Fuentes and afternoon interludes at Adam's place. They were beginning to become very good friends and passionate lovers. Sara was falling in love and Adams felt the same but they didn't speak of it. In her eyes, she was committing a mortal sin. Adams didn't believe in sins or religion at all. He knew the difference between right and wrong and he knew what he was doing was wrong, but he had never felt this way about a woman before. He didn't ever want it to end.

It was 8:45 in the morning and Adams was waiting in his office for a 9:00 meeting with his team. They had kept in touch over the past few weeks, but had not discussed the case in detail over open lines. Ten minutes later they were all seated.

"How's everyone doing this morning?" Adams asked.

They all acknowledged him.

"Okay. We haven't met for almost a month and I'm anxious to get started. Marty, you have been working on the boat and information regarding the cargo and the customs logs for Albatross Corporation. What have you got?"

"The name of the ship is the *El Conquistador*. It is 569 feet long and weighs just over 60,000 tons. The (HS) classification number is MX3664120, and it is expected to port in Mazatlan in eight to nine weeks. I tracked the ship through the World Maritime Organization and it is now in the Yellow Sea. It mostly transports textiles from China, just as we thought the logs would read. There have been no violations registered with the World Customs Organization or NAFTA. They appear to be clean."

"Is that all?" Adams asked.

"Yeah, for now."

"Bobby, what about the paper trail?"

"I've been able to link Albatross Corporation to two companies in China through accounts payable, Chi'nak Corporation and Sientsi Corporation. Both are located within a hundred miles of North Korea. The money transactions are all conducted through Bank Niaga in the Cayman Islands. I was also able to link Albatross to a company in Iran called Shiekan Inc., located just northeast of Tehran. They also do their transactions through Bank Niaga. As far as his local banking, that is done through the Bank of Mexico. His accounts receivable are from textile and retail companies in Mexico and the U.S."

"Have you been able to get any information on the names of the people that own the Corporations?"

"So far just one, and his name is," Bobby was going through his notes, "Cheng-foo Ping of Chi'nak Corporation in Ji'an China."

"Okay, good work. As you know, Sara and I went to Mazatlan to investigate Fuentes and see what we could learn about where he lives and anything regarding his business and personal life. We weren't able to come up with much without blowing our cover. Here are some photos of his compound." Adams put them on the table and they began passing them around. "We did find out that he is well-known in that area and widely feared. One shop owner referred to him as, El Diablo. I will be speaking with my contact in the CIA this week and hopefully we will get some information regarding his friends abroad. In the meantime, keep digging and see what else you can find out. I know it's hard following the money trail when it's in the Cayman Islands, but keep working on it, Bobby. Marty, we need to know exactly when that boat is coming in. See what you guys can gather on the remaining names of the owners of those two companies. Let's do it."

The agents left the office with notebooks in hand. Sara stayed and locked the door behind them.

Chapter 39

▼

A cloud of smoke billowing into the sky was hidden by the blackness of night. The house on Stoneridge Drive was completely engulfed in flames. The once well architectured colonial Tudor was now an oversized bonfire quickly being reduced to ashes just as midnight brought Pinehaven a new day.

Maryanne Goodman's charred body lay in the bedroom on the second floor overlooking the back yard. The cigarette that caused her death had disintegrated in the scorching heat that climbed up to 370 degrees. It wasn't the first time she had passed out with a cigarette burning between her finger's, and a bottle of vodka on the nightstand, but it was the last.

Her younger sister Dianne, and her husband Stephen, sleeping on the first floor escaped the flames unharmed, at least physically. Emotionally they were walking zombies. Their four-year-old daughter, Wendy, who was fast asleep on the second floor, wasn't as lucky. Two firemen had taken her out through her bedroom window that faced the front of the house. She had been trapped in her room by the flames and her parents were unable to get to her. Her father's attempt to reach the top of the stairs was unsuccessful. The heat was so intense the hair on his arms singed down to the skin. If it weren't for his wife pulling him away from the flames, he would have perished attempting to rescue his little girl.

Both fire trucks in Pinehaven were fully manned with every volunteer firefighter in town. As they attacked the fire from both sides of the dwelling, Dianne and Stephen Corerra watched in horror as the Emergency Medical Technicians hoisted their daughter's burnt body into an awaiting ambulance. Her beautiful long red hair was completely burned to the scalp and the cute freckles she once displayed on her beaming face was now a black, bubbly mess. She had third degree burns on 90% of her body and her life was hanging on by a thread. Diane felt guilty that she wasn't as bereaved about her drunken sister as they took her out with a sheet covering her face. Deep down inside she figured Maryanne had most likely caused the fire.

Three days later Maryanne was buried and Wendy was barely alive, fighting for her life. The prognosis was not favorable for her and, if she did survive, she would be scarred forever, and would need to undergo many surgical procedures throughout her remaining days. Her face and most of her body were burned to the bone. She would spend her life trying to avoid the stares and subtle comments from people who found her appearance to be hideous. She may never have a boyfriend and lover, never be able to marry and experience the gift of having a child. She most likely would never have a family of her own.

Sunday service was dedicated to Maryanne and Wendy. The townspeople gathered to support Stephen and Diane. They held a fundraiser and prayed together for Wendy's recovery and for the soul of Maryanne. The preliminary investigation concluded that the fire had started in Maryanne's bedroom and Diane resented her sister for her recklessness and the damage and pain she had caused. She wasn't prepared to pray for her sister's soul. She wasn't ready to forgive her; she doubted that she ever would.

Diane made sure she attended the service. She wanted to thank people for supporting her family with donations and all the prayers they said for Wendy. Stephen was at the hospital in Clarionton sitting outside the intensive care unit hoping and praying for his daughter's recovery. One of them made sure they were always at the hospital. They took shifts at night and during the day they stayed together, looking in on her and holding her bandaged hands. She was on life support and her entire body was covered with bandages. Her doctor had told them that she most likely would not survive, but they kept praying and didn't give up hope.

Justin was speaking to a crowd of people when Diane approached him in the church lobby.

"Justin, may I speak with you for a minute?"

"Yes, of course."

"Wendy is my daughter. She is dying at the Clarionton hospital. Please, can you help her? I have heard you can do miracles. I don't want to lose her; she is only four years old. Please, can you help us?"

"The only one who performs miracles is the Lord our Father. Only He can save her. Through Him I have performed miracles. He makes the choice."

Diane reached out and took Justin's hand into hers. "Please, Justin, can you try?" He could see the pain in her eyes. Her strength was intriguing and her faith unquestionable.

"Yes, I will go and see her."

"Thank you. Thank you so much." She had a feeling of relief over come her. She had heard rumors about an incident that had happened years ago, about how Justin had saved a girl's life that had been attacked by a swarm of bees. She wasn't sure she believed the story, but she was hoping it was true.

Stephen had been sleeping for about an hour. It was 3:00 AM when he felt a hand touch his shoulder. He looked up to see Justin sitting next to him, on the leather couch he had grown accustomed to in the waiting room outside the Intensive Care Unit.

"Stephen, do you know who I am?" Justin asked.

"Yes, I do."

"Let's pray for Wendy. And then I will go and see her."

They prayed together for five minutes and then Stephen showed him the way to his daughter's bed. Justin asked Stephen to go to the washroom and run a tub of warm water. He started to ask why, but after looking into Justin's eyes, he walked away without saying a word. Justin knelt down next to Wendy's bed and held her hand while he prayed. There weren't any nurses or doctors nearby as he began taking off her bandages.

"What are you doing?" Stephen had returned to find Justin taking off his daughter's dressings.

"Trust me, Stephen. Help me with the bandages."

Stephen began assisting him with the bandages. They started at her feet and worked their way up to her head. Stephen worked hard to fight back the tears as he was witnessing for the first time what the fire had done to his child.

"What are you doing?" a nurse called out interrupting them.

"Please, allow me to help her," Justin insisted.

"Get away from her right now!" The nurse grabbed Justin by the arm.

Stephen pulled her away from Justin and tried to talk to her, but she was becoming irate. Finally she ran off threatening to call security.

Justin had taken the last of the bandages off and he looked at Stephen who was now shaking uncontrollably, his eyes were filling up with water. The person he was looking at wasn't his little girl. He had never understood the true meaning of pity until now. Justin reached out and took Stephen's hand.

"I have to unhook her from life support now." Stephen nodded his head in agreement. Justin removed the mouthpiece from her and unhooked her from the machine. An alarm sounded and he knew they didn't have much time before security arrived. Justin took her naked body in his arms and made his way to the bathtub, with Stephen following.

"Close and lock the door," Justin demanded. Stephen did as he asked.

Justin handed Wendy to her father. She was not breathing and Stephen was experiencing uncompromising agony while holding onto the lifeless body of his daughter. Justin was on his knees praying over the tub when the commotion outside the bathroom door began.

"This is security, open this door right now!"

After he finished praying, Justin reached down into the water with both hands cupped together and brought it up cleansing his face. He took Wendy from her father and submerged her into the water. Stephen was now crying, his hands covering his face. The chaos outside the bathroom was getting louder and louder. Justin ignored the security guard and nurse who were threatening to have him arrested for murder. He just continued praying with the little girl submerged under the water. He finally stopped praying and pulled her from the water. Stephen looked down at his daughter and she was dead.

"What have you done?" he asked.

"Please hand me that towel," Justin asked. Stephen did as he asked. Justin wrapped Wendy in the towel and then he took another and wrapped her whole body so that none of her body was exposed. He kissed her on the forehead and handed her to Stephen. Just then the security guard, who was extremely angry, opened the door. There were four guards and five nurses waiting outside the bathroom. Two guards grabbed Justin and he just stood there offering no resistance.

"Wait!" Stephen called out. "She's moving!"

"Daddy?" A voice sounded from beneath the towels.

Stephen slowly pulled the towel down exposing his daughter's face. He suddenly began sobbing like a child as he looked down to see her blue eyes and freckled face looking back up at him. Her red hair was long and flowing over her smooth and creamy shoulders. He had his daughter in his arms and there were no burns or scars. She was completely healed. He turned to Justin.

"Thank you. My God. Thank you." Justin smiled at him. The guards immediately released Justin's arms. The room had gone silent. The ICU duty nurse got on her knees and began praying as she stared directly at Justin. Another nurse joined her, and then another.

"Hello, Wendy." Justin rested his palm against her face. "Welcome back," he said.

Stephen set his daughter on the floor. Wrapped in her white towel she walked over to Justin and embraced him.

Chapter 40

It was Friday, early afternoon, when the phone rang. Adams was in his office.

"Agent Adams."

"Hey. I need to talk to you." Ryan Wysocki sounded excited. "You need to find a secure line and call me at this number, 301 334-9989."

"Give me fifteen minutes." The line went dead.

Ryan was waiting for the call and, exactly fourteen minutes later, he picked it up.

"Adams, are you on a secure line?"

"Yes, Ryan, what have you got?"

"John met with me this morning. He has been working his ass off to break this code. He has spent six to eight hours a day for the past month working on it. With this guy it's personal. It's like he's at war with the guy who wrote the code."

"Did he read the code?"

"Yes, he told me it was some of the hardest code he has ever worked on. This guy can usually break code in a week or two. The code is written in Latin backwards, and it's just sentences of words and numbers that make no sense. He figured out that the third letter of every word is the key. When he took the third letter of every word and put it together he was able to decipher it. The numbers were also written backwards with every third number being the key. This guy is brilliant."

"What does it read?"

"De Lorme was instructed to meet with two people in Russia to expedite the packages. Adams, it also refers to a day that is arriving soon. This looks big. I'm not sure what you have gotten yourself into, but all I can say is, be careful Adams, be very careful.

"Ryan, I want you to overnight the package today."

"You got it, chief."

"Ryan, I owe you one. Thanks."

"Anytime, my friend."

The next day Adams was home waiting for the package to arrive. Sara was with him when it was delivered at 11:35 AM.

"Are you ready for this?"

"You bet I am." He had the package in hand. He opened it and began reading the decoded message.

Contact Ruslan Bakov and Cheng-foo Ping at 5:00 PM 11/15, 474 Pushkinskaya St. Vladivostok
D115545N3736E, D124310N132OE, D135956N3018E,
D143955N11625E, D153110N12128E
Expedite the packages. Our day will arrive soon.

Adams handed the message to Sara. "Look at the Chinese name."

"Looks like Ping gets around," Sara said.

"This is bigger than I thought. De Lorme and Fuentes are connected through Ping. Ji'an China and Vladivostok Russia are both near the border of North Korea. What the hell are they up to?"

"Whatever it is, it appears to involve North Korea," Sara concluded.

"Yeah, or at least someone from there. Take a look at these numbers. These look like longitude and latitude locations. I have a world map. Hang on." Adams went into his office and returned with a map. Sara read the numbers, as he found and marked the locations on the map.

"We have Moscow, Vladivostok, St. Petersburg, Beijing and Shanghai. Five major cities in Russia and China."

"What do you think D11-D15 means?"

"I'm not positive, but it could mean that these were his five destinations."

"Five destinations to do what?" Sara looked at Adams obviously concerned.

"I don't know, but we will definitely be in Mazatlan when El Conquistador arrives."

Chapter 41

The church was completely full and flowing out the door with people. Justin stood at the altar, speaking of selfless love for others and for all to rid their hearts of hatred and envy. Cardinal Zupra and Monsignor London worked their way through the crowd and stood in the rear of the church listening. When Justin finished speaking people began filing out. Justin stayed to answer questions and bless people who had unresolved issues. Most people had cleared out when Zupra and London approached Justin.

"Hello, Justin." Cardinal Zupra bowed his head.

"Hello."

"Do you remember us?"

"Yes."

"We have been searching for you for quite some time. You disappeared a long time ago without a trace."

"And now you have found me," Justin said.

"Yes, Father McCarthy from our parish in Clarionton contacted us and told us of a young man who had a God-given gift. That he was in Pinehaven preaching the word of our lord. We came as soon as we could."

"Let's pray together then," Justin said. He took both of them by the hand and began praying for all the lost souls in the world. Both Zupra and London had never heard such an original, precise and beautiful prayer before. Without a word wasted, Justin ended the prayer with an Amen.

"Thanks for coming." Justin blessed them.

Cardinal Zupra cleared his throat. "Justin, we spoke with the Pope and he has invited you to come to Rome and visit with him at the Vatican. We have arrangements to fly out next week and we would like you to accompany us."

"Please thank the Pope for the invitation, but my work is here now. Tell him my Father is proud of what he has done, and to continue his good work."

"Justin, do you truly believe you are the Son of God?" Monsignor London looked puzzled as he spoke. There was a brief hesitation as both men looked deep into Justin's eyes.

"I am."

"Then you must come with us so there can be no mistake," Cardinal Zupra suggested.

"There is no mistake. Walk with me." They followed Justin outside. People were still outside kneeling and bowing their heads as Justin walked by. Zupra and London were surprised by his reception. Justin reached down and picked up a dead flower. He cupped it into his hands while closing his eyes. A few seconds later he opened his hands and inside his palms laid a beautiful, fully-bloomed flower. He handed it to Monsignor London.

"Please give this flower to the Pope, for it was born again. This is the lesson we must teach as many as we can. It is time for all to be born again and live without sin."

Justin went on to help the people awaiting him outside the church. Zupra and London went back into the church to pray.

Chapter 42

The conference room was magnificent, located at FBI headquarters in Washington DC. Adams sat waiting for the rest of the government officials to arrive. He had called Book to arrange the meeting and Book was reluctant until Adams gave him a summary of the situation. Book had arrived just before Adams and they were the only ones seated in the room. Adams could tell by looking around that this conference room was used for very high-level meetings. A few minutes later the gentlemen entered the room and took their seats. Adams recognized most of them.

"Good morning, gentlemen. Let me introduce everyone and then we can get started." FBI Director William Morris stood up while introducing the group.

"The meeting was called by FBI Group Supervisor James Adams." Adams nodded his head. "This is FBI Deputy Director Ronald Kemper, FBI Agent In Charge of the D.C. office, Leonard Book, Deputy Director of the CIA, John Sands, Associate Director of CIA Homeland Security, Brad Conway and Deputy Assistant Director for Counter-terrorism, Andrew Woodrow."

The men had all been called to attend the meeting on very short notice, and they all assumed it was of a serious nature. They had all been advised of the urgency of the matter and therefore had canceled other previously scheduled engagements.

"Agent Adams." Director Morris sat down and Adams stood up. He had never spoken in front of such an important group of men before and his sweaty palms were a constant reminder of it.

"Good morning, gentlemen. I'll get right to the point. A few months ago while on assignment in Paris, I was heading up a surveillance of a known terrorist

AKA Rene De Lorme, who was known to be associated with the Alherita terrorist network. De Lorme was wanted for murder and many other serious crimes in the U.S. and Great Britain. While conducting surveillance we spotted him and moved in for an arrest. De Lorme and four of his associates engaged us in a firefight and they all ended up dead. After securing the parameter with the assistance of the French, we took into evidence a laptop which had a message written in code." Adams pulled down a screen and put on the overhead. He walked over and switched off the set of lights located directly above the screen.

"This is the message that was decoded."

Contact Ruslan Bakov and Cheng-foo Ping at 5:00 PM 11/15, 474 Pushkinskaya St. Vladivostok
D115545N3736E, D124310N132OE, D135956N3018E, D143955N11625E, D153110N12128E
Expedite the packages. Our day will arrive soon.

"What concerns us is Mr. Cheng-foo Ping. Ping owns an import-export company called Chi'nak Corporation, headquartered in Ji'an China, which is located right on the border of North Korea. The message you see here indicates five locations. These numbers are longitude and latitude locations of five major cities in Russia and China. De Lorme was directed to meet with Ping and Bakov in Vladivstok also near North Korea to 'expedite the packages.' Gentlemen, my group and I have been investigating a man by the name of Rojas Fuentes, a Mexican citizen and businessman who imports textiles from China and Iran. He owns a company called Albatross Corporation." Adams clicked the remote and changed the screen. "Here are documents that link Fuentes to Chi'nak Corporation, owned by Mr. Ping. They are doing business together. The accounts payable records here show Albatross Corporation is paying Chi'nak Corporation millions of dollars through Bank Niaga in the Cayman Islands."

"Let me get this straight." The Deputy Director of the CIA stood up. "You're investigating this Fuentes character and he is importing textile goods from a Chinese Company owned by Ping, who was supposed to meet with a known terrorist in Russia near the border of North Korea to expedite some packages. These are the five locations listed and it reads, "Our day will arrive soon?"

"Yes, sir," Adams answered.

"Where are the five destinations?" Director Morris asked.

"Moscow, Vlasivostok, St. Petersburg, Beijing and Shanghai." Adams was now sitting.

"You have just named some of the largest and most populated cities in the world."

"Yes sir, I'm afraid so, and Albatross Corporation owns a ship, El Conquistador, which has been confirmed to be sailing back to Mazatlan Mexico from the Yellow Sea."

"When is it arriving?" asked the Deputy Assistant Director of Counter-terrorism.

"In a few weeks, we are trying to narrow down an exact date. We will know more when it gets closer to Mexico. They can't give us an exact date due to the inability to predict future weather patterns."

"What do you think is on that ship?" FBI Director Morris was looking directly at Adams.

"I'm not sure, sir, but I would bet it's more than just textiles."

"As far as I'm concerned, we have enough evidence for a thorough search of the ship. Customs has the authority to inspect all cargo through the World Trade Organization's fair trade agreement act, anyway, right?" asked Director Morris.

"Yes sir." It was music to Adams' ears. "The only problem would be if they were hiding something on the ship that wasn't considered part of the cargo," Adams said.

Director Morris stood up. "Gentlemen, this is a matter of international security. After observing the evidence that Agent Adams has presented here this morning, I am highly concerned that there may be a plot involving the distribution and possible detonation of weapons of mass destruction at the hands of terrorists. North Korea is a rogue nation that cannot be trusted regarding the exportation of dirty bombs and possibly even nuclear weapons. I will contact the appropriate parties to assure full cooperation from the Mexican government to make all necessary arrangements for a complete search of the ship."

"Sir, I would ask that we wait until the day the ship arrives, to avoid the possibility of someone tipping off Fuentes."

"I'll do what I can. Agent Adams, I take it you will be in Mexico several days before the ship is to arrive, in preparation for the search?"

"Yes sir, I'll be there."

The meeting continued for another hour and a half before they adjourned with their individual instructions regarding the matter at hand. Adams booked a plane back to California. His mission to Washington was a success.

Chapter 43

The only hardware store in Pinehaven was fully equipped with nearly everything one would need for the repair and maintenance of their home and garden. When a town resident needed to buy a snow shovel, they would go to Will's Hardware store because William Foley, the owner, enjoyed a monopoly on selling hardware in Pinehaven. There was a blizzard in the forecast and it was expected to hit Pinehaven the following day.

Justin was shopping in the hardware store and overheard a town resident haggling over the price of snow shovels with Foley.

"You go and double the price of shovels just because there is a blizzard heading this way?"

"If you don't like it, you can drive to Clarionton and get one," said Foley, a wealthy and greedy man who lived alone in his big house on the lake. He owned a thirty-eight foot boat, three cars and motorcycle. He was not very well liked or respected in the community. He was a selfish man who believed material possessions brought happiness.

"Good afternoon." Justin approached Foley.

"What can I do you out of?" Foley chuckled to himself.

"I see that you have doubled the price of your snow shovels."

"What, are you going to complain, too? Then you can go with Baker to Clarionton and buy one."

"I didn't come here to complain. I was wondering what you will do with the profit you make from selling your shovels?"

"I don't think it's any of your business, pal, but if you must know, I'm going to buy a new snowmobile."

"I see," Justin said. "And that will make you happy?"

"It's a start," Foley replied.

"Alright then, have a nice day." Justin said, as he exited the store.

The winter storm had dropped twenty-two inches of snow on Pinehaven and the roads had finally been cleared off. Foley was pulling into his parking lot to get prepared for another day of business, when he observed a brand new snowmobile parked in front of his store. He jumped out of his truck and nearly slipped and fell while running to the recreational vehicle. When he got close enough, he noticed a big red bow with a note that read, "Congratulations, William. Enjoy Your New Snow Mobile." The key was hanging from the ignition. Foley was bewildered. Who would do such a thing for him? Nobody ever gave him anything. Everything he had ever gotten he had to take. After admiring his new gift he took the key, put it in his pocket and opened the store.

It was closing time on Saturday when Justin came by the store.

"Hello, William."

"Good afternoon. Just getting ready to close up for the day. How can I help you?"

"I was wondering how you like your new snowmobile?"

"It's a beauty. Hey, are you the one who brought it here?"

"Yes, the gift is from me. I have no use for it and I knew it was what you desired."

"Okay. What's the catch, pal?"

"There is no catch. If it's all right with you I would like to take a ride on it with you tomorrow. I have never ridden on one and I'm not sure how to operate it."

"Does that mean you want it back?"

"No, it's yours to keep."

"Okay. I'll meet you here tomorrow at 10:00 AM." Foley said.

The next morning Justin was on the back of the snowmobile while Foley raced through the woods. He was like a little kid with a new toy.

"Go this way." Justin directed him down a long driveway where there sat a little run-down shack in the middle of the woods.

"Let's stop here for a minute."

"Okay," Foley said. "Who lives here?"

A woman came walking out of the house with two youngsters following.

"Hello," she said.

"Hello. I'm Justin and this is William."

"I'm Ellen Green and these are my two sons, Derek and Austin. Would you like some hot chocolate and banana bread?"

"I'm all set," Foley answered quickly after seeing the rags they were wearing.

"Yes, that would be nice," Justin replied.

"Come inside then." The woman's weathered face concealed her natural beauty.

After spending ten minutes in the old shack, Foley was ready to go. The place was rundown and primitive. It was obvious they were very poor. The woman had treated them so kindly, yet Foley couldn't wait to leave. Justin finished his bread and thanked Ellen Green and the children. They mounted the machine and rode off through the woods. When they reached their destination, Justin turned to Foley.

"William, when you bought your house, were you truly happy?" Foley thought for a couple seconds.

"No, not really."

"How about when you bought your cars. Were you happy then?"

"No."

"And when you bought your boat. Did that make you happy?"

He thought for a moment before responding. "No, I don't think so."

"Why, then, would you think owning a snowmobile would be any different? Material possessions will not make you happy. Once the novelty has worn off you will just move on to the next possession for temporary fulfillment. The Greens are very poor people, but they were happy just to invite us in for bread and a hot drink. They asked for nothing in return. Their happiness is reflected in their smile and generosity. What made them happy today was to give to others. You shall never find happiness in owning material possessions. True happiness is achieved by opening up your heart and purse to others. Greed is a sin. Ask the Lord for forgiveness and show generosity to your fellow man." Justin rested his palm on top of William's head and prayed.

Monday morning arrived, and Will's Hardware store was open for business. There was another snowstorm in the forecast and Foley had his shovels on display. This time they were marked down to half price.

The Greens woke up that morning and found Foley's snowmobile parked in front of their shack. It had a card that read, "Please accept this gift as a gesture of good-will. It will sell for a fair price."

Chapter 44

It was like old times. Adams and Sara were naked, lying in the bed adjacent to the sliding glass doors that opened to the balcony, which overlooked Puerto Viejo Bay. Adams had decided to stay in the same hotel. He figured everything went so smoothly last time why change and break good karma. They had received a call early that morning from Marty, who notified them of the date the ship was scheduled to arrive. Adams was pleased it would be delayed an extra day. He could spend the day sailing with Sara. The ship was arriving in three days and that would give them plenty of time to make love and enjoy the tropics, he thought. Marty and Bobby were staying at the Playa Satanio.

Mazatlan is called *La Perla del Pacifico* and hosts over one million visitors per year and one could easily get lost in the crowds. Even with this in mind, Adams couldn't be too careful. He had to keep his affair with Sara a secret, and if Marty and Bobby were staying at the same hotel, it would be more difficult to hide. He wasn't fooling anyone, though. Marty and Bobby already knew about the affair. They were FBI agents and that was their job, to observe things.

Marty and Bobby were situated and conducting surveillance on Fuentes's villa. They had to be discreet and set up a stakeout quite a distance from the villa because they didn't want to take the chance of alerting anyone to the investigation. It was a long, tedious assignment and much of it was spent complaining about Adams and Sara. How they were on vacation, getting laid, and sailing, while Marty and Bobby were stuck sitting in a car trying to keep their asses from sticking to the leather seats.

"What a way to spend a morning. What do you say we eat breakfast in bed?"

"I thought I already had," Adams said.

Sara smiled. "How about something a little more filling? Like eggs."

"Okay, scrambled with bacon well done and rye toast. Don't forget coffee and spring water. You call it in while I use the bathroom. When I come out we should have just about enough time for round two before the food arrives," he said with his chest inflated.

"You are an animal," Sara said.

"Is that good or bad?"

"It's so good," she answered.

"How's this for an animal?" Adams sprang out of the bathroom wearing only a shower cap and a semi-hard on. He started dancing around in circles on his toes and singing the "Sound of Music." Sara busted out in laughter. Unable to contain herself, she rolled off the bed onto the floor. Adam's yanked off the shower cap and crawled on his hands and knees across the floor until his body was on top of hers. They began kissing and she reached down grabbing onto his manhood. She guided him to her and he moved forward. He felt so good, she thought. He was perfect.

After breakfast they took a long walk along the beach. They held hands and talked about where they were in their lives and where they wanted to go in the future. They stopped along a deserted stretch of beach and took off their suits and sprinted to the water. They held each other's naked body and allowed the soft current to carry them while they engaged in a kiss that seemed to last an eternity. Sara looked up and down the beach and could see two people far away in the distance and she thought it was within her comfort level.

"Lets go to the water's edge. I want to make love with you right here, right now."

Adams was pleased with her spontaneity and her libido. After rolling around on the beach, they put their bathing suits back on and went back to the hotel and showered. Sara had showered first and was lying naked on the bed when Adams came out.

"How many orgasms do you think you're behind?"

"I'm not keeping count," Adam's responded.

"I'm not either, but I had two on the beach and you didn't even have one, so I think I owe you."

"Can I ask you something?" Adams asked.

"Sure, anything."

"Does your husband please you in bed? It seems like you are deprived and are playing catch up."

"Lets just say he is not an animal like you. He is more concerned with pleasing himself."

Adams laid down next to her and took her in his arms. "Do you love him?"

"I guess I love the idea of him. The security he offers."

"Is that enough for you? Can you live the rest of your life like that?"

"I don't know. I never thought about it until I met you."

"I'm falling in love with you, Sara."

Sara looked into his eyes and knew he was already there. So was she. She kissed him without saying a word and rolled over on her stomach.

"I want it like this." She was on her hands and knees. He made love with her from behind. She closed her eyes and didn't think about her husband at home. She was in another place.

Chapter 45

El Conquistador was due to arrive the next day. The manner in which Fuentes' compound was situated made it difficult to set up surveillance. The road to the villa was a secluded windy road with palm trees on both sides of the street. There wasn't a place to set up without being noticed. Marty and Bobby set up a half mile down the road and would drive by from time to time and take photos and look for anything suspicious.

Adams and Sara rented a boat and once again sailed south to observe the villa from the water. They had already determined where the ship would be porting and posted two undercover customs agents there to observe anything out of the ordinary. Once again it was a beautiful day on the boat, and Adams placed a couple of life jackets behind them to act as pillows.

"Do you want to make love?" Sara asked.

"Are you kidding? Aren't you sore?"

"A little, but not enough to stop me from being with you again."

"If you need it, I'll do it, but it will be for you. I'm all set right now."

"I don't need it. I was just making sure you're all set."

"Thanks for caring. I am content just having you in my arms. The serenity and beauty here is more than enough for me. I wish this moment could last forever."

"Me, too." Sara kissed him.

"Life is funny. One minute you're covered with blood fighting for your life, caught up in the most ugly and horrible, situation one could imagine. With a blink of an eye you're here in paradise. How can we go from one extreme to the next in such a short period of time? And how can you ever go back to the ugliness and horror after being here like this?"

"Your assignment in Paris was a tough one, wasn't it?"

"I really didn't think about it until I saw them carry out the bodies of my men. That's when it hit me. One minute you're having a conversation with them and the next they're dead."

"There was nothing you could do. It was just their time. God takes people when He feels they have completed their work here on earth."

"I don't believe in God. I believe in this." He kissed her. "I believe in the moment."

"You really took it hard, didn't you?"

Adams didn't answer. He just lay there with Sara, watching the clouds above, slowly pass by.

The word had been passed on to all agents involved in the operation. El Conquistador was arriving at approximately 1:00 PM. The Mexican Federal Police were notified the day before. Agents from the FBI, ATF, Customs, NNSA and the Mexican Police were in place waiting for the ship to port.

Adams and Sara were sitting at a dockside café having lunch. Every few minutes he would put down his fork and pick up his binoculars. In the distance he could see the ship approaching. It was massive, he thought. He handed the binoculars to Sara and he signaled to the waiter who was standing erect by the gazebo entrance. He paid the check, made sure he got his receipt and they got up and moved closer to the dock. Adams and Sara approached a Customs agent who was standing nearby.

"Agent Adams and Kimball, with the FBI. How are you doing?" Adams asked.

"Good, I'm Agent Tom Sockolowski with Customs." They shook hands.

"Nice to meet you, Tom. Could you direct us to the agent in charge of Customs here?"

"Sure. That's Nick Garvey, the guy standing over there with the ATF Agent." He pointed down the dock.

"Okay, thanks."

Adams and Sara went directly to where Garvey was standing and they introduced themselves.

"Nick, can you tell me how many agents you have here to conduct the search?"

"We have seventeen Customs people here."

"Have you been briefed as to what we are looking for and the background of El Conquistador and its owner?"

"Yes, we are very familiar with Rojas Fuentes. If there is anything illegal on that ship, my people will find it."

"That's what I like to hear. We'll be coming along with you, if you don't mind," Adams suggested.

"That's alright with me," Garvey said.

"Make sure your people are locked and loaded. We don't know how they will react to this search."

"We're ready for whatever comes our way," Garvey said with confidence.

"Good. One more thing, we need to keep our eyes open for Fuentes. Alert your people and if anyone sees him, he is to be held. If he is spotted, I want to know immediately."

"Consider it done."

"Thanks, I appreciate your help."

As El Conquistador approached port, the sound of the ships horn resonated so anyone within five miles knew it was coming. The orders from the Mexican military commander in charge of the operation read that no person or item was to be allowed off the ship until cleared. This was a matter of international security and took the highest priority. It had taken some convincing, but once the Mexican government received in detail the possible threat that existed, they agreed to cooperate with all agencies involved as long as it was understood that they were in charge.

As the ship reached port, the Mexican military soldiers were lined up in columns in parade rest formation. The Customs agents were in the ready position alongside of the soldiers. Agent Garvey, who spoke fluent Spanish, was discussing the search with Colonel Ruben Hernandez of the Mexican Army. He was the officer in charge of the operation and he took it very seriously.

Agents from the FBI and ATF were waiting in the rear and preparing to assist in the operation.

There were half a dozen representatives from the National Nuclear Security Administration, with their plutonium and uranium detection devices secured in what appeared to be large aluminum cases.

After the gangway had been secured, Mexican soldiers were called to attention and ordered to file into the ship. They were followed by the assisting agencies that boarded the ship in a less formal manner. Once aboard El Conquistador, the ship's Captain, Ramiro Guerrero greeted Colonel Hernandez. It was immediately evident by the show of force that this was not a routine inspection, and Captain

Guerrero appeared nervous. Adams and Sara accompanied Garvey and other Customs agents as they ordered the crew to begin removing large steel containers off the ship, one at a time. The Mexican soldiers armed with automatic weapons stood by in the ready position in case of any unexpected trouble. Each container was thoroughly inspected by Customs and then NNSA inspectors, who had state of the art nuclear detection sensors. The devices they used had the capability to detect plutonium and uranium as well as the existence of any radioactive material.

The effort was a long tedious inspection that went on throughout the day and into the next, before it was complete. When they finished, every container and the personal luggage from the crew had been thoroughly inspected. All containers removed from El Conquistador were packed with textiles and other assorted retail items. Customs agents seized two kilos of heroin, that they determined had been smuggled in by a member of the crew. There were seven handguns and other items that concerned the Food and Drug Administration, removed from the vessel. Adams, agitated at the lack of progress, insisted he be allowed to accompany the NNSA inspectors aboard the ship, while they inspected the interior.

The galley had been cleaned spotless and the aroma of ammonia lingered throughout the entire area. The inspectors slowly paraded around with hand-held detection devices going through the walk-in freezer. Adams and Sara were standing outside where it was warmer, when a call came over the radio to all inspectors.

"They have found something on the bottom level near the boiler room," said an inspector as he exited the freezer.

They all headed directly to the bottom level where they found several inspectors anxiously waiting.

"What have you got?" Adam's didn't waste time asking.

"We have detected plutonium along these walls," answered an inspector, who looked as if he had just discovered a lost treasure. He showed the device to the agents, displaying the level of activity on the gauge.

"So what do you think, it's behind the wall?" Sara was asking now.

"It looks that way."

"So let's tear it down," she suggested.

Garvey arrived on the scene and was advised of the situation. He immediately got on his cell phone and called Colonel Hernandez who gave him permission to proceed. Two agents armed with crowbars began prying off the wooden panels, one by one. As they removed several large sheets they were astounded at what they uncovered. They immediately made it clear to everyone in the area that this was an emergency. Garvey made a call and ordered that the ship be cleared of all non-essential personnel. He then made a call to Colonel Hernandez advising him of the situation.

The wall constructed of hard wood was a fake. The true wall was erected seven feet behind it. The space between the walls housed five tactical nuclear bombs with a radio frequency detonator. Each bomb had enough energy to kill all living creatures within the radius of a city the size of Los Angeles, California. The Mexican National Guard was put on full alert. The bomb disposal team, along with the emergency disaster unit, was activated. Fire and police units were dispatched to the area and Colonel Hernandez set up a command post in one of the local restaurants. The entire area surrounding the dock had been cordoned off while experts from the NNSA were called in to deactivate the bombs.

Adams had been given the green light to execute a search of Fuentes' villa. He called Marty on his cell phone and gave him the news that they got a thumbs-up on the search.

"Good thing Mexican law doesn't afford criminals as many rights as the U.S.," Adams said.

"We don't need a search warrant, right?" Sara knew the answer.

"That's right." Adams had the smirk on his face she knew so well.

The police arrested Captain Guerrero. During their initial line of questioning they asked him the whereabouts of Fuentes and he stated, "I don't know." They also asked him if Fuentes usually meets the ship when it sails into port and he responded, "Most of the time."

Everyone was in position. Soldiers from the Mexican army rammed the front iron gates with a two-ton truck and they came crashing down without resistance. One of the guard dogs was immediately killed, being instantly crushed by the gate as it came down. A Mexican soldier shot the other dog dead on the spot as soon as it displayed hostility. The soldiers moved toward the house and came under fire by two of Fuentes' guards. They were both quickly shot dead after wounding a Mexican soldier. As soldiers surrounded the premises, Adams and his team followed the soldiers as they bashed in the front door with a ramming rod. They entered the house and found two more guards in the lobby standing completely still with their hands in the air. The house was empty with no sign of Fuentes. The search of the villa was underway as Adams moved into the library.

A mahogany and glass display case ran along the corner wall. There were books and small trinkets lined up on the shelves. As Adams approached, he felt a chill run down his spine. Sara noticed his expression and asked him if he was okay. He turned and looked at her with a blank look on his face. Then he turned back, looking into the case at an old dagger with a gold handle and a serpent with seven snakeheads on the end of it, laid out on display. Adam's waited until he was alone then with a quick elbow strike he broke the glass and removed the dagger and hid it in his lower back waistline.

They continued to search the villa and found many satanic cult related books written in Spanish. The house was decorated with several eerie paintings and sculptures. There was a commotion in one of the walk-in closets and the agents followed two soldiers in to see what was happening. They located a trap door on the floor and pulled it up to find a staircase that led underground. The villa had been built on a slab, as all homes in the area, for flood prevention purposes, so the house didn't have a basement. As they followed the soldiers down the steps, they heard weeping sounds. Sara's first thought was they had found another dog. After reaching the bottom of the stairs they had realized the tragedy that laid beneath the house. They found a young Mexican girl sitting naked chained to a wall. Her mouth and eyes were covered with duct tape and her wrists and ankles were shackled. Next to her was a large seven-foot wooden bench with shackles on each corner where many before her had been systematically raped and tortured. The bench had blood stains so deeply embedded they couldn't be scrubbed out. The torture chamber had the stagnant smell of death lingering in the air. For a few seconds they all stood in silence witnessing unbelievable horror. A soldier quickly called for bolt cutters and a blanket for the girl.

"Take me out of here!" Sara demanded.

"Come on, she's in good hands now." Adams took her by the arm and assisted her back up the stairs.

The entire house was searched and anything Adams felt was pertinent to the case was booked into evidence and taken into custody by Colonel Hernandez. Adams asked Hernandez for permission to accompany him to his compound to inventory the evidence, and he agreed. The whereabouts of Fuentes was still unknown and Adams was growing concerned. There was an active warrant for his arrest and a nationwide All Points Bulletin had been called out on him.

It would only be a matter of time before they caught him, Adams thought. But he had to be taken in alive and able to talk. He had information that was critical to the security of the world.

Chapter 46

The room was small and stuffy and without air conditioning. Evidence taken from Fuentes' villa was spread out on three tables. A Mexican soldier armed with a rifle stood by the entrance to the room holding his weapon in place without moving, like a toy soldier. Colonel Hernandez sat next to one of his men, who was logged onto Fuentes' computer.

Adams was looking over the soldier's shoulder at the screen. There were spread sheets and itemized logs with company names and locations that Fuentes had done business with.

"Adams, take a look at this book."

Sara had been thumbing through books found in the library. She could tell by the binding the book was very old. She had worked in the University library when she was in college and had been exposed to rare books and recognized one when she saw it. The book was written in Spanish. Sara searched for a copyright date but couldn't find one. There were no dates to indicate when the book was written, only brittle pages that had yellowed with time and a binding which appeared to be crafted at least three hundred years ago, she thought.

"Look at this." Sara pointed to a picture in the book. It was a picture of a dagger with a serpent and seven snakeheads on the top of the handle.

"Let me see that." Adams took the book and brought it to Colonel Hernandez. "Colonel, what do you make of this?"

Hernandez muttered out in Spanish but it was quite understandable, "El Libro del Diablo."

"The book of the Devil." Sara repeated.

With his index finger, Hernandez made the sign of the cross on his forehead and across his body.

"Can you read this page for us?" Adams asked.

Hernandez began reading, "And the black angel was cast out of the Heavens. With hate in his heart and blood in his eyes, he dwells on earth as a serpent. He will choose seven disciples. Each will be given a dagger with the sign of the beast. And together they will rule for eternity."

Adam's looked at the book and then at Sara. He couldn't speak. He had an uneasy feeling inside that he couldn't explain. Sara knew him well enough to see something was wrong.

"Can I speak to you outside for a minute?" she asked.

"Okay." He closed the door behind them.

"What is it Adams? Something is wrong. Tell me."

"When we hit De Lorme's place in Paris, I found a dagger in his safe. It's exactly like this one." He took the dagger out from his waste band and handed it to her. "I took this one from Fuentes' library. They are both identical to the one in the book."

"This is getting pretty weird, Adams."

"Too fucking weird, Sara."

They went back into the room.

"Mira esto," said the Mexican soldier behind the computer.

There was a document written in code.

"Print it out for me please?" Adams requested.

He sat down with the document and began to decode based on what he had learned from De Lorme's document. He began to circle the third letter of every word after reversing the letters in each word.

When he was finished he looked at Sara and said, "This isn't good." The code read.

Contact: Cheng-foo Ping in Tonghua China at 11:00 AM, 12/12, 441-498-0098-7899
D1128S4829W, D2432N7415W, D31028N672W,
D43328S7045W, D51926N997W
Your packages await you. Our day will arrive soon.

Colonel Hernandez looked at Adams puzzled. "What does it mean?"

"Do you have a world map?"

"Yes, follow me." They went into a large room that looked like it was used for military meetings. There was a map spread out on the wall. Adams went to work and began writing on a pad.

"These series of numbers represent the longitude and latitude locations of these cities. Belem, Brazil; Bogotá, Columbia; Caracas, Venezuela; Santiago, Chile; and Mexico City.

Hernandez looked at the cities scribbled on the pad and then up at Adams. He spoke out in disbelief, "Cinco ciudades, cinco bombas nucleares."

"Five cities, five nuclear bombs." Adams said.

Chapter 47

Not long after the girl was taken to the hospital and everyone had cleared out of Fuentes' villa, the high-pitched screams once again bounced off the inner walls of the torture chamber.

Under the orders of Colonel Hernandez, several soldiers escorted two of Fuentes' guards down to the chamber at gunpoint. The first guard was tough and defiant refusing to crack under the excruciating pain of having his fingers broken one at a time. With three fingers on his left hand mutilated, he was thrown into the corner and the other guard that was sweating profusely was hoisted onto the bench to take his place.

The burley soldier who had the task of inflicting the pain on the guards, noticed the fear in the second guard's eyes and figured he would break much sooner than the former. Three soldiers held him down as he struggled and cried out in an attempt to talk them out of hurting him. As he looked into the dark eyes of the large soldier, he saw no remorse, no pity. The soldier picked up the bolt cutters that had been used to free the girl a few hours earlier. He placed the sharp edges of the blades far up the length of his finger stopping at the large knuckle. Clutching both handles firmly, he spoke with conviction.

"I am only going to ask once. Where is Rojas Fuentes?"

Without hesitation the guard began spilling his guts.

"Catemaco, he fled to Catemaco. That's where he's from. You'll find him there."

The guards were taken into custody and a call was immediately made to Colonel Hernandez. He was still in the conference room going through the evidence with Adams and Sara when his cell phone rang. Adams was not fluent in Spanish but he knew enough to understand that the conversation was regarding the whereabouts of Fuentes. When the call was finished, Hernandez clipped the phone on his belt and turned to Adams and Sara.

"We have information that Fuentes fled to Catemaco. Apparently he grew up there. I will assemble my troops and we can go out and find him."

"With all due respect, Colonel, I think it would be better if we hand select a few of your men and go out a little less conspicuously. We need to take him in alive. He has information that may help us to prevent an international catastrophe. Also, we don't want to take the chance of tipping him off and losing him. I suggest we keep a low profile until we locate him. Once we locate him we can call for reinforcements, if we need too."

"Alright, I can see your point, Agent Adams. As long as you understand this is my investigation and I am in charge. I will be going with you," Hernandez insisted.

"That's fine. Let me suggest that you bring three of your best men along. If you have someone from Catemaco or someone who knows the area well, that will be helpful. Try to get men who speak English"

"I will assemble my men and we can leave in the morning. Let's plan on meeting here at 6:00 A.M. and we can brief the team before we leave."

"Okay, Adams said, I will have my men Marty and Bobby join us."

"Will she be coming along, too?" Hernandez looked at Sara. "It may get very dangerous."

"Don't concern yourself, Colonel. I am perfectly capable of taking care of myself." Sara said, obviously offended.

"Make no mistake." The Colonel slammed his palm down on the table making a loud thump, commanding everyone's full attention. "Rojas Fuentes is a very powerful and dangerous man. He has many people who will support him, and even die for him, including police officers. We may not all make it out alive."

The room was quiet as the magnitude of the situation settled in the minds of the agents.

Adams broke the silence. "So that's it. There will be eight of us. I would suggest that we take three vehicles. I would like to have your man who knows the Catemaco area ride with me. I don't know the place at all. We will have Sara with us. Marty and Bobby can ride in a car with one of your men and you and the other soldier can ride together."

Hernandez was disturbed that Adams was already calling the shots.

"If that makes sense to you," Adams said, redeeming himself.

"That sounds alright to me," Hernandez Replied.

"How far is it to Catemaco?" Sara asked.

"It's on the other side of the country, in the south on the gulf coast." Hernandez pointed it out on the map. "We can take route 185 south to Cosamaloapan, cut across just north of the rain forest on route 175 east to Lerde, and then head south on route 180 to Catemaco." He traced along the map with his pen while he spoke. "It should take us about Twelve hours."

"Okay, we will be ready to roll first thing tomorrow morning. Let's get some rest," Adams suggested.

Chapter 48

The golden rays of the sun were nearly in full spectrum and reflecting off the hood of the black sedan that Adams and Sara were slumped down in. They had arrived early and were awaiting the arrival of the rest of the team. Adams spent most of the night tossing about with his mind racing, as if he were in the open sea on a sailboat competing for the America's Cup. He had unsuccessfully attempted to convince Sara to pass on the trip to Catemaco and go home to her kids, and the defeat weighed heavily on him.

Adams rested his coffee on the dashboard, as he observed Marty and Bobby approaching through his rearview mirror. They were in a red sedan and he wondered if it would have been wiser for them to be a little less conspicuous. They pulled up along side him and rolled down their window.

"Good morning, you two are up bright and early," Bobby said.

"Can't say the same for the Mexicans," Adams responded while looking at his watch, it was 6:02 A.M.

"No wonder they lost the Battle of Cerro Gordo," Marty offered in a low monotone voice. They all started laughing. Bobby was wondering what the hell he was talking about.

"Listen," Adams spoke up. "We don't know these guys so we need to watch out for each other very closely. Who the hell knows where their loyalty lies. I think we can trust Hernandez, but we don't know anything about the rest of his team. Keep one in the chamber all the time."

"Here they are now," Sara announced.

They pulled up in a dark green car moving in next to Adams and Sara. At first, Marty thought they were going to drive right past them up the embankment and crash into the fence. Abruptly, the driver slammed on the brakes skidding to a complete stop right next to them. They all exited their vehicles and started toward the building. It was the first time Adams had seen Hernandez in plain clothes. He appeared awkward, as if the clothes didn't fit right. He wore them like his older brothers hand-me-downs. He looked much more comfortable in his uniform, Adams thought.

The meeting lasted less than fifteen minutes. Adams wanted to make it clear that Fuentes was to be taken alive. He didn't explain the magnitude of the situation to the three soldiers, but he did articulate that it was a matter of international security. Ramiro was the soldier who was assigned to ride with Adams and Sara. He was a thin man who couldn't have been more than twenty-five, but his face was weathered and dry from the sun and it added a few years to his appearance. Out of the three, he spoke the worst English, but he knew Catemaco the best. He had lived there for six years just before joining the army. Juan was a pudgy man a few years older than Ramiro who had a symmetrical-shaped head and a mustache that was in desperate need of a trim. Adams thought he might be related to Pancho Villa. He was riding along with Marty and Bobby. The last new member of the team was Ernesto. He seemed to be the quiet one. He was older than the others and appeared to be well seasoned. He was an observer with black, deep-set eyes that gave him the disposition of a man who had been to hell and back. Adams knew the eye of the tiger when he saw it and there was no denying it in Ernesto. He understood why Colonel Hernandez chose to have Ernesto ride in his car and he didn't blame him.

The day grew hotter and hotter as they drove across the desolate countryside with the sun in their eyes the whole way. Sara made sure she applied sun block on her face and arms to avoid sun burn right through the car windows. The conversation was minimal, which allowed for much anticipation on what was to come in the next few days. Sara rode in the back while Ramiro rode shotgun pointing the way for Adams. Their vehicle led the three-car caravan along the deserted strip of pavement that seemed to be an endless abyss of sand and sun. Sara had to use a rest room but there weren't any in sight, so she crossed her legs and thought about yoga postures and holiday gatherings with her family. She was almost tempted to stop and squat behind a cactus plant but she would shoot herself in the foot first, she thought. Finally they came upon a spot they could stop. It was a gas station sitting alone, along the roadside like a scene in a bad horror movie. Sara raced to the attendant, asking him where she could find the restroom. He didn't understand a word she muttered, but he could tell by the way she walked and the look on her face what she was desperately searching for. He pointed her in the right direction and she flew into the room. After seeing the toilet, she almost wished she had used the concealment of a cactus in the desert. When she finished her business, and it was done in record time for Sara, she joined the rest of the team outside for a cool drink and rest.

"Feel better?" Adams asked, with a slight grin. "Here you go." He handed her a bottle of coke.

"What's that over there?" Marty pointed toward the wood line.

"I'm not sure." Adams responded, while looking at the Mexican soldiers anticipating an answer.

Hernandez began speaking to Ramiro in Spanish. When they stopped talking, Hernandez smiled at Marty. "That is our history. Let's go take a closer look." They all made their way over to the wood line and as they got closer, Sara's curiosity got the best of her.

"My God," she said. "How old is it?"

Interpreting for Ramiro, Hernandez answered. "About 1500 BC. It was erected in that era."

They all stood at the base of a colossal stone head that had been relatively well preserved considering its age. Pieces of the head had fallen off over time or had been desecrated by people with lack of respect for ancient culture and artifacts. The head was round with a flattened nose, wide lips, and a capping headpiece. They all took a seat near the enormous head and listened to Ramiro ramble on in Spanish, echoed by Hernandez in English.

"This is the work of the Olmec tribe. They ruled this land nearly 2000 years before Christ was born. These heads were once thrones used by Olmec rulers. After they died they were converted into a colossal portrait head of the ruler." Ramiro kept talking and Hernandez repeated his every word in English. It was obvious by the way he followed along he was getting a history lesson as well. As they sat sipping their drinks in the shade staring up at this six-foot tall head, it was clear that everyone found the story to be interesting, except for Bobby. He could care less and it was very obvious by the way he was sleeping.

"It is said that the Olmecs practiced Shamanism, and that's where it originated. Shamans believed they had the ability to assume the powers of animals, particularly the jaguar. It is said that the heads represent sacrificial offerings. There are many heads like this situated throughout Los Tuxtlas."

"What is Los Tuxtlas?" Sara inquired.

"Los Tuxtlas is our rain forest. This is where it begins and it stretches all the way out to the coast and down towards the border of Central America. It is a very famous area in Mexico," Ramiro continued. "The movie 'Medicine Man' with

Sean Connery was filmed here. Some of the heads have a human face with a jaguar mouth; these are called "were-jaguar" (as in werewolf). This suggests a change from Olmec religion to Shamanistic worship which practiced human sacrifice, including that of infants."

"Sounds pretty sick to me," Adams said. Hernandez repeated his words in Spanish.

"Yes", Ramiro continued. "And it is said that the sacrifices continue today in Catemaco. There have been many children who have disappeared over the years, never to be found again. You must understand, Catemaco is where la maldad negra, the black evil is found. This place is known as the devil worship capital of the world. Some say this is where Satan resides. It is said his throne is an alter located in the mountain of the white monkey."

Bobby had awoken and began listening to Hernandez as he interpreted Ramiro's story. He had captured the attention of everyone at this point. Except for Ernesto, who was cleaning his handgun, everyone else sat in silence listening. "There are many witches here who practice black magic and cast spells on others, whom they despise. They have maimed and even killed people through the use of toxic herbs, poisonous bat droppings or the slashing of the jugular vein with extracted jaguar's teeth."

"Give me a break," Bobby said. "You expect us to believe in all this hocus pocus bullshit?"

"You believe what you will. I will tell you that Shamans live here today, by the thousands. I have seen what their spells can do."

"Well when you see one, you be sure and point him out, so I can bust a cap in him, if he starts sticking a pin in a Bobby doll," Bobby said.

Marty started laughing. "If he does, hopefully, he'll stick the pin in its head so he can deflate your fucking fat head ego."

"Fuck you, Marty."

"Okay boys, calm down," Adams said as he pushed himself onto his feet.

"I won't have to point them out. They all dress in black robes. You will know them when you see them. Understand something, this is not a hoax, this is for real. Do not underestimate the Shaman. There have been many people murdered here who also did not believe. I left here soon after five people were found murdered in the mid-1990s. The town has a population of 20,000 people. Five murders occurred in a span of six months and residents were afraid to leave their houses. Since then, people have been disappearing every few months without a trace. Believe what you will, but keep your eyes open." Hernandez finished interpreting.

"Thanks for the heads up. We better get moving now," Adams said. They all started walking back towards their cars. Sara stood alone staring into the face of the enormous head. It was apparent she believed what Ramiro said to be true. She felt uneasy, yet curious.

Chapter 49

▼

Mile after mile the drive south began to reveal the unquestionable beauty of the rain forest. The wetlands were filled with thick vegetation and beaming plant life. Birds were obnoxiously loud and singing out of concert. The smell of rotting vegetation lingered throughout the thick, humid air. Along the road were over-ripe mango, papaya, and melon. Herds of cattle were moving about, grazing on the fertile landscape.

Soon they arrived to the edge of town and Adams pulled over and stopped. Colonel Hernandez pulled up along side of him and Marty got out on foot and walked to Adam's vehicle.

"Well, here we are," Adams said. "What do you say we find a place to stay and get some chow before we start looking for Fuentes?"

"That sounds good," Hernandez responded. He spoke to Ramiro in Spanish and they agreed on a motel in town they could check into. Continuing into town with Ramiro pointing the way they pulled into a motel that was in desperate need of two coats of paint and a few bottles of Windex. As luck would have it, they were able to get four rooms. Adams made sure he booked his room with Sara. He wanted to make love with her, and at a glance, he knew she felt the same.

After a shower and a roll between the sheets, they were dressed and ready for dinner. The room didn't have a telephone or air conditioning, just a ceiling fan that made a squeaking sound at every turn. Neither of them were thrilled with the accommodations, but acknowledged, it was only for the short term. They collected the rest of the team and started into town searching for a decent place to eat. They found a place called El Ojo Del Gato (The Cat's Eye) and settled in to a spot in the corner. Pulling two tables together, they sat and began browsing the menu.

"Fish, fish, and more god damd fish!" Marty complained. "Don't they have any steak in this toilet?"

"Fish is good for you. It will keep you light on your feet," Adams said.

"Lots of protein, Marty," Sara offered.

"Yeah, there's plenty of protein in a steak too," Marty said, while tossing the menu down.

After dinner Hernandez asked them to stay put while he and Ernesto paid a visit to the local authorities to see what they knew about Fuentes. Adams asked if he could accompany them, and Hernandez agreed. With assistance from the waiter, they were able to locate the police station, which was walking distance from the restaurant. The station house was a small brick building that stood alone on the intersection of two main streets. The town was busy with people moving around peering in store windows and bartering with local shopkeepers. There seemed to be fortune tellers and people claiming to be witches ready to cast spells, situated all over the town.

Adams noticed many people wearing black robes and he thought about what Bobby had said. They entered the building. "Buenas," Hernandez shouted out. A man wearing a raggedy uniform walked out from around the corner wall.

"Si, Señor."

"I am Colonel Hernandez." He displayed his identification and Ernesto did the same. "Do you speak English?"

"Yes. Who is this?" He looked at Adams.

"FBI Agent Adams," Hernandez responded.

"How can I help you?" He had a medium build with black hair that could easily pass for a bad toupee.

"We have a warrant for the arrest of a man we believe fled this way. He is wanted for very serious crimes. His name is Rojas Fuentes. Do you know him?"

"No," the officer responded without hesitation. Adams noticed that the officer's eyes shifted to the upper right, when he answered. From that moment forward, he seldom looked Hernandez in the eye, when speaking. It was apparent to all of them, he was hiding something.

"Are you sure you don't know this man?" Hernandez produced a photograph of Fuentes and placed it on the table in front of him.

"Yes, I'm sure. I'm very busy. Is there anything else?" He was getting edgy.

"Yes, Señor Lopez, there is." His name was displayed on a name tag out of line with his shirt pocket.

"How long have you lived in this area?"

"My entire life," Lopez answered.

"I'm not the best at guessing one's age, but I would say you're at least forty-five years old."

"Forty-nine," he responded, feeling a little better.

"Well, Rojas Fuentes is almost the same age as you and he grew up right here in this town. He is a well-known and respected businessman who has made millions in textiles. I find it hard to believe that you have never heard of him or recognize his photograph. Have you had your head up your ass, your entire life?" Hernandez was getting agitated and it became apparent when he reached out and grabbed the officer by his badge and pulled him across the table. At the same time Ernesto retrieved a blackjack from his inside jacket pocket and placed it on the table.

"I don't have time to dance with you. This man is a threat to the security of our country and I have full authority from President Fox, to do whatever it takes to find him, and if that means busting your head open and having your brains spill out all over this nice mahogany table, so be it."

"I don't know him," the officer insisted with a stuttering response.

"Wrong answer," said the Colonel. He reached down grabbing the officers left wrist pinning his hand to the table. Simultaneously, Ernesto picked up his blackjack and came down with a fierce force crushing the back of Lopez's hand. He let out a scream that could be heard for a quarter mile.

"I am told there are many, many bones in the hand. How many will I have to break until you start telling us the truth?" Ernesto raised the leather-covered steel weapon over his head once again.

"Bueno!" he cried out. "Don't hit me. He has a house on Lake Catemaco."

"That's better. Thanks for your cooperation," Hernandez said.

After getting the address they walked out leaving Lopez on the floor, in pain, favoring his broken hand, thinking how glad he was that it wasn't his gun hand.

"Well, you two certainly have a charming way about you," Adams said.

"We do what is necessary. We don't have time to waste."

"I couldn't agree more," Adams said as he discretely re-snapped his gun holster.

Chapter 50

The day was nearing its end as their car tires shot gravel projectiles into a cooler air, while pulling out of the motel lot. It was a short ride to the lake that was nestled in the Tuxtla Mountains of Veracruz. The sun was barely peeking its head out from behind the mountains that surrounded most of the lake. The sky was illuminated light blue with shades of white reflecting off the water, which seemed to reach out like an ocean's hand. The rugged volcanic ridges reached from sea level up to the lake, which sat nearly 6,000 feet above sea level.

The beauty was undeniable to anyone with clear sight and sound faculty. The lake was quiet and desolate. It offered an eerie kind of peacefulness, as one might find in a graveyard.

"Muchos pájaros viven aqui. Hay más que quinientos clases." Ramiro said, hoping they understood him. Using his hand gestures like wings of a bird and Sara being able to count in Spanish, she repeated to Adams what she interpreted, that there were 500 species of exotic birds living near the lake. Ramiro appeared delighted that they understood him. He mistakenly assumed there was progress in their communication gap. As they approached the lake house, darkness was falling and the sound of the frogs began to pick up, where the birds left off. They all exited their vehicles and got into a huddle to discuss a strategy.

"The four of us will take the front and you four can take the back." Hernandez was calling the shots. "When you hear us hit the door, you do the same. If there are any guards surrounding the house, we will need to try and take them down quickly and quietly, ¿entienden?"

"Agreed," Adams said. The rest of them showed acknowledgement. Adams, Sara, Ramiro, and Bobby made their way around back while the others went to the front. There wasn't any resistance as they moved into position. The house was dimly lit and not a sound from within could be heard. A minute later, Adams and his team heard the front door being kicked in. At that moment, Adams smashed the door window in with the butt of his handgun and reached in to unlatch the bolt. They entered with flashlights resting over their gun hands moving tactically from room to room clearing each room as a team. While moving deeper into the house they met up with Hernandez' team who finished clearing their sector of the house.

"It looks like the first floor is clear," Bobby observed, and was hoping he could pop a cap into someone's ass that resisted them.

"How about we take the basement and you take the upstairs?" Adams suggested.

"Alright," Hernandez responded.

As they moved into the basement, Sara found the light switch on the wall at the top of the stairs, which allowed them to put away their flashlights. As they moved through the basement, Sara stopped to look at a large corkboard, set up in an office area of the room. There were photographs pinned up next to each other covering the entire board. As she gazed into the array of pictures she began to tremble with fear. She just stood looking at the board as the rest of the team finished clearing the basement. She didn't speak, she couldn't. Adams called out for her, as he made the corner into the office area. He looked at her standing there like a statue staring at the wall. She appeared to be shaken up. Adam's turned to see what mesmerized her, so.

"Oh no!" was all he managed to say.

Chapter 51

▼

The rest of the team entered the office area and each person became silent as they peered up at the wall. The first picture that caught Sara's eye was one of her husband and two children playing in their front yard. There were photos of her and Adams having intercourse on the beach in Mazatlan. Other photos of them having dinner in San Diego and kissing outside the restaurant.

There were so many shots of them in the United States and Mexico. How could he not have noticed someone taking pictures of them, Adams thought. There were pictures of Bobby and Marty playing golf, and Marty playing baseball with his son at the park. Until that moment, none of them really knew what it felt like to be truly vulnerable. Sara had a chilling nausea that seemed to creep right to the very marrow of her bones.

"While we were attempting to watch him, he was watching all of us," said a defeated Adams.

"Yeah, and our kids too," Marty added.

Without saying a word, Sara reached up and took down the photos of her and Adams on the beach. Then she took down the ones that showed them kissing and finally the family pictures that had her so very scared.

"I have to make a call," she said, and walked out of the room.

"Lets take down these pictures, and then lets find this son of a bitch." Adams said, through gritting teeth.

As they toured the house, they saw a wolf's head mounted on a wall. Several pagan ritualistic pictures hung about the house and antique furniture made of the finest wood and fabric. There were ancient swords and daggers laid out on display and a three-foot tall, black onyx sculpture resting on a pedestal of the most hideous looking creature Adams had ever seen. It had bulging eyes and a scorned frown. Short pointed horns were erected from either side of its head, over sized fangs protruding from its jowls, which secreted down to a long pointed chin. Its hair consisted of thin snakes entangled in frenzy. There wasn't a doubt in anyone's mind, that if there were a Satan, he could definitely look like that.

Ramiro stopped to pick up an old book that sat alone on a marble table. It was constructed with a black leather binding and cover. "El Libro Supremo," Ramiro muttered. "El Anti-Cristo," he continued.

Hernandez looked at Adams and repeated what was said in English. "The Supreme Book of The Anti-Christ."

"Let's get the fuck out of here," Marty said. "This place gives me the creeps."

As they walked outside, Adams put his arm around Sara. "Are you okay?"

"I called my husband and told him what we found."

"What?" Adams responded.

"It was the only way I could convince him to take the kids and leave town."

"What did he say?"

"He said, if I didn't quit the Bureau he wanted a divorce."

"You didn't tell him about us, did you?"

"If I did that, he would have already retained a lawyer."

"Why don't you catch the next flight out, then?" Adams suggested.

"No, I'm staying. I want to nail this evil prick and pin the picture of my family to his eye."

"Now, that's the spirit," Adams said. Sara didn't laugh nor did she cry. She was totally numb.

The team met outside for a few minutes at the request of Hernandez. He ordered Ernesto and Juan to stay behind, conceal their vehicle and watch the lake house in case Fuentes returned. The rest of them would go back to Catemaco and shake up the town to see what would fall out. They were back to square one in locating Fuentes and they didn't have much time. Adams and Sara, more than anyone, were suffering from a sense of frustration in the effort. They were becoming extremely determined.

The next morning had arrived and it was already 81 degrees and humid. The four Americans sat at a breakfast table overlooking the water. It was a dingy little restaurant with a very strange looking staff of two. Neither of them spoke English, or they pretended not to. The waitress was frail and had long graying hair banded into a ponytail. Her eyes were deep-set into her face and she seemed to walk in a gliding type motion. The embedded dirt under her fingernails made

Sara uneasy, as she browsed through a menu she couldn't understand. From what they could all put together, the consensus was that everything on the menu consisted of fish. They ordered coffee and breakfast while looking out over the water.

"This place is like paradise lost," Sara mused. "It is so beautiful, yet so desolate."

"Well, yes, look at the fucking menu," Marty said. "Not the first place I'd consider for a family vacation, especially with all these assholes walking around in black robes."

"Grim Reaper wannabees," Bobby said.

"When we find this asshole, and I'm hoping it's alive, you better be ready for some extreme measures on this one. We need information from this guy and we need to do whatever it takes to extract it. We may even need to torture the bastard. And I'll tell you, I have seen Hernandez in action and I think he may even like it," Adams said.

"If torturing one man means saving the world, I'll tape the wire to his balls myself," Sara said.

Everyone just looked at her without responding. They could see she had hardened since they hit the lake house. Adams was worried she may not be thinking as clearly as she should. He knew it had something to do with her maternal instinct to protect her children. Not having children of his own, he could not truly understand the emotional bond and deep-rooted unconditional love a parent has for their children. But he had an idea, and he was hoping it wouldn't interfere with her judgment.

The food arrived in bowls. Everyone ordered the same thing, rice with fish on top. Adams was hungry and didn't waste anytime digging in. Marty sat drinking his coffee not moving toward his fork. Bobby and Sara began eating and they continued talking about what they had found at the lake house. Not a word was mentioned about the photos of Adams and Sara on the beach. A few minutes later Sara began toying with her food.

"What's this?" She jumped onto her feet and began spitting out what was in her mouth. She had noticed that the rice in her bowl was moving. Adams pulled her food closer and looked into the bowl to find maggots crawling around in her rice. Sara began rinsing her mouth out with water, totally disgusted. The rest of them began searching through their food for white worms or anything else that was moving, but found nothing. Adams began calling out for the waitress to exit from the shack where the food was prepared. There was no response. He got up and walked into the wooden hut to find it empty. He looked around and then walked out the back door onto the dock, but there was no sign of the waitress or the cook.

"Let's get the hell out of here," Adams commanded. "They disappeared. They must have seen what happened and got scared."

Sara remained quiet. She wasn't enjoying Catemaco, at all. They all went back to the motel to find their two Mexican friends, Hernandez and Ramiro, who were sipping coffee, sitting on the motel porch.

"Buenos días," Hernandez said. "Where did you four go?"

"Breakfast," Adams answered.

"Did you enjoy our Mexican cuisine?"

Sara just looked at him and went to her room. "Not really," Adams responded.

"It sucked!" Marty sounded out.

"Sara found larva in her food."

"Rotten fish," Hernandez said, as if he had experienced it first hand.

"Where was the place? I want to make sure I don't eat there," Hernandez said.

"The shack by the water. So what is the plan?"

"I paid a visit to Officer Lopez this morning. He doesn't know the whereabouts of Fuentes."

"Are you sure?" Bobby asked.

Hernandez looked him in the eye and said, "Yes, I'm sure." Bobby had a feeling he was right.

"Did you ask him if he tipped Fuentes off, that we were coming?" Marty asked.

"He didn't do that. He was too busy at the doctors office." Hernandez answered, with a smug look on his face.

"So what do you think? Where should we go from here?" Marty asked.

"First of all we need to go back to lake Catemaco and find out why my men aren't answering their cell phones."

"You haven't heard from them since last night?" Adams asked with a look of concern.

"No, I haven't."

"Well, let's get going then."

Adams stopped into his room and Sara was in bed lying in the fetal position. He sat next to her and stroked her hair.

"Are you alright?"

"I don't feel well."

"Let me guess, your stomach?"

"Yes."

"Can I get you anything?" He offered.

"No, I just need to rest for a while."

"Sara, I'm sorry you had to see those pictures hung up in everyone's view."

"Yeah, me too."

"I love you, Sara." He kissed her on the head. "I have to go. We aren't able to contact Ernesto and Juan, so were heading back up to the lake. Will you be alright?"

"Yes. Adams, be careful."

"I will. Make sure you keep the door locked after I leave. I'll see you in a couple hours."

He walked out leaving her on the bed, making sure he secured the door on the way out.

During the ride out to Fuentes' lake house they tried calling the two soldiers several times, at no avail. As they approached, they didn't see the vehicle or the men anywhere. Exiting their vehicles they searched the parameter of the house and found nothing. Both men had vanished.

"Over here!" Bobby called out.

They all hurried over to where Bobby was standing. He was looking down at the ground.

"What is it?" Hernandez asked.

"Looks like blood." Bobby answered.

Hernandez knelt down and touched the red substance that lay splattered on the sand. He rolled it between his fingers thinking, they were most likely dead. "Vamonos," he said.

"What are we going to do?" Marty asked. Ramiro was making the sign of the cross across his body.

"We are going to drink tequila and have conversations with the nice people of Catemaco," Hernandez responded in a firm determined voice.

"That is the best suggestion I've heard in two days," Marty said.

Adams was quiet. He was deep in thought. When he saw the blood of good men being spilled, it put him in a different place. It was a place you wouldn't want to be, if you were on the other team.

Chapter 52

Over the years Beth had mastered gardening. The assorted vegetables were lined up, growing ripe for the picking. She had strategically grown flowers around the vegetable garden to allow for a beautiful display. Outside the windows in her house she placed flowers that matched the wallpaper inside that particular room. Gardening had become therapy for her and it gave her solitary time to reflect on her life.

It had been a long time since she ran the Boston marathon and her speed and distance had decreased over the years. She thought back and was pleased that she had finished the race in three hours and twenty-one minutes, but realized those days were a distant memory. She had kept running, but her body was beginning to change like never before.

Watching Justin grow from an infant into a man had been the best years of her life. Learning that he was the savior sent from God had scared her at first, but she learned to realize there was nothing to fear. She was blessed to be chosen to bring him into the world. Beth believed everything was written and meant to be, that everyone had a path in life and if they changed the direction in which they traveled, it was because they were destined to.

While pruning in her garden, Beth thought about her ride back from the doctor's office the day before. She knew that most people would have been frightened to death while making that drive home. But she wasn't afraid. She didn't cry or get angry. She wouldn't ask God, "Why me? Why so young?" She didn't fear death because in her heart she knew the place she was going was a place without pain and sadness, a place free from hunger and war. There would be no hate, envy or greed. Where she was going, there would only be love and peace. She would miss the people she loved on earth but she would see them again in the kingdom of God. Beth thought about her days as a child and young woman, how she was afraid of death. She was happy to be at peace with death now. She even welcomed it.

It had been five months since Beth had started feeling differently. She knew her body and felt something was wrong, so she decided to go to the doctor. Blood tests had determined she had cancer and the doctor recommended she start chemotherapy treatment. Beth asked him if she underwent the treatment, would it cure her disease or just prolong her death. As convincing as he tried to be, she knew by the look on his face there was little hope of recovery. She was in stage four. On the last visit to the doctor she learned the cancer had spread to her liver. She didn't have to tell Justin; he already knew. She wondered why he didn't heal her. She knew he had the power to heal.

Chapter 53

Adams unlocked and opened the door to his motel room to find Sara sweating profusely. She was burning up and had broken out with soars all over her body.

"Adams, something is wrong here. I am so cold," she stammered.

Adams immediately got Ramiro into the room and asked him where the nearest hospital was. Ramiro knew of a clinic and offered to drive them. Adams carried Sara to the awaiting car and they took her straight to the clinic. After the examination the doctor came out and suggested she stay there until they got her 105-degree temperature down enough, where she could travel to a hospital in Mexico City. He had no explanation, other than a viral reaction to the food. Ramiro knew better, he had an idea of his own, but didn't share it. He kept to himself that, he had seen these symptoms before. When he lived in Catemaco several years back, a local merchant who was taking advantage of the villagers had been cursed by a local witch and after many days of suffering, he died at the hands of a Shaman devil worshiper. Someone had put a curse on Sara and continued to chant daily, pushing her to the brink of death, Ramiro thought.

Adams offered to stay with Sara, but she insisted he continue in his search for Fuentes. She knew time was running out and he had to be found. Adams told her to call his cell, if she needed anything. He also gave his number to the doctor and asked him to call if her condition got worse. He didn't like the idea of leaving her behind, but he had no other choice. Besides, he knew he could work better without worrying about watching her back.

"I'll be back to take you home," Adams promised.

"You find him and get what we need." Sara said behind trembling lips. 'This may be the most important thing you ever do."

Sara reached out to take his hand, and as they touched, she slipped her crucifix necklace into his palm.

"Please wear this." Adams looked down into his palm at the silver cross.

"You know I don't believe in this stuff, Sara."

"Please wear it for me, okay?"

He dabbed the perspiration from her forehead and placed the cloth down.

"Alright." He fastened the necklace around his neck and put it under his shirt.

"I love you Adams," Sara whispered.

"Thank You," he said, as he bent over kissing her. "I'll be back soon."

He walked out of the room wondering, if he would.

Chapter 54

The five of them walked through town like Doc Holiday and the Earps. They had an agenda and nothing was going to stand in their way. Adams gave them a quick pep talk articulating the severe nature of the matter at hand. Bobby's chest seemed to expand several inches as they walked through the busy streets of Catemaco.

"Black robes everywhere," Bobby noticed.

"Where do we start?" Marty asked.

"There." Adams pointed to a place across the street. "Seven Witches Tavern."

They entered the tavern and walked straight to the bar. The place was busy with people playing billiards, darts and just sitting and sipping on beverages. They all immediately noticed that many of the patrons were dressed in black robes. They also noticed that none of them made eye contact with the team.

"Cinco cervezas, por favor," Hernandez ordered. The bartender didn't say a word. He put the bottles on the bar and Adams laid down a twenty. The first beer went down fast and it was the first of many. They raised their shot glasses several times toasting to everything from the waitress with big breasts to President Fox. The tequila was beginning to take effect and Marty was getting edgy.

"Do you know a guy named Rojas Fuentes?" Marty asked the bartender loud enough to draw the attention of several people near the bar.

"No." he responded.

"Are you sure? He has a house on Lake Catemaco. He is a very well known man." Adams put a photo of Fuentes on the bar.

"Take a look," Adams insisted. The bartender avoided looking at the picture. Hernandez reached over the bar and grabbed the bartender by the lapels.

"My friend asked you a question. Look at the picture." The colonel grabbed him by the back of his hair and slammed his nose onto the bar.

"Have you seen this man, Rojas Fuentes?"

"No lo he visto," the bartender said with blood running from his nose.

Hernandez released the bartender and turned to face the crowd. Now they had caught the attention of everyone in the establishment. The people wearing the black robes went on with their business, avoiding eye contact. Several people started walking out leaving their glasses half empty sitting on the tables.

"Who can tell me where I can find this man, Rojas Fuentes?" Hernandez started walking into the crowd with the picture held high. The rest of the team began moving around asking the same question.

"How about you?" Bobby demanded of a man wearing a black robe. The man ignored him. "Hey, I'm talking to you." Bobby reached out and pulled the hood down from the man's head exposing his face. He looked directly into Bobby's eyes and what Bobby saw were black eyes filled with hatred. Just then a knife came turning through the air and lodged into the wall an inch from Adam's head. When he realized what happened it was too late. A robed man had thrown another knife and it found its destination in Adam's left shoulder. He felt the razor sharp blade, as it tore through his shirt and skin and lodged against the bone in his shoulder. As soon as he was hit, he charged his attacker before the man could get another knife in flight. He tackled the man to the ground and started punching him with his right fist, smashing in the perpetrators eye socket with a series of quick right punches, like an angry hockey player. Several men wearing black robes began surrounding the team as they drew their weapons.

"Come on, mother fucker. Make a move and I'll blow the hood right off your sorry head." Bobby yelled out.

Marty helped Adams drag the bloodied man out through the back door, as the rest of the team covered them, with their guns leveled at the hooded patrons. Adams ignored the blood as it continually poured from his open wound. Hernandez took the blade that had cut into Adams and held it to the robed man's throat. Ramiro was covering the door with Marty and Bobby.

"I will ask you one time and if I don't get an answer I will cut your throat right here and watch you die." Looking into Hernandez's eyes, the man knew he meant it.

"Where is Rojas Fuentes?" Hernandez was pressing the blade so hard against the mans throat it was cutting through the skin.

"The Mountain of The White Monkey," he cried out.

"I know where that is, Ramiro said."

"If you're not telling the truth, I'll find you." Hernandez threatened. He released the man and handed the knife to Adams and got back on his feet.

"I believe this is yours," Adams said. He took the knife into his right hand and came down with a sudden force burying the knife into the man's thigh. The man let out a scream that could only be caused by unbearable pain. Adams turned and looked back as they walked down the alley toward the main street. Several people wearing black robes had come to the aid of their friend. For a moment they all just stood, motionless, staring at Adams. It made him feel uneasy and he wasn't exactly sure why. It was one of those unique moments in time, that a person captures, that stays with them forever.

The clinic was quiet and Sara was one of the few people there seeking treatment. Adams, Marty, and Bobby walked in and Adams insisted he see Sara before receiving care for his wound. The doctor was in her room, as he entered.

"How is she?" Adams inquired. The doctor looked at him standing there with a blood soaked shirt.

"Her condition has worsened. Let me take a look at your arm," the doctor suggested.

"Wait, what do you mean? She is getting worse?"

"Yes, her temperature is not dropping as we had hoped."

"What else can you do for her?" Adams asked.

"She really needs the kind of care a hospital can offer."

"Then get her to a hospital, now!" Adams demanded.

"There is a risk involved, if she were to travel," the doctor said.

"And what is the risk, if she stays here?" Adams asked.

"She may die."

"Well, that answers that question. Let's get her moving, now." Adams demanded.

"I will make the arrangements to have her transported to Santa Maria Hospital in Mexico City. You will need to be taken care of, before you lose anymore blood," the doctor insisted.

"Doctor," Adams clutched onto his arm. "Make sure you get a vehicle that takes bumps well and moves fast. I want her there fast and safe."

"Yes, of course," he responded.

Adams kissed Sara on the forehead, as she lay unconscious. He watched as they moved her into an ambulance that resembled a hearse. As they drove off, he held her cross between his thumb and forefinger. For the first time in his life, he was really scared. For the first time he knew he was totally in love.

Chapter 55

As Adams opened his eyes and the blurred vision began to clear. He saw Marty and Bobby sitting in his room playing cards.

"Aren't you going to deal me in?"

"Hey, boss," Bobby said with a look of delight.

"Are you just going to lay around all day while a bad guy is out there trying to blow up the world?" Marty said with a huge grin attached to his face.

"I'm ready." He felt dizzy as he sat up. "Well, maybe in a day or two."

"Hernandez says were going to the mountain without you," Marty said.

"You tell Hernandez, he can kiss my ass!" Adams said in a raised tone.

"He wants to leave tomorrow, first light," Marty said. "You took quite a few stitches and the doctor says you will be sore for a while."

"Yeah, how many stitches?" Adams asked.

"Inside and out, twenty-three. Lucky for you, he didn't sever any arteries."

"I'll be fine. You get Hernandez over here, so I can speak with him."

"Okay Boss," Bobby said.

"One more thing, any news on Sara?" Adams asked.

"No, not yet," Marty answered.

"All right, thanks guys. Hey, were you two sitting here all night?"

"Yes we were," Bobby said. We didn't want any black robes stopping by to pay you a visit while you were sleeping."

"Thanks, I appreciate it."

Adams convinced Hernandez to wait an additional day so he could gain some strength. The Colonel was anxious to climb the mountain to search for his men and the people responsible for their disappearance. Morning had arrived and they were packed and ready to go. Ramiro knew the mountain since he had hiked it a couple times in the past. He would lead the way for the five of them. They parked their cars at the base of the mountain of the white monkey, and began ascending up the gradually inclining landscape.

"Look, Ramiro said. He pointed to a bird sitting on a tree branch. "That is a Yellow-Winged Tanager. There are so many rare birds up here. Over there he pointed, once again. See that pair of birds? Olive Sparrows," Hernandez was repeating his words in English.

"How does he know so much about birds?" Adams asked.

Hernandez asked Ramiro the question in Spanish.

"His mother used to bird watch. She had a book on birds of the rain forest and Ramiro used to study it."

"I see, we can learn so much from our parents, if we just take the time to listen." Adams said. Hernandez repeated in Spanish what Adams had said. Ramiro nodded his head in agreement.

They had walked up the mountain for nearly a half hour when Adams suggested they stop for a rest. He wouldn't admit it, but he was not feeling well. They found a spot in a clearing and sat in the shade for a drink of cool water. The chatter in the trees grew louder and louder as they moved toward the summit.

"What is all that noise? Marty asked.

"Those are Monkeys," Hernandez answered.

Ramiro began speaking and Hernandez interpreted in English.

"The white monkeys are said to be the evil pets of Satan." Ramiro began. "Legend has it, they are the eyes of Satan and the protectors of his followers."

"Here we go again with this horse shit," Marty said. "Tell this hammerhead we don't go for all that shit."

"You should listen to him," Hernandez suggested. "He has lived here and he has knowledge of the people and their culture."

Ramiro continued. "The Shamans have been here for thousands of years. They believe, if they sell their souls to Satan, they will have the power to cast evil spells on their enemies. They can cause people to endure bad luck throughout their lives or make them very sick. In some cases they can even cause the death of their victims through illness or fatal accidents."

"Adams, do you believe this voodoo shit?" Bobby asked.

"No, I suppose I don't. But, a lot of weird shit has been happening since I came to Mexico, that much I believe."

"The men dressed in black robes are Shamans. They have been at odds with the Charlatans for years. They are the ones you saw dressed in white robes. They are Christians who believe all the bad things that happen in Catemaco are caused by the Shamans." Hernandez was learning himself, as he interpreted for Ramiro.

"It seems like there are a lot more people in the town dressed in black robes than white," Bobby remarked.

"Most Charlatans don't wear robes. It is the Shamans way of commanding fear from the local population. Even in the hottest of days they keep their hoods on, covering their heads."

"Let's just catch this fucking guy and get the hell out of this shit hole," Marty insisted. "I just want to go home where people wear shorts and a tee-shirt when it's a hundred fucking degrees out. These people have serious mental problems," Marty offered.

"Many people have climbed this mountain searching for Satan's alter. It is said there is a cave somewhere on the mountain and a furious red devil rages above a black alter. The evil spirit is so ugly that you cannot look him in the eye because you will be paralyzed with fright, and then he will take your soul. It is said, people who have found the alter have never returned."

"Okay, kids, what do you say we keep moving," Bobby suggested while standing up.

"Lets go, thanks for the update on the locals, Ramiro," Adams said.

Ramiro once again nodded his head. Adams couldn't help but notice how serious Ramiro was when telling the story. It was somewhat bothersome. They all got back on their feet and continued up the mountain. The sun was moving through the branches making it's way to the treetops. As they reached a plateau there was a rustling in the thick brush. Marty looked to his left and out sprang a white monkey.

"What the fuck!" Marty sounded out, alarmed, as he ducked, falling to one knee.

The monkey flew past him grabbing onto Ramiro's leg, sinking her two-inch fangs deep into his flesh. Ramiro began screaming as he attempted to pry the animal off his leg. After what seemed to be an eternity, the monkey finally let go and vanished into the brush sounding out with a loud, victorious roar.

"Holy shit!" Marty shouted. "What the hell was that?"

For a brief moment there was no response. "El Diablo," Ramiro said, as he tended to the bleeding wound on his left thigh.

The team gathered around and assisted Ramiro in bandaging up his leg.

"Are you going to be able to make it?" Hernandez asked.

"I don't know," Ramiro said. "I'll try."

"Colonel, I think we are going to need reinforcements. Maybe you should call for help," Adams suggested.

"I already have," he responded.

"When did you do that?"

"This morning. They are a couple hours behind us."

"You have told them we need Fuentes taken alive, right?" Adams asked in a concerned tone.

"Yes," Hernandez said.

"Good, lets get moving." Adams helped Ramiro onto his feet.

"Hey Boss," Bobby was speaking.

"Yeah."

"Permission to blow the head off any fucking monkey that comes near us?"

"Granted."

The pace up the mountain slowed with Ramiro favoring one leg. The team that stood in a huddle on the lake had quickly deteriorated from a strong eight to a weak five. Adams wasn't sure how many men Fuentes had in his ranks and he hoped it was enough to help them in their quest. He thought about Hernandez' men, who by now would be ascending the mountain. There were many trails leading to the summit. He hoped they would follow their trail.

"I hate this assignment," Marty said. "Sara's lying in a Mexican hospital half dead from some viral infection. Adams has a hole in his shoulder. And we are humping our asses off, up Monkey Mountain, looking for a devil worshiper." Bobby was listening as he picked up the point. "I just want to get home to the wife and kid. This case is just too fucking weird," Adams said.

"I hear you partner. I miss my dog, Sam. He's locked up in some dog kennel, probably cursing the day he was born," Bobby said.

"Yeah, just like me right about now," Marty said.

"Will you just stop your crying and…"

Bobby's sentence was cut short by a loud bang from fifty yards away. It was the last sound he would ever hear. A thirty-caliper round had entered through Bobby's right eye, and exited out the back of his head, causing his blood to splatter across Marty's face and chest. Marty's knees seemed to give out and he hit the ground in an instant. The rest of the team did the same.

"Bobby's hit!" Marty cried out. "He's hit real bad!"

Marty knew from the first look at his friend it was too late. He just lay there holding his friend in his arms weeping. Adams low crawled up to them.

"Son of a bitch!" Adams hissed.

Just then, shots rang out. Rounds were sweeping through the bushes and trees above their heads. They all returned fire, popping rounds off into the woods that had just taken the life of their brother. Marty was screaming the whole time his finger was squeezing his trigger. He wanted to get up and charge the mountain and kill every one of the bastards responsible for taking away his best friend. He was afraid to leave the rest of his team behind, so he stayed, just continuing to fire with tears blurring his vision. Suddenly the shots subsided. It was quiet again, but more quiet than before. There weren't any sounds coming from the trees and jungle like before. Emptiness filled the air. The birds and animals had stopped singing and chanting. It was an eerie silence.

Colonel Hernandez crawled up to Adams and Marty. He looked at Bobby and offered his condolences to his comrades.

"I think this is a good time to wait for my men," Hernandez said looking down at Bobby's corpse.

"Yes, I agree." Adams said.

All four of them lay motionless looking up the mountain. Not knowing the summit was just through the trees ahead. Marty thought about Sam. He would adopt the dog and treat him like a king for the rest of his days.

Chapter 56

Low crawling uphill didn't do any good for the wound on Adams's shoulder. A few of the stitches had popped open causing the bleeding to continue. Ramiro had to bare the pain of a bite wound and the thought of disease wasn't far from his mind. Marty was totally bereaved and nearly in a state of shock. Hernandez was ready to kill. None of them were of complete sound mind and body. Charging the hill was out of question at this point and it made Adams feel helpless. He thought about Sara and her well-being weighed heavily on him. He started to fantasize about being able to retire, alive and healthy.

From a distance shots rang out. It sounded like a grand finale at a Forth of July fireworks display. The firing continued as they all lay fixed in their position wondering what was happening.

"What the hell is going on up there?" shouted an alarmed Adams. "Your men breached the summit." It was apparent he was very angry.

"No," Hernandez responded. "They are still behind us."

"Then who the hell are they battling with?" Adams asked. "Let's move out and see what's going on."

They got on their feet and started up the mountain. As they continued up the hill the shots became less consistent and more sporadic. Finally the shots stopped except for a few here and there.

"Halt!" A voice sounded out from the summit. Once again they hit the ground.

"Who goes there?" the voice sounded out in Spanish.

"Colonel Hernandez, Mexican Army," he responded.

"Alright Colonel, show yourself."

"Whom am I speaking with?" Hernandez asked.

"My name is Juan Cabrera. I represent the Charlatans. It is safe now, we have beaten the Shamans."

Hernandez turned to Adams. "It is the Charlatans, they have taken the Shamans. It is safe to proceed."

"Who the fuck are the Charlatans?" Adams inquired.

"They are the tribe that have been fighting with the Shamans. You know, what Ramiro was talking about before," Marty said.

They finally had made it to the top, ragged and weary and without victory of their own. Bodies were everywhere riddled with bullet holes. Men dressed in camouflage fatigues moved about, hovering over black robed bodies. Cabrera offered his hand to Hernandez and re-introduced himself. They shook hands and began exchanging dialog.

"Ask him about Fuentes," Adams demanded.

"Rojas Fuentes?" Cabrera responded in English. Adams was relieved.

"Yes, do you know him?" Adams asked.

"Yes, he is the leader of the Shamans. We have been waiting to find him for a long time. Until recently no one knew who led them. When we found out he was their leader we learned they were up here on the mountain. We started up the mountain yesterday and waited for the right time. You distracted them and that's when we made our move."

"Where is he?" Adams asked.

"Follow me."

They followed Cabrera to an opening in a cave on the mountainside. Adams was the first in. What he saw was the most gruesome sight he had ever witnessed. He turned back to Hernandez.

"You may not want to come in here," Adams said.

"Let me through," Hernandez insisted.

What he saw made him extremely angry and as he got closer, sadness set in. Hernandez was a man who didn't show emotion, but Adams could see by the look on his face he actually had a heart somewhere beneath his façade of stone. Ernesto and Juan had been hung upside down by the ankles. Their carotid arteries had been cut and they were drained of all their blood. There were two large earns situated on an alter. As Hernandez suspected, they were filled nearly to the brim with blood. The cave smelled of death and just as Ramiro's story had been told, the alter was black.

"This is where all the children were taken," Cabrera said. "People have been vanishing for years without a trace. No one knew where they were or what became of them until now. We had suspected the Shamans but could never prove anything. Now maybe their souls will be at rest." He made the sign of the cross and walked out. Adams followed him.

"Cut them down!" Hernandez ordered.

Adams put his hand on Cabrera's shoulder. "I'm sorry about your people. I need to know what happened to Fuentes." Hernandez joined them outside the cave opening.

"Over here." He walked over to a robed corpse and kicked it over with his foot. The body had been shot several times and had a knife protruding from the center of its chest. Adams pulled the hood down to reveal his face. Rojas Fuentes died with his eyes wide open. Adams turned and faced Hernandez, and then he looked at Cabrera.

"You have no idea what you have done." Adams sat down and began rubbing his forehead.

Chapter 57

It was like a bad influenza epidemic. Once the first story hit the news, reporters were swarming around Pinehaven, so they wouldn't miss out on covering one of the biggest stories since the attack on the twin towers. Just as Beth had figured, word had spread fast about Justin and what was happening in Pinehaven. The way he helped so many people to change their lives in a positive way. Rumors of the miracles he performed had intrigued people from all over the world and even the Pope was considering a visit to Vermont. Justin refused to give interviews to the media. Instead he would invite them to worship with him, and he asked that they respect his request to leave the cameras outside of the church. The story had international coverage, and people from all over the world had begun pilgrimages to Pinehaven. Beth was concerned about the safety of her son but he assured her everything would be fine. Pinehaven was not the same quiet little town it used to be. It never would be again.

It was six-thirty AM when the alarm clock went off. Adams slapped the snooze button as he did every weekday. He wasn't one to wait for it to sound off ten minutes later so he got up and turned it off. He looked into the mirror, thinking how much he had aged. The scar on his shoulder resembled a smooth caterpillar. He filled his kettle of water and put it on the stove for his morning coffee. He switched on the TV for the morning news and went to the front porch in search of his USA Today newspaper. As he made his way back into the kitchen the TV reporter caught his attention. He turned it up and listened. The breaking news was on a man who claimed to be the Son of God. They cut to clips of people who were interviewed and who claimed to see miracles performed, and many who had become enlightened by Justin's word. Adams glanced at the front page of his paper and it was the same story. He picked up the phone to call Sara. As he dialed he thought about how grateful he was that she had recovered fully in Mexico City. It was ironic that she completely snapped out of her sickness in one day. And Adams still wondered if it was a coincidence or if it was related to the death of Rojas Fuentes. The day she became instantly better was the day Fuentes was killed.

"Hello." Sara answered her cell phone.
"Sara, have you seen the news?"
"No, why?"
"Put on channel six and meet me at the office in an hour."
"What is it Adams?"
"Just watch the news. Bye." He hung up.

Adams went into his storage unit where he kept hundreds of books. He thought he had a bible somewhere, or did he throw it away years ago? He wasn't sure but he needed to find one.

He began to turn boxes upside down. Books flowed out onto the floor, and as they fell the titles he saw brought him back to a particular place in his memory. He emptied box after box and books fell like snowflakes from the clouds of time. He saw Last of the Mohicans, Catcher in the Rye, The Old Man and the Sea, Treasure Island, Fountainhead, Master of the Game, so many books he had enjoyed throughout his life. It was in one of the last boxes he turned over, The King James Version of the Holy Bible. He looked at the mess he had created and left the room as it was. He sat down at the kitchen table and turned to Revelation and began reading.

"So the great dragon was cast out, that serpent of old, called the Devil and Satan, who deceives the whole world; he was cast to the earth, and his angels were cast with him."

Adams had never read the Bible but had overheard passages from time to time. He kept reading.

"We give thanks to you O Lord God Almighty, The one who is and who was and who is to come, Because you have taken your great power and reigned. The nations were angry and your wrath has come, And the time of the dead, that they should be judged. And that you should reward your servants and the prophets and the saints, And those who fear your name, small and great, And should destroy those who destroy the earth."

He turned the page and continued reading.

"In the same hour there was a great earthquake, And a tenth of the city fell. In the earthquake seven thousand people were killed, and the rest were afraid and gave glory to the God of Heaven. The second woe is past. Behold the third woe is coming quickly."

An hour later Adams was waiting in his office for Sara when she shuffled in.
"When are we going to Vermont?" she asked.
"Tomorrow morning. Take a look at this."
He handed her the bible with the passages he read, highlighted.
"How many people died in the earthquake in Iran last month?" Sara asked.
"A little over seven thousand."
"Adams, I'm getting a little scared."
"Me too."
"Lock the door. I want you to make love to me right now. Right here."
Adams locked the door and turned off the lights.

Chapter 58

It was 6:48 AM and Adams was seated next to Sara. He had always requested the aisle seat when flying. He never told anyone the reason. He had always kept to himself that he wanted a clear shot down the aisle at any bastard who tried to hijack a plane that he was flying on. They had both been cleared by airport security to carry a side arm on the plane. He also had brought along the dagger and advised security of that prior to boarding. Adams was reading the Bible and Sara was going over the file on Fuentes.

"Look at this." Adams handed her the open book.

And many of the people believed in him, and said, "When the Christ comes, he will do more signs than these which man has done."

Then he handed her the morning paper, which had an article about Justin and the miracles he had performed since he was a child.

"Do you really believe this guy is the Messiah?" Sara handed him back the paper.

"No, I don't. But there are a lot of coincidences."

"Do you think the story will ever make print?" Sara asked.

"Probably someday. How can you keep five nuclear bombs set to go off in five major cities quiet forever? Someone will leak it eventually. Then you will see a huge White House scandal and the FBI will be the scapegoat." Adams said.

"Yeah, and it will point right to us."

"Hey, it wasn't our decision to put a lid on it." Adams said.

"Do you really think that will matter when the shit hits the fan?" Sara asked.

"No, but I'll be able to sleep at night."

"How many agents has the bureau put on this case since Mexico?" Sara asked.

"Two hundred, give or take. They are seeking cooperation from North Korea as we speak."

"You can't deal with the devil. It reads that way right in that book doesn't it?" Sara asked.

"In so many words, yes." Adams said.

When they arrived at the airport they had a rental car waiting. After retrieving their luggage they were on the road driving toward Pinehaven. Adams had booked them a room in Clarionton. They planned on spending the night making love. Adams couldn't wait, so they found a secluded area off a country road and pulled over. Sara was wearing a skirt and the only obstruction was her panties, which Adam's had off in less that five seconds. Sara felt like a schoolgirl making out in the front seat of a car. It turned her on so much they had sex twice. Her husband would never do it in a car. She had thought long and hard and had decided she was going to ask him for a divorce. She was in love with Adams and he was in love with her. She couldn't bear to have her husband touch her anymore. Sara had to completely detach herself when he crawled on top of her. She imagined him to be Adams, even though his body was puny and without muscle. This was the only way she could get through it without crying. She didn't love him anymore. All she thought about was Adams.

Chapter 59

Autumn had arrived and the leaves were in full bloom showing off their colors. This was Beth's favorite season. Every year in October she felt as if she was starting a new life within her own.

Beth was glad she decided to spend her life in New England. Although she felt winter dragged on longer than she would like, she loved the four seasons. She was sitting on her front porch swing when a car drove up. She figured it to be another reporter or another follower looking for absolution or miracles from Justin. Adams and Sara had gotten the address from the local sheriff. He was reluctant to give them the address until Adams told him it was business related and might help him in his investigation. The sheriff wanted details but Adams told him it was confidential information and he wasn't allowed to share any details at that time. The sheriff wasn't happy with his response but cooperated anyway.

"Good afternoon." Adams and Sara approached Beth.

"Hello, may I help you?"

"Yes, I am Agent Adams and this is Agent Kimball. We're with the FBI." Adams displayed his credentials. "We are here to speak with Justin. Is he available?"

"I'm Beth, his mother." She stood and shook hands with them. "What does the FBI want with Justin?"

"We are investigating terrorists that have satanic beliefs and would like to speak with Justin regarding these matters."

"What kind of matters?"

"Murder."

Adams noticed a look on Beth's face that told him she knew something.

"I have read about your son and some of the things people say he has done. Some believe he is the second coming of Christ."

"What do you believe, Agent Adams?" Beth asked.

"I believe in catching bad people and putting them away."

"There are too many," Beth said it as if she had experienced them first hand.

"Has anything strange happened to you or your son recently?"

"No, not recently. Many years ago when we were living in Massachusetts I was dating a man who was murdered in a hit-and-run. Before the police could question the suspect, he killed himself. It turned out that he was plotting to get to Justin through me."

"What was his name?" Adams had his pen and pad out.

"George Farkis. But that was not his real name."

"What was his real name?"

"Nobody knew. He didn't exist, not on paper anyway."

"What department investigated him?"

"Cambridge."

"Do you remember the investigator's name?"

"Yes, Ken McLaughlin."

"When exactly was that?"

Beth hesitated in thought before answering. "Fourteen years ago."

Justin came walking around from the side of the house.

"Hello Sweetie. These people are from the FBI. These are Agents Adams and Kimball."

"Good afternoon," Justin said.

"Hello," Sara said as she reached out and shook his hand. He had a soft and comforting way about him, she thought.

"Nice to meet you," Adams said. They shook hands.

"Have I broken any laws?"

"No, of course not," Adams said.

"Then what brings you to our home?"

"We are investigating a group of terrorists. One of them was wanted for very serious offenses. He was a very dangerous devil worshiper."

Justin interrupted him. "You continue to refer to him in the past tense."

"Well, that's because he's dead. He was shot to death in Mexico. We are attempting to locate his accomplices. His name was Rojas Fuentes. Does that name sound familiar?"

"No." Justin answered.

"I was speaking to your mother who told us about the incident that occurred when you were a child. We are investigating all leads hoping to get to the center of the terrorist cell."

"I don't see how that has anything to do with me."

"Justin, may we sit for a few minutes?"

"Of course, please." Justin gestured toward the chairs on the porch.

"Can I offer you something to drink?" Beth asked.

"No thanks," Adams said. Sara concurred.

"Justin, I am going to get right to the point. We think this guy is part of a group of people who believe they are disciples of Satan. They may also be plotting some very devastating terrorist attacks. We have read about you and what people have said regarding miracles you have performed and such. I personally don't believe in those type of things but I had to meet with you to be sure there is no link between what you are doing and what the terrorists are up to. Have you noticed anything strange, or has anyone threatened you?"

"No." Justin responded.

Adams reached into his bag and pulled out the dagger. "Does this mean anything to you?" He handed it to Justin. He took it and held it laying flat in his open palms.

"This is the dagger of Satan. He is here."

Adams looked at Sara then back at Justin. "How do you know this?"

"Because I do. I am the son of man."

"I'm sorry, Justin, but I don't buy that," Adams responded.

There was an uncomfortable silence as Justin peered into the eyes of Adams.

"You two are committing sins of the flesh." He looked at Sara and then back at Adams while handing the dagger back to him.

"What are you talking about?" Adams asked.

"Thou shall not covet another man's wife."

Sara's face turned white. At that moment she believed that he was who he claimed to be.

"I can't help you. It's not too late to help yourselves. Go and pray to our Lord for forgiveness and fornicate no more." Justin walked away. They said goodbye to Beth and got back into the car.

The ride to the hotel was traveled without a single word spoken. Adams didn't understand how Justin knew about their affair. Sara believed she knew and was overwhelmed with guilt. When they arrived at the hotel they didn't have sex, they just slept in each other's arms.

Chapter 60

The drive from Pinehaven to Cambridge had the most spectacular foliage scenery either of them had ever experienced. They were in northern Massachusetts on Route 2 headed east when Sara turned down the car radio to speak.

"Adams, doesn't it bother you that Justin knew about our affair?"

"Yes, it does."

"How could he know that?" Sara asked.

"I don't know, maybe he's a psychic or something."

"I don't think so. Hasn't it ever crossed your mind that maybe he is Christ returning? He looked at the dagger and knew right away it was evil. He said it was Satan's dagger. How could he know that by looking at it?"

"Well, doesn't it appear evil with the serpent on it? I don't know anymore, Sara, I'm confused. I have never been a believer in God and the devil, but there are so many coincidences and unanswered questions. I am not sold on any of it but I guess anything is possible."

"I don't know about you, but I have a real bad feeling about this case. I just want to hug my kids." Sara said.

Adams looked at Sara and saw she was really scared. He would never admit to being scared about anything. He was tough and a realist. There wasn't anything he couldn't deal with, even the loss of his soul mate.

"May I help you?" asked the officer sitting behind the bulletproof glass in the lobby of the Cambridge Police Department.

Adams had the phone up to his ear. "I am here to see Detective McLaughlin. He is expecting me. I am agent Adams with the FBI."

"Please hold on while I call him," said the officer behind the glass. He looked as if he had passed retirement age a decade ago. "He will be right down."

"Thanks," Adams said.

A few minutes later Ken came down and Adams saw him through the glass. Ken pointed to a door in the corner of the lobby and met them there.

"Agents Adams and Kimball?" Ken asked.

"Yes," Adams responded and put out his hand.

"I'm Lieutenant Ken McLaughlin."

"Nice to meet you," Sara said.

"My office is on the third floor. We can talk there."

They sat down in Ken's office. "Can I get you a cup of coffee or water?"

"Coffee would be great," Adams said.

"Water for me, please." Sara was thirsty after the long drive.

Ken picked up the phone and asked his secretary for the drinks. He also had a coffee. Adams started the conversation. "Lieutenant I want to thank you for seeing us on such short notice."

"Please, call me Ken."

"Okay, I go by Adams, but you can call her Sara. Ken, we are investigating a terrorist cell that is involved in a very serious and dangerous plot that may include bombings in the United States and abroad."

"Alright, how can I help?" Ken was puzzled.

"What brought us here, Ken, is a woman named Beth who used to live in Arlington, Massachusetts. She now resides in Vermont with her son Justin."

"Ah, yes, the miracle boy," Ken responded. "He is all over the news these days."

"We went to visit them yesterday and she told us about a case you were investigating fourteen years ago that involved the murder of her boyfriend."

"Yes, I remember that case like it was yesterday. It has haunted me for a long time. It was tragic and we never uncovered the identity of the perpetrator. He killed himself by ingesting cyanide during a foot chase. I watched him die. We ran him through NCIC and Interpol, checked his prints, dental, and even his DNA and we came up with nothing."

"His identification was listed as Farkis, right?" Sara asked.

"Yes, let me pull the file on him." Ken picked up his phone and called for his secretary. She came right in with their drinks.

"Donna, would you please have records pull the file on this person and bring it right over?" He handed her a slip of paper.

"Sure, Ken," Donna responded.

"How do you link Farkis with your case?" Ken asked.

"One of the terrorists we we're investigating was a devil worshiper, and with all the press on Justin being the second coming, we decided to meet with him to see if he could help. We thought we would take a shot and see if something may have occurred with him recently that might point us in the right direction. The terrorist we are speaking about was killed in Mexico while we were moving in to apprehend him. He has accomplices that we must locate." Ken could tell it was serious by the expression on Adam's face.

Justin's mother told us the story about Farkis and that's what brought us here. Can you tell us more about the case?"

"It was very strange. My partner Horace Washington", Ken pointed to a picture on the wall of him and Horace posing together in their younger days.

"He died three years ago. We were investigating the hit and run murder of a young man who was dating Beth. The case was going nowhere and about six months later we got a break in the case from a homeless guy who witnessed the murder."

There was a knock at the door. Donna brought in the file.

"As I was saying, this bum remembered the plate and we traced it to a rental company and we were able to get an ID on the guy. It's right here." Ken opened the file. "His license ID was Assad Madul. We showed his photo to Beth and she identified him as a guy she worked with at her school. She was a teacher and he was a substitute. They had been dating for a while. He was teaching under the name George Farkis. We went to his apartment to question him and serve a search warrant and he took off on foot after breaking Horace's nose. That's when he poisoned himself."

"Did you find anything on him or at his place?" Adams asked.

"I remember this guy was a health nut. That's why the theory that he had a heart attack during the foot chase didn't make sense. We searched his place and didn't find anything unusual except a document on his hard drive that was written in some type of secret code. It was written in text I couldn't make out. I downloaded it onto a disc and sent it to the FBI."

"What happened?" Sara asked.

"It was strange, because a few days later I had a visit from four FBI agents. They came and confiscated the computer and asked me if there were any other copies made. I remember they were real concerned about that."

"Do you remember any of the agent's names? I might know them."

"How could I forget? The agent that was in charge is Secretary of State Fred Connors."

"This was fourteen years ago, right?" Adams asked.

"Yes."

"President Rockwell was the deputy director of the Bureau fourteen years ago. Did they ever tell you what was on the disc?" Adams asked.

"No, I asked and they said it was nothing. That is what I found so peculiar. If it was nothing, why did they send four agents to collect the computer and why all the concern over the possibility of there being another copy?"

"I wish you had kept a copy. Was there anything else about the case that was out of the ordinary?" Adams asked.

"No, just the fact that we never found out who Farkis really was. And there was the old dagger."

Adams grabbed Ken by the arm. "Dagger! What dagger?"

"I found an old gold dagger with a platinum blade. I had it appraised and it's worth thousands."

"Ken, does the dagger have a serpent with seven snake heads at the top of the handle?"

"Yes, how did you know that?"

Sara looked at Adams. Ken could see something was wrong.

"Because I found two daggers with the same markings, one in France and the other in Mexico, and both of them belonged to two of the most dangerous terrorists in the world. We think there is a conspiracy that is a serious threat to the security of United States."

"Can I trust you two?" Ken appeared apprehensive.

"Yes, you can trust us," Adams said.

"I have a copy of the disc. I've had it locked up for fourteen years and never had the chance to find out what is on it. It has plagued me for a long time."

"Where is it?" Adams asked.

"I have it in a safe at home with the dagger."

"Let's go and see what is on that disc." Adams said.

"Alright, lets go." Ken grabbed his jacket and opened the door.

Chapter 61

The safe in Ken's basement was a gun safe almost the size of a refrigerator. It weighed four hundred pounds and was bolted to the wall. With a few turns of the dial Ken opened the safe and pulled out a wooden box and handed it to Adams. He opened the lid, took out the knife and handed it to Sara.

"It's exactly the same as the others," Adams said.

Ken took the disc out of the safe. "The computer is in my office upstairs."

They were all anxious to see what the disc contained, yet they were afraid of what they might find. Ken downloaded the disc and printed the document.

Adams retrieved the paper from the printer and went to work circling every third letter in from the end of each word. Sara and Ken sat in wait as Adams decoded the message.

"Oh no!" Adams looked as if he saw a ghost. He handed her the decoded message and she began to read. With every word she was trembling more and more. The message read:

Behold seven daggers. One for you and the remainder to be given to my other six disciples who you must seek out and find. Each disciple will be given instructions for the final day.

Thirty-five cities will burn. I will soon lead the most powerful nation in the world and I will reign for seven years until the last season. The winter to end all winters.

Ken read the message and handed it back to Adams.

"Adams, what the hell is going on?" Ken asked.

Adams looked at Ken and Sara. "Next year is an election year. President Rockwell has been in office for seven years."

"Adams, tell me what is happening here." Ken was growing impatient.

"One of the terrorists who owned a dagger just like yours had a shipment arrive in Mexico last month. Aboard his ship we uncovered five tactical nuclear bombs. The instructions on his hard drive listed five major cities in South America and Mexico. Another terrorist I killed in Paris this year also had the same dagger and his instructions listed five cities in China and Russia. There are four disciples still out there and thirty bombs. That means there are thirty cities targeted for destruction."

"Jesus Christ, help us!" Ken said. "Thirty nuclear bombs would devastate the world."

"No", Adams said. "It would completely destroy the entire planet. What the actual explosion doesn't kill the nuclear winter would."

Adams looked at Sara. She had a look he had seen on other people before her. It was the look of hopelessness.

"Rockwell was deputy director and he squashed the message fourteen years ago. Now he is the president of the most powerful nation in the world. My God, Adams, he has been in office seven years." Sara said.

"He wrote the message," Ken said.

"Winter is only a few weeks away. What are we going to do?" Sara was looking for an answer.

Adams didn't have one. He just stared at her, once again rubbing his forehead.

Chapter 62

The five hour flight back to San Diego seemed to take forever. Their plane landed and they disembarked and walked to the baggage claim area. They sat down and waited for their bags to circle around the conveyor belt. People were impatiently waiting to retrieve their luggage and retreat to the comfort and safety of their homes. People were greeting each other with hugs and kisses. Adams could hear the laughter and light conversations between family and friends. They were just people going about their every day lives, he thought.

One by one, they cleared out with luggage in hand. When they were all gone there were just two bags left going round and round the carousel. Adams and Sara just sat there watching their bags turn after turn.

"What are we going to do?" Sara asked.

"What can we do?"

"We have to tell someone." She said.

"Yes, that would be a start." Sara answered

"Who would believe us? Winter is almost here and the bombs are already in place. It's too late." Adams said.

Sara began to cry. "What are we going to do, Adams?"

"Go home to your husband and children."

"What are you going to do?" she asked.

Adams didn't answer. He just sat watching his bag.

Adams stood in front of the church looking up at the tall stone steeple, which rested under a large golden cross. After a minute he started toward the 20 foot oak doors designated as the main entrance. Making his way up the isle, he glared at the huge stain glass windows spread out on both sides of the cathedral. The colors were brilliant and detailed, he thought. Along the walls were a series of pictures starting with the last supper, continuing with Jesus dead on the cross, and finally the resurrection. He made his way to the pew outside the confessional doors and sat alone in wait.

A few minutes later a confessional door opened and an old woman shuffled out undistracted, and hurried toward the alter to kneel. Adams looked at the door that awaited him and then at the large oak doors that seemed so far away. He reached for the closer door and walked in.

Adams knelt down in the confessional feeling uncomfortable and embarrassed. He listened to the prayers from the priest who was on the other side of the wall. He tried to make out what the priest was whispering, but wasn't able to. There was a silence before a calm voice resonated through a small metal speaker that sat to close too his lips.

"You have come to confess your sins?"

"Yes."

"Go on my son."

Adams was stumbling in thought.

"Forgive me father for I have sinned."

"When was your last confession?"

"About twenty-five years ago." Adams wanted to get up and run out of the church. He felt like a child that had been caught skipping school.

"Have you come to repent?"

"Yes, Father."

"Go on." The priest said.

"I have sworn and stolen."

"Go on." The priest said as if it were routine.

"I have had sexual relations with a married woman,"

"Continue, my son."

The fire was getting hotter and hotter as Adams continued. He cleared his throat.

"I have killed many people."

The confessional was dead silent. Adams broke the silence with the sound of his shoe accidentally bumping the door.

"Is there anything else?" The priest asked in a different and uneasy tone.

"Yes, please ask the lord to forgive me for what I am about to do. Most people will remember me as one of the world's worst tyrants. But what I must do will be a gift to mankind everywhere."

"First you must pray for your sins of the past. Then you can ask God to guide you in the right direction to live free from sin going forward." The priest added.

"I don't have time right now." Adams said with conviction. "There will be plenty of time to pray later, thank you, father."

Adams opened the door and walked out of the confessional without stopping for prayer or anything else. He walked directly down the isle toward the entrance hoping for some kind of relief or weight lifted from his shoulders. He felt nothing.

The other confessional door slowly creaked open and the priest popped his head out and watched Adams as he opened the tall oak doors and disappeared.

Chapter 63

▼

The presidential motorcade was traveling to its destination in Chattachoochee National Forest, Georgia. Seven black motor vehicles, proudly displaying American flags on their car antennas, traveled twenty miles per hour, following behind several marked police cruisers. Somewhere in the middle was the car that occupied President Rockwell. Secret service agents were alert and prepared for anything that may occur out of the ordinary. They had been briefed on the probability of environmentalists protesting the arrival of Rockwell. The President had his writers prepare a speech addressing his concern over environmental issues in our state forests. Like most presidents before him, Rockwell had a poor track record of implementing real steps toward improving the environment.

Adams was situated in a prone position in the thick brush of the national forest, five hundred meters from where President Rockwell's podium sat. He lay on a hill with a clear view and the sun to his back. The ground was still damp from rain that had fallen a day earlier. The wind whistling through the treetops offered a serene peacefulness, that until now, he had taken for granted. The detachable butt of his Iver Johnson AMAC 1500 high-powered sniper rifle, rested on his right shoulder. His back was aching and he was itchy from dirt that had found its way into his fatigues.

Three days earlier Adams had entered the park anticipating the arrival of the secret service advance team. He was equipped with his weapon, three fifty caliper rounds of ammunition, and enough rations to survive three days. He had a custom-made, straw-like, breathing device that he used to take in air. Adams had buried himself under the earth and lay there for nine hours, while secret service agents patrolled the forest with dogs. To avoid detection, he covered himself with the smell of a rotting animal carcass. He knew the dogs were trained to sniff out people and bombs, and may overlook an animal scent.

As he peered through his high-powered scope, he spied the area watching for anything out of the ordinary. He slowly moved the cross hairs around the staging area, in preparation for his target to arrive. Adams did all he could to remain awake. He had very little sleep in the past seventy-two hours and his head was beginning to get heavy. He thought about Sara and their time together in Mexico. He thought about how much he missed her. He fantasized about lying in bed with her in the hotel overlooking Puerto Viejo Bay, but quickly dismissed his feelings. He knew he would probably never see her again, and he couldn't let that thought distract him.

The motorcade pulling up and then finally stopping at its final destination was, in Adam's mind, like a roaring train screeching to a halt. He tried to remain calm and focused as he followed the president who popped in and out of his site, while making his way to the stage. Sweat was running down his brow just as it had the day before, as he lay buried under a foot of soil.

The president was waving his hands high at the cheering crowd as he walked onto the stage. Only Adams could see the evil in his eyes, as he positioned himself behind the podium. Adams could hear his heart pounding like African war drums. His hands were slightly trembling, as he firmly clutched his weapon. He fixed his site on the center of the presidential seal embedded in the front of the podium. The cheering had subsided as the president began speaking. Adams raised his site up until the crosshairs were centered on the president's chest. He took in a deep breath, let it out, and stopped breathing for a brief moment. As he slowly squeezed his trigger, his mind drifted back to another place with a different podium. The recoil took him back to a stage with a podium that had a seal of the Department of Justice on the front. It was a day much like this day, many years ago in Quantico, Virginia, and he was graduating from the FBI academy. It was a day he remembered taking an oath, to protect and serve the United States of America.

978-0-595-67252-3
0-595-67252-3

Printed in the United States
33899LVS00003B/130-177